da Vinci's Parachute

DAVID HARRY TANNENBAUM

Red Engine Press
Fort Smith, AR

Library of Congress Control Number: 2026935665

ISBN: 979-8-9985192-3-9

Disclaimers

Everything in this book, except for the establishments frequented by Detective Leslie Hodges, is purely fictional.

Lee County Acronyms

ASA	Assistant State Attorney
CIA	Criminal Investigation Assistant
COD	Cause of Death
DFU	Digital Forensics Unit
ROR	Release on Own Recognizance
RTIC	Real Time Intelligence Center
SOU	Special Operations Unit (SWAT)

DA VINCI'S PARACHUTE

THE SEMINAL SOCIETY

Thomas A. Edison
Phonograph
1847-1931

Ernst Chladni
Acoustics
1756-1827

Sir Isaac Newton
Greatest Ever Scientist
1643-1727

Galileo Galilei
Father of Science
1564 to 1642

Leonardo da Vinci
Artist- Inventor
1452-1529

Oswald Von Wolkenstein
First Song Composer
1376-1445

ONE

LEE COUNTY SHERIFF'S DEPUTY, Detective Leslie Hodges was angry with herself as she passed through the guarded entrance to Miromar Lakes. She turned left toward where a small dock jutted out into a lake mirroring the deep blue of the Florida sky. She silenced the siren, allowing the cruiser's alternating blue and red lights to continue saturating her surroundings. Her anger stemming not so much from the fact that she had caught a drowning; actually, a man found floating just beneath the surface, but rather from the fact that her partner, Simeon Cox, had beat her to the scene. That now meant that he would have day-to-day operational control of the investigation, assuming there was to be an investigation.

Petty, she knew. But she was pissed, nonetheless. Cox held a two-year seniority to her in the department, but she had been a cop, a street cop, in Tampa for six years before moving to Lehigh Acres after Junior, her husband, a Tampa detective, was shot and killed in the line of duty.

"There's a boat waiting for you down there," a uniformed deputy, the name Hendrix pinned to his uniform blouse, called to her when she emerged from her car. "You can go around that way," he offered, pointing to the white sand to her right. "This way is congested; lookie-loos at the bar. Nice place they have here."

That was an understatement, at best. There probably wasn't a home in this section of the community under two million. "You can say that again," Leslie confirmed. "Who found the body? And how long ago?"

"A teen, from what I've been told. About fifteen minutes ago. I believe she was out on a paddleboard and bumped into a foot. She's freaked to say the least. That's her over there." Hendrix nodded to Leslie's right in the direction of a teenage girl sitting in a lounge chair under a white cabana. A woman appearing to be in her mid-twenties was standing over her.

"Who's that with her?"

"Sherry. Boat instructor. I believe they're waiting for the girl's mother to arrive."

"I see a pontoon boat out there. I presume that's where the floater was found. Who's that on the boat?"

"Another staff guy. Didn't get his name. He runs the boats and stuff. From what I could gather, that pontoon belongs to the club."

"Floater been identified?"

"Not that I know."

"Your source?"

"Your partner, Detective Cox. He's the one said for you to go on out and secure the scene."

"Where's Cox now?"

"Around the corner. Interviewing potential witnesses."

"At the bar?"

"There. And at the pool. It's spring break, everyone's grandkids are here." He rolled his eyes as if to share in a secret about spring break.

Leslie didn't respond. Instead, she hurried around the building and crossed the small beach area to the dock where she stopped, taking a moment to turn her head back toward the bar area. Hendrix had been right about the crowd. They were packed four deep around the circular bar. She spotted Cox off to the side, standing by a large swimming pool, talking to a cluster of bikini-clad young women.

Cox wasn't exactly her partner. Neither was he not her partner. When Daryl Fischer, the only assigned partner Leslie had worked with since joining the Lee County Sheriff's office as a detective, retired, her boss, Captain Karen Stetson, known to all as Boots, had said, "I'm allowing you to float for a while, work with different people. Eventually it will all work out." That had been over a year ago, with no permanent assignment in sight. The dispatcher, on the other hand, seemed to think she and Cox made a good team, seldom missing an opportunity to pair the two of them on an investigation.

"ETA for the ME team?" Leslie asked the dispatcher a few minutes after entering the pontoon boat assigned to ferry her the three hundred yards out to where the first pontoon boat was idling, presumably at the site of the floater.

"Fifteen more minutes," came the dispatcher's reply. "Need me to move them along faster?"

"No need. This guy's not going anywhere in any hurry. And neither, it seems, am I."

TWO

LESLIE TRANSFERRED OVER to the boat with the instructor, whose name, he said in answer to her query, was Henry Hernez. The man was only too happy to be relieved from keeping his eye on the dead guy. "Hey, listen," he said the moment her feet hit the transfer boat, "this is freaking me out! A few minutes ago a big air bubble popped and he turned over. Caught a glimpse of his face before he went back under! I know him! Lives over there," the instructor pointed toward the south end of the lake. "Name's Jacobi. Goes by Tac."

"Cox," Leslie said into her comm a few minutes later. "It's Leslie, here. I'm on scene with the floater. ME team's fifteen out."

"Any identification yet?"

"Nothing official, if that's what you're asking. But the guy you asked to maintain watch on the deceased, instructor guy by the name of Henry Hernez, says the deceased lives on the south shore of the lake. Name's Jacobi. Goes by Tac. Don't know it that helps, but it's all I got so far."

"More than I have. Not one of these coeds saw anything. No boat's been reported missing. Nobody's been reported missing. Nothing's been seen floating. Unless this Tac guy was going for a swim, don't know how he got out here. I'll follow up on Jacobi."

"Ten-four," Cox finished, his comm going quiet, apparently anxious to get back to his interviewing duties.

"Nobody swims in this lake," Hernez volunteered. "Not with the alligators and all!"

"Steer the boat as close to the body as you can without hitting it," Leslie directed. When the young man announced that he was as close as he could get without hitting it, Leslie hung over the side as far as she dared and peered into the water. She saw only a bare outline. Suddenly, the body flipped, as if it had come alive. "Gas!" she exclaimed. "Tac, or whatever the hell your name is, you're wearing clothes! Hernez was right. You weren't out for a casual swim. Maybe you simply fell off a dock."

Leslie quickly motioned for the boat to be moved further away, not wanting to bump the body and contaminate the investigation. She wasn't yet convinced this was a crime scene—

but why take a chance? She had the instructor shift out of gear when she was satisfied that they were far enough from the floater to not cause damage, yet not so far that she couldn't protect the scene. When the boat came to a stop, she focused her attention on the beach where several men were now moving a power boat across the sand. Large rollers were being used, such that when a roller escaped from under the boat's stern, one of the men quickly retrieved it and ran it around to the front, placing it under the bow so that for all practical purposes the boat was moving smoothly across the beach on a continuous cushion of rollers. Leslie was pleasantly surprised to read the name, **LEE COUNTY MEDICAL EXAMINER** on the starboard side of the boat. Disappointment set in when she realized her friend, Chief Investigator Langston Williams, was not among the crew on the beach.

"Leslie," Cox's voice sounded on her communicator, "the ME will be out there on scene in a few minutes. When you're free, we'll take Star's statement. I'll meet—"

"Star?"

"Young woman who found the guy. Orion Skyler. Goes by Star. I'll meet you on the dock. I understand she's over in the beach area by the boats."

"That she is," Leslie answered. *Why,* she asked herself, for perhaps the hundredth time, *does that guy bother me so much?* Before any answer came, the medical examiner's boat pulled up alongside.

"I'm the new ME Investigator," a suntanned man in his early forties announced. I'll be working alongside Lang Williams, I will. Answer to Brat. On paper my name's Bratton, but that's a real mouthful, it is. I assume you're one of the coppers assigned to this unfortunate man?"

"I am indeed. Leslie Hodges."

"Nice to know you, Hodges. How about we trade places. I mean our boats trade places. In fact, you can go back to shore if you wish. I'll signal for you when I'm ready. That work for you?"

"Matter of fact, it does." She nodded to the instructor, who, without hesitation, pushed the throttle forward and moved away from the floating body as fast as he safely could.

"That's her over there," Cox said, when Leslie stepped onto the dock a few minutes later. He was pointing in the direction of a white cabana a hundred yards or so down the beach. "Only thing I know about her, she's visiting her grandfather. Man sold his shoe-store chain for a 'Godzilla pile of money'—and that's a direct quote from one of Star's friends—and bought several multi-million-dollar homes. At least two in the U.S. and one in the hills of Italy. No one I spoke to knows anything about a wife. Apparently, Star was out paddleboarding this morning with some friends she brought down here from Sag Harbor—that's on Long Island, New York, case you're wondering—when she bumped into Mr. Tac."

"Any more on Tac's identity?"

"No one I spoke with knows anybody named Tac."

"You interview anyone other than women at the pool? What about the staff? Check with the office?"

"You implying something? Out with it."

"Just trying to determine the scope of your investigation. No need to get all defensive."

"I'm not def—"

The conversation was cut off when a gorgeous blond woman, no older than early twenties, appeared in front of them. "If you two are detectives, it's about time! I only have one more day down here and I don't intend to spend it grounded! I've been waiting over an hour as it is!"

"I'm Detective Simeon Cox," Cox said, his eyes coming alive, his demeanor clearly communicating that he was in charge. "This is my partner, Leslie Hodges. Sorry to keep you waiting. Hopefully, you can answer a few questions and be on your way."

"I don't know anything!" the defiant young woman spit out. "We were paddleboarding and my paddle hit something under the water. I looked down and saw a man's arm. It freaked me out! At first, I thought he was swimming underwater. He rolled over and I screamed! That's all I know! Can I go now?"

"What's your name?" Leslie asked, studying the young woman who obviously was accustomed to getting what she wanted, when she wanted it.

"Orion Skyler. I go by Star."

"Star. Where do you live?"

"When I'm in Florida? Or where?"

"Start with Florida?"

"In my grandfather's house."

"And that's where?"

"Around on the back part of the lake. Don't know the actual address. His name is William Paxter Skyler!" She said the name as though all who heard it would tremble. "They can tell you in the office!"

"You live there or what?" Cox asked.

"Taking a quick break. A week. Maybe two. Then off we go."

"We, who?"

"My friends and I, that's who."

"These friends, where are they now?"

"Last I saw, you were talking to them over at the pool. That's where they still are, working on their tans. We're off to Belize first of the month. And then on to Antigua for a few weeks."

"Your grandfather here now?" Leslie inquired, taking an instant dislike to this obviously over-pampered woman.

"Oh, we're never here when he's here. Not allowed. No, he's off in Italy, or somewhere, at one of his many houses, chasing his latest itch."

"What kind of itch are you talking about?" Cox asked. "Women?"

"Oh, he has all the women—and girls—he wants," Star spit out, rolling her eyes and curling her lips. "Ever since grandmama died—and even before that, if truth be known. Grosses me out, you want the truth. Women fall all over him. No, his big itch is his interest in art. Original art. Firsts, he calls them. He's right now chasing after Michelangelo—or is it da Vinci? No, it's da Vinci. Something about a trove—I think that's the word I heard—a trove of artifacts he found. Been sending his Firsts back here. His dressing room has a lock on it. That's where he keeps his art."

"These Firsts. Have you seen them? What, exactly, are they?"

"I don't have a key."

"Who does?"

"I know a neighbor does. Maybe more than one. Don't know."

"Any guess what he has in there?" Leslie pressed. "Paintings? Books? Medical sketches?"

"Some paintings. Saw them being delivered. That's how I know the neighbor has the key. Also, something wrapped up in paper. I thought it was a large blanket, but that made no sense. Ski-looking sticks hanging out. The material, whatever it was, had a sketch, several sketches, of a man with outstretched arms and legs drawn on it."

"Where exactly is he doing this chasing?" Cox asked.

"Italy."

"Where in Italy?"

"How would I know? I didn't book his trip! Besides, he doesn't fly commercial. Uses his own jet. Just goes where he wants, when he wants."

"You don't seem happy about him being in Italy," Leslie commented, picking up on Skylar's dramatic flip of the head.

"Don't care a darn for Italy. Only... only we'd been planning to use his plane to head down to the Caribbean. Had it lined up and all. This place is too, well, confining, with all the... the people and everything. The plane was all set, then he decided to fly to Italy and off he went." She wrinkled her nose. "Now we'll have to fly commercial!"

Leslie was sure Star had been about to say 'old people,' but had thought better of it.

"Can I go now? Friends are waiting. Morning sun won't last forever." She turned and gave a little wave in the direction of the pool. Several bikini-clad friends waved back.

"Go," Cox said. "I have all their names and I know where to find you should the need arise. Don't leave Miromar Lakes without checking with me first."

"Before I go, is there anything more I should know? About any relationship you have with the man out there?" Leslie pointed in the general direction of the lake behind her. "Or any relationship your grandfather has?"

"I saw him at the house a few times. I think he was there about some packages he handled for my grandpa. That's all I know."

"If you recall any..."

"Oh, just remembered. France as well."

"What about France?"

"Grandpa has a place in France. He often goes back and forth between Italy and France. I think some of his packages have come from France. Can I go now?"

"I said you could." Cox replied. "But as I said, don't leave town without permission."

THREE

"WE DREW THE NEW GUY," Cox informed Leslie on the way out to the floating crime scene. "Not much on him, other than he appears to play it by the book. Name's Bratton Goodrich. Aussie, I'm told."

"I know. I already met him. Just to say hello. When he arrived at the scene, I came ashore at your command. Other than being friendly, I have no idea what he's like."

The detectives didn't have long to wait. When they came alongside the ME's boat, a deep voice, with a distinctly Australian accent, said, "Tie up alongside, mates and come on aboard."

Stepping onto the ME's relatively small boat, Cox introduced himself, making certain to add that he was leading the investigation.

"As I told your partner, I'm the new ME Investigator. Be working alongside Lang Williams. I answer to Brat. Bratton's a bit much. You're the other copper assigned to this case. That matches what Dispatch said. Pleased to meet you, Mate." Brat then threw what passed for a salute. "Permission to come aboard."

"Do we get whistles and pipes, as well?" Cox whispered to Leslie as she stepped carefully from the pontoon boat down into the wobbly ME skiff.

"Welcome aboard," Goodrich boomed, when the two were safely in the workboat. We're just about to bring the poor man onboard. Been in the water, about four hours, judging from body temperature, and assuming for now he went in alive."

"Cause of death?"

"Can't be certain until we take a look inside and study the toxicology. I'd say from the bruising on his face, and the angle of his neck, he died from wounds incurred when he hit the water."

"As in jumping off a dock?" Cox asked. "Or—"

"If he went off a dock, someone bashed him in the face with a shovel. Real dog's breakfast his face is. Then took the shovel to the rest of his body. No, this man hit the water from altitude."

Leslie reached for her phone.

"Detective Hodges, I presume you are about to enquire what planes were in the vicinity four hours ago, let me save you the trouble. The answer is none. This is less than five miles from the airport. Air traffic controllers know who's in the vicinity of the airport. According to them, only aircraft overhead were two commercial craft, one at twenty-thousand feet and the other at twenty-four thousand. Also, there were three F-35s out of MacDill up at fifty-thousand, and a refueling tanker at thirty-five thousand, just offshore. The fighters returned to base with all personnel accounted for. Don't know about the commercial flights, but I presume if they had lost anyone, we would have known it by now. Seems a baby can't blow wind without it going viral."

"If there were no aircraft then any idea where he fell from?"

"Won't even take a swing. Remember, everything I just said is preliminary. Autopsy will help sort it. Man could have been tossed in dead for all we really know at this point. Any reason you have for not bringing the alligator's breakfast on board?"

"Not that I can see," Cox answered. "You okay with that, Les?"

"Okay," Leslie said, still processing the information they already had received. Dead man, middle of a lake, apparently killed on impact from a high altitude, with no known planes overhead. "Bring him on up. Hopefully, he'll have ID on him."

For all Brat's bluster, he instructed his team to extract the floater slowly, pausing several times so he could examine the body as it came out of the water. "Ok, then," he finally said, "over the gunnel, easy. No need to add misery to what's already been done. There, there. Piece-a-pudding."

Under what appeared to be one, or possibly two collapsed parachutes, the dead man had on shorts and a white T-shirt. No shoes or socks.

Cox observed. "He's dressed for swimming, I'd say."

"It appears that way, Mate. Appears that way."

"Nothing in his front pockets." Goodrich gently rolled the corpse onto his side and checked his back pockets. "Nothing here either. Miromar Man, then?"

"Might be. Haven't confirmed yet. Told he lives over there," Leslie said, pointing to the south end of the lake. She then took a picture of the distorted face, and several more of the dead man's body. When she finished, Goodrich announced that he was almost finished and would bring the body to shore in short order. The suggestion was that their continued presence was unnecessary.

Cox, operating from Goodrich's clear signal, motioned Leslie to get back aboard the pontoon boat, which took longer to do than it should have because the operator, a college student from

Florida Gulf Coast University, was hanging over the side vomiting up the waffles he had eaten for breakfast. By the time they arrived back on the dock the earlier crowd had mostly dispersed, prompting Cox to comment, "Wouldn't it be just great to have nothing to do but sit around and drink fancy drinks and shoot the shit all day?"

"Don't know about you, Cox, but I'd go out of my mind," Leslie replied.

A tall guy with a name badge that read Greenford helped them into the slip. When the lines were secure, Greenford asked, "What happened out there?"

"Man found deceased," Cox responded. "Your guess is as good as ours at this point how he got there. Most likely jumped from a plane." Showing Greenford a cell phone image of the deceased, Cox asked, "Ever see this guy before?"

"Hey, I'm new working here. Don't know a soul."

Handing his card to the guy, he instructed, "If you hear anything, please call. If you remember something, do the same."

"Yes, Sir."

"You a student at FGCU?"

"Second year. Drama."

"Good luck," Leslie said.

"Same to you with this guy. Hope you find out what happened."

"Oh, we will," Cox said. "We will. Just a matter of time."

"And luck," Leslie said as they walked up the stairs, heading for the bar. "What a nice place this is. Circular bar, eating area looking out over the lake. White sand. What can be bad?"

Before Cox could respond, a nicely proportioned bartender approached. Her name tag reading Crystal. "Mind telling me what's—"

"Man found deceased out in the water." Cox immediately answered, toning down a notch the usual deep smile he reserved for good-looking women. "Can't say much more than that. Do you know this man?"

Leslie held up her phone. "Ever see him around?"

"That's Tac! He's been in here a few times. Quiet guy. I put him down for a scientist. Loved art and... and come to think of it, jumping from planes. No! No. Got that wrong! Not so much jumping as the parachutes. He was into parachutes."

"How do you know that?" Cox asked.

"He was in here—sitting right over there," She replied, pointing to a table just behind where the two detectives stood."

"How do you know about the parachutes? And the art?"

"As I said, he was sitting over there with another member, Mr. Donatello Andino. Believe he was called Andy. They got to arguing. Got loud. I had to ask them to tone it down."

"About?"

"About a parachute. Whether it was genuine or not. Andy said it was, Tac claimed it wasn't. Something about wrong color—or pattern. Something like that. I thought the two of them were friends. Seen them in here a few other times. They didn't seem like friends when they left, tell you that much."

"When was that?"

"Two nights ago, it was."

"And what exactly did they say about the parachutes?" Leslie asked.

"Didn't really hear any more than I just told you. Sorry."

"Does that mean they both live here? In Miromar Lakes?"

"Sure as hell does! Tac's member number 33—"

"Don't need his number," Leslie interrupted. "Need his full name—and address—if you have it."

"Marino Jacobi. He lives in that house over there." The woman pointed in the general direction of south. "The one with the stone wall facing the beach.

"You know his number. I assume you can look up his address."

"I don't know if I'm allowed. Could get in big trouble if I—"

Cox leaned across the bar. "Crystal, there'll be even more trouble if you don't give us the address. Understand me?"

"Take me a minute. Be right back." She hurried over to a computer, entered a few keystrokes, wrote something on a piece of paper and returned. Handing the paper across the bar, she said, "Just don't say where this came from. Need my job, Man. Know what I mean?"

"Mum's the word," Cox played along, his I'm-just-a-great-ol'-guy smile now fully in place. "Can't do better than that."

On the way out of the bar area, Leslie informed her partner that a search warrant for the Jacobi house had already been obtained.

"Don't really need it, you know. Man's dead from indeterminate causes. Search of his house is proper."

"Perhaps. But as you know, it's almost automatic in cases of suspicious death. Could save our butts. In fact, we only have speculation for the deceased's identity. Name could be wrong. Address could be wrong. Who the hell knows. Judge bought Beth's probable cause argument. Asses are covered. Say, thanks,

Team." In this case the team was led by Lizbeth Hillard, their Criminal Investigative Assistant.

"Thanks, Team. Happy?" Cox said.

"I'm always happy. Now let's get on over there and see what there is to see."

Cox rang the bell, waited a moment, then rang it a second time. Nothing seemed to be moving inside the house. He called out.

Still nothing.

He slammed into the door with his shoulder. "Shit! That hurt! Like near broke my collarbone!"

"What did you expect in this neighborhood?"

He reached for his gun.

"Put that away! You're not shooting the lock off! And you're not breaking the window."

"How the hell—"

"Try the back door!"

Without a word, Cox disappeared around the corner of the house and return a moment later. "No luck. I say we—"

"Call the locksmith. That's what we do. No indication that time's critical. Knowing Beth, I bet she has one standing by. I'll check." Leslie pressed the comm button, explained to the dispatcher what she needed, then added, "Send a couple uniforms over here. This could be a crime scene. Don't need looky-loos contaminating the site until we know what we have."

"Fifteen minutes," Leslie informed Cox. "Gotta cool your heels for fifteen minutes. I was right. Beth had already ordered one. I suggest we canvas the neighbors while we're waiting."

Reluctantly, Cox fell in behind Leslie as she started down the slightly curving driveway.

They hadn't made it to the street when, from off to the side, they heard, "I see sheriff cars!"

From that direction a tall, slender man was approaching. He was wearing a Tommy Bahama straw safari hat, a yellow T-shirt with Go Tigers printed across his chest, and shorts that covered his knees. His open-toed sandals revealed a missing toe on his left foot. "Did something happen to Tac?" he yelled.

"And who are you?" Leslie responded.

The man straightened his back before responding. "Name's Bill Baxter. I happen to be President of the Homeowners Association. And a friend of Tac."

"When did you last see him?"

"Yesterday. Afternoon it was. Why? Is something wrong?"

"What makes you think something's wrong"

"You two being here! Tac doesn't usually have a lot of visitors. He keeps to himself mostly."

"Something didn't have to happen to him for us to be here. Maybe something happened to someone else—or to his house."

"Could be, I suppose."

"Do you recognize this man?" Leslie asked, holding up her phone.

"That's Tac! But what the hell happened to his face? Looks like he got hit by a Mack truck!"

"You have his full name?" Leslie asked, all business.

"Marino Jacobi."

"The name Tac? Where'd that come from?"

"No idea. Can you just tell me what happened to him?"

"That's what we're here to find out," Cox said, entering the conversation. "Any thoughts?"

"God, no! Tac's a quiet guy. Too quiet at times. Good neighbor."

"What's that mean? Can you tell us about him?" Leslie asked.

"Not a lot. As I already said, man keeps to himself. Liked to work in his garage, building things."

"What kind of things?"

"I don't know. Wooden projects. He built a kite last month. Flew it over on the golf course once or twice. Things like that."

"Did you happen to see him fly it?"

"He asked me along one time. Neat kite, I must say. Cloth wings above a box-like base. Reminded me of an air balloon carrying a... a, what do you call it? A basket thing. The cloth wings were above the basket part."

"Did it work?"

"Gandola! No, gondola's the word I was looking for. Gondola."

"Did it work?"

"He went up in a small plane and came down in the... Gondola. Brought him down perfectly. Well... almost perfect I'd say to be perfectly honest."

"What was wrong?"

"Landed in a Royal Palm. Bit of a mess that was. Scratched hell out of him, the tree did. But he called the landing good. 'As well as anybody could expect,' were his exact words. Ripped hell out of the gondola... tree did."

"Did he rebuild it?"

"I'm not sure. But last week he was working on something. I think it was another kite. Only this one was mostly cloth, not wood. And that's all I know."

A small truck with **ALMOST ALWAYS AVAILABLE LOCKSMITH** written on the side rolled down the street, coming to a stop a few feet from where Leslie stood.

"If you think of anything more," Cox said, handing Baxter his card, "please let me know. Oh, I forgot to ask, is there a Mrs. Jacobi? Or anyone else living with him in this house?"

"Not that I'm aware of. Haven't seen anyone. No one is on the guest register. As I said, that's all I know."

"Just in case, you have my card."

"I can't imagine what else I could possibly know, but I'll keep your card just in case."

FOUR

IT TOOK THE HEAVILY BEARDED LOCKSMITH less than five minutes to open the front door. While he was working, Leslie retrieved a large spool of tape from the trunk of her car forbidding anyone from entering the crime scene. "Here, tie this end to that tree near you and I'll secure the other end over there by the window," she instructed Cox. "That should be enough for the front. I'll have the uniforms cover the rest of the house."

"Did you change the lock?" Cox inquired of the man who was already packing up his tools.

"No need to. The original works perfectly well. Same key and all. The order didn't say anything about rekeying."

"Don't worry about it. If the ME wants it rekeyed she can jolly well get it done. Thanks for coming out so promptly," Leslie added.

"Pleasure to serve," the man replied.

The two detectives put on paper booties and latex gloves and were about to go inside when a sheriff's car, it's lights flashing, slid to a stop at the end of the driveway.

"Keep everyone off the property until further notice," Leslie instructed the officer. "And I mean everyone, except for the ME team. Tell them we're inside. When you get reinforcements, crime-tape the entire house. I left a roll over by the side door."

"Oh, hell!" Cox exclaimed to himself, "I didn't give Brat an update." He reached for his comm. "Cox here," he said to the dispatcher. "Inform ME Inspector Bratton Goodrich that the deceased's name is Marino Jacobi. Hodges and I will be on scene for at least an hour, maybe two."

Joining Leslie inside, he confessed. "Forgot to give Brat an update on the name and address of the vic. Just called it—"

"No worries. On the way here, I let him know. When he finishes up on the beach he said he'd join us. He's still of the opinion, Tac—Jacobi—died from a fall. He's estimating five to seven thousand feet."

"Gives new meaning to Mile High Club."

"You got a one-track mind, that's all I gotta say."

"Serves me well."

"I bet. Now pay attention and let's give this place a thorough looking at before the ME team gets here. I promised Brat we'd not touch anything until the house is released to us. At this point we don't even know what we're looking for, so hopefully we'll see something that will trigger a search direction."

"Garage's where I'd start," Cox suggested. "Seems he was into parachutes of some kind. Like to know what that's all about."

Crossing the kitchen, they spotted a wallet and cell phone neatly stacked on the marble surface of the kitchen island. "Love to get my hands on that phone," Cox said. "See who he was communicating with."

"Soon enough," Leslie said, calming her own desire for information. "Right now we wait for prints to be taken. Less chance of smudging anything?"

"I'm with you on that, partner. Here's the garage door," Cox called. "Let's see what Tac's been up to."

The garage held a full workshop with just enough room in the middle for a red, 60's vintage MG. Over the car, a liftable platform held strips of wood, piles of fabric, and several large spools of rope of varying sizes, some labeled Dacron, others labeled nylon. The spools were mounted so that they would rotate when their respective line was pulled. Nine canvas harnesses hung on the far wall with a spot open for a tenth.

"Unless I miss my guess, that platform over there," Cox commented a moment later, pointing to a second platform up against the ceiling in the far corner, "has over a hundred parachutes of all sizes! And over there," Cox now pointed to a set of shelves against a wall, "are plastic bins with buckles and all sorts of connectors and stuff. This guy was really into jumping."

"Looks that... We're in the garage," Leslie yelled. "That you, Brat?"

"Didn't hear him enter," Cox said. "You sure they're here?"

"That's because you were talking," Leslie called over her shoulder, already back in the kitchen, walking in the direction of the tall Australian.

"Your mate here with you?" Goodrich asked when he saw Leslie, his hard face softening as she approached. "Or did you ditch him?"

"In the garage."

"Car buff is he, now?"

"Looking over the parachute material. This Jacobi guy was a... well, I don't know exactly what he was. He liked to make parachutes—or so it appears. He obviously likes kites. Garage's outfitted very professionally. Even has spools of rope and lots of canvas straps."

"Hey Brat," Cox called from behind Leslie, "how about dusting his wallet and phone. Like to see who he last called. Check for messages, as well."

"In due course. First things first," the crime scene investigator answered, bristling at being told how to conduct his job.

"What's that mean? Time's a wasting."

"Been a long day, mate. So don't be going off on me. We'll get on it soon enough. Why don't you and your partner go about your business. I'll have the phone, and whatever else we gather, brought over to your office when we're finished here. How's that work for you?"

"I don't think—"

"That'll work just fine," Leslie interrupted, knowing that she and Cox needed the county investigator more than he needed them. Squabbling would only delay the investigation. "We'll just do a quick walk around and get out of your way. Call us, if you will, when you're ready and we can arrange to meet."

Not being able to move anything, they found nothing further of interest in the house. On the way to their cars, Cox, walking briskly to keep up with Leslie, called, "Why'd you let that Aussie off the hook? He could have dusted the cell first."

"We're going to need him down the line. Break his ass now, he'll bust yours later. Goes with the territory, and you know it only too well. What's really eating you?"

"Frig'n guy falls out of the sky and nobody sees anything! That's what! People don't fall from nowhere! There had to be a plane, something. Someone saw something!"

"Devil's Advocate. Do we really know when Tac hit the water? Maybe it was dark out? When we know how long he was in the water, we'll know what to look for. Maybe it was yesterday? Middle of the night? You're getting ahead of yourself."

"We know one thing!"

"And that one thing is?"

"There's a chute missing."

"How'd you know that?"

"That platform. The one over the car."

"Yea."

"Had a space all cleared out. And... and it had tie-down bolts. And an open lock!"

"When Brat's finished with the house we'll go back and see if we can scare up anything. Love to know what the lock—"

"Ten-Thirty-Three! Ten-Thirty-Three!" Both of their coms came alive at the same time. "Active shooter! Costco parking lot! All available units! Use extreme caution. Repeat. Use extreme caution!"

"Hodges and Cox!" Leslie responded running to her car. "We're on our way! Three minutes out!" Turning to her partner, she yelled, "I'll drive! Leave your car. We're coming back here any way!"

Cox jumped into the already moving car. Out through the exit gate they flew, her right bumper slighting nudging the slowly opening gate, lights and siren blaring.

"You almost bought it that time!" Cox chided. "Sheriff won't be happy, getting your car nicked up. Or for that matter, having the HOA lodge a complaint."

"Make yourself useful. Provide our location and ETA to dispatch."

The massive main Miromar fountain, spewing water upwards as it did all year long allowing it to trickle down over a depiction of the four seasons, was mostly a blur as Leslie sped past. She turned right onto Ben Hill Griffen avoiding the vehicles that had haphazardly stopped for her. A moment later she turned left into the Gulf Coast Town Center. She suddenly braked hard, throwing them both hard against their seat belts.

"What the hell you—"

Her door flew open. "Get your protective gear on! Who the hell knows what's going on over there!"

Cox followed his partner to the trunk, which, by pre-arrangement, held his protective gear as well as hers stacked neatly for each of them. They were both back in the car within a minute. Cox strapped his vest in place, then asked Leslie if she wanted help with hers.

"I'm fine, thanks," she answered, concentrating on maneuvering her car around cars again randomly pulled to the side to let her pass.

"Have it your—"

"Ten-Thirty-Three! Ten-Thirty-Three!" the radio blared. "Shooter's location is now the Costco gas pumps! Repeat: Shooter's location is the Costco gas pumps. Use extreme caution. Two down. Ambulance dispatched. Four uniform cars, ETA three minutes. Also, two detectives, Hodges, Cox, street clothes, ETA less than one minute. Repeat: Use extreme caution! Scene is active. One shooter confirmed, possibly two!"

"Sounds like we'll be first on scene," Cox said. "Be sure your vest is snapped before you exit the car."

"Ten-four to that, partner. This isn't my first rodeo." Leslie said, turning left just before reaching the gas pumps. "Gas pumps are over there," she said to Cox, nodding to their right. "Just on the other side of those hedges. Inform dispatch we're on scene. See the shooter yet?"

"Nothing yet."

Leslie slowed as she turned right into the area where cars lined up for the pumps. Only a few cars remained, their drivers and passengers crouched low behind their dashboards, trying to protect themselves. "See anything?"

"Nothing," Cox replied. "Oh, there he is! See only one!" Cox pressed his comm button. "Shooter in sight! Standing near the pump furthest south, away from the building. He's waving cars away! Don't see a second shooter."

"Third person reported shot," the comm announced. "White Lexus. Male. Forty-five. Head wound."

"Over there!" Leslie yelled, pointing to an area twenty feet from the pump. "White Lexus! New York plates. I'm positioning our car between the shooter and the Lexus. That should shield medical!"

Cox instructed Leslie to stay low, adding, "So he can't get you through the windshield!"

A bullet glanced off the hood of their car almost at the same instant that the words had come out of Cox's mouth. Leslie slammed her foot on the brake. The cruiser slid to a stop ten yards from the shooter just as the windshield exploded, spraying shards of glass over them. Both doors flew open in unison as the officers prepared to dive to the ground.

"Stay low!" Cox continued to remind Leslie as he threw himself out of the passenger-side door to the pavement.

"Permission to engage!" their comms announced. "Repeat: You have permission to engage the shooter. Medical is one minute out and has been advised not to approach any closer until instructed. Cox, you're senior on site. It's your scene!"

"Roll out, Leslie!" Cox called from his position on the ground behind the passenger door.

"Can't! My vest's stuck!" It had caught on the turn signal lever as she had attempted to leave the vehicle. The unexpected sudden tug had turned her sideways and held her head high enough to be exposed to the shooter. Her body hung against the car, her left knee just scraping the ground as she struggled to free the vest.

A shot rang out, the slug again ricocheting off the car frame, this time embedding itself in the driver-side headrest where her head had been a second or two earlier. Leslie did her best to keep her head as far down as possible while she slowly worked her way back into the car to free her vest. From the sound of the approaching sirens, she knew not to expect help for at least another two minutes—an eternity with an active shooter. What she knew, she assumed the shooter knew as well. She braced for a barrage of shots.

"Sheriff!" Cox called in a loud deep voice. "Drop your weapon!"

Immediately, in answer to his demand, a bullet slammed into the door he was positioned behind. Then a second. Followed immediately by a third and a fourth.

"Assault weapon!" Leslie called to Cox, lifting her head from the seat so she could be heard. She reached for the turn signal to free her vest and a bullet buried itself in the seat back less than an inch from her head. The smell of burnt gunpowder filled her nostrils. She forced her arm upward so that her fingers could slide the vest free of the signal control lever. Twice her hand slipped, causing her chin to slam against the steering wheel. Each time that happened the shooter fired a round. The second bullet came within an inch of her hand.

A sheriff's car came to a sliding stop behind her, just off to the left. Before their passenger door was fully open, two shots hit it mid-center.

"Drop your weapon!" Cox again shouted.

He was answered with two bullets hitting the door, this time near the bottom.

"Shit!" he yelled, "he's aiming for my legs!"

"You're surrounded!" called a uniformed officer who was now crouching behind the car door of the cruiser that had just arrived. "This is the Lee County Sheriff! Drop your gun! Put your hands—!"

Leslie looked back in time to see, and hear, several rounds hit the asphalt under the door in the location where the officer was kneeling. Sucking in her breath, she gathered her strength. *Go!* she commanded herself, lunging upward at the sound of her own voice.

Her vest slid over the end of the lever allowing it to slip free. She tumbled out of the car while at the same time managing to pull the vest tight around her body.

"Officer under fire!" Leslie yelled into her comm. "Civilian in the line of fire! Return fire is unadvised!"

The comm didn't respond, but the shooter did. Two rounds hit the car door just above where Leslie was kneeling. She moved to her right closer to the cab so she could see though the hinge area between the door and the body of the car. The shooter held a woman hostage in front of him. Leslie had no safe shot. "Shit," she exclaimed in exasperation. "Shit, shit, shit!"

A third sheriff car joined them, this one parked thirty yards further away and off to the left.

"Car three-eighteen, now on scene," the comm announced. "Five minutes until three more cars arrive. Tactical is also five minutes out."

The passenger-side door of car three-eighteen opened, but before the officer could exit the vehicle, two shots rang out. One smashed into the windshield, causing it to explode as Leslie's had. The other slug hit the open car door.

That was the bad news. The good news, as observed by Leslie from her perch behind her car's door hinge, was that the shooter had turned slightly sideways just before he shot at the newly arrived sheriff's car. When he turned, he moved slightly away from his hostage, opening a line of fire between himself and the terrified hostage.

"Car three-eighteen," Leslie said into her comm, "on my command, count to three and then yell, *Sheriff! Drop your weapon!* You'll take fire, so observe all precautions."

"Ten-four," came the immediate reply from car three-eighteen.

Leslie steadied her Glock on the car door's hinge and carefully aimed her weapon as she had practiced so often in the comfort of the firing range. She focused the sight several inches to the shooter's right. That's where she anticipated the center of his head would be when he fired at the officer behind her in car three-eighteen. Calming herself with several deep breaths, she said into the comm, "Car three-eighteen. Begin your count!" Her eyes remained glued to the target as she silently began the count down.

Remembering her instruction, she took a deep breath on the count of One. She let it out on Two. She was steady now, but the shooter's head was directly behind the hostage. Three! A round hit the asphalt in front of where Leslie was positioned and slammed into Leslie's right leg. But the shooter hadn't moved. Pain shot up through her body, almost blocking out the sound of the officer in the car behind her yelling, "Sheriff! Drop your weapon!" The shooter twisted slightly to his right and a shot rang out. Then a second. Both hitting the car door of the deputy who had just yelled.

The shooter could not have fired a third shot; his head had exploded, covering his hostage with blood and brain matter.

Leslie Hodges didn't see her bullet hit home. She had already passed out.

FIVE

SERGEANT HUDSON OAKMORE, Leslie's immediate superior, along with Captain Karen Stetson, her commanding officer, had been waiting for nearly three hours to talk with her. Leslie had not arrived at the hospital unconscious as the TV news had reported but had regained consciousness by the time the first paramedic had arrived at her side in the Costco parking lot. That allowed her to flash a thumbs-up to Stetson outside of the hospital. Stetson's return salute raised her spirits.

"I hope you know you're one lucky woman," the young emergency room doc informed her after examining her right ankle. Why your Kevlar vest was down at your ankles I don't know. But it essentially stopped the bullet. You passed out when the vest slammed into your peroneal nerve. Had the bullet itself struck you, your foot would be gone. Most likely, you would have bled out before the paramedics arrived. As it is, it'll be tender for a week or so, but nothing permanent."

"Will I have limitations? Long term? Or even short term?"

"None. Might need a bit of pain management for twenty-four hours or so. Beyond that, you're good to go. Between you and me, how you got that shot off is beyond me. Great shot as well. Guy didn't have a chance. We're putting you in a private room. Let me know when you're ready for visitors."

Lying in her bed, Leslie struggled to understand exactly what had happened, who had done what, and when. She thought she had it right, but the time frame nagged at her. When had she been hit? Before she had discharged her weapon? Or after? She recalled the pain, but it felt like she was dreaming pain. A nightmare dream happening, but not happening, all at the same time. She remembered pulling the trigger of her weapon, then nothing. Yet, from what she had overheard, the shooter died instantly from her bullet, so she had to have been shot *before* she pulled the trigger. Perhaps, they had each shot at the same time. Unlikely, but nothing else made sense.

She knew from prior experience that the discharge of her weapon meant that suspension would be automatic until Internal Affairs cleared her. She also knew that she would have one chance, and only one chance, to tell her story. How the words came out of her mouth the first time would determine her future. And nothing she could ever say again would change how Sheriff Radcliff would define her actions. That definition was key to a range of options, beginning with her possible dismissal from the force and being prosecuted for murder, and extending all the way to a public commendation. Any false or equivocal fact she uttered would be used against her. Today's police environment was a far cry from what it had been when she first went through the academy in 2009. Then, she would have been innocent, until proven otherwise, with all presumptions going her way. Today, in most situations it seemed as if the presumptions would go against her. Taking a deep breath, she pushed the call button, suddenly anxious to get the show on the road so she could get out of the hospital and go home.

"I'm ready," she told the nurse. A moment later, a tall stocky woman with shoulders that would make a football lineman proud, hurried to her side. "Let them in," Leslie instructed. "I'm as ready as I'll ever be."

"I don't think you know what all's out there," the husky-voiced nurse replied. "On this floor alone there're about a dozen people who want a piece of you. The auditorium downstairs is full. Don't want to think about what's outside."

"I heard the shooter's dead. Was anyone else hit—or dead?"

"Sorry, Detective, I've been instructed to say nothing other than answer your medical questions. Doctor ordered one at a time be allowed in here. You can stop the parade any time you wish. Just push the call button. I'll be just outside your door."

"You have your work cut out for you. No one can stop that bunch. Seen it before."

"Don't bet on that, young lady. Doctor took a liking to you. That's why he assigned me. Played rugby in college. Former Navy Corpsman. Served two tours in Afghanistan. Helmand Province. This, my dear, is a piece of cake."

"We'll see about that. Let them in."

The nurse disappeared through the door. A moment later Captain Stetson took her place. "Nurse said you're ready for visitors. How you are doing?"

"Other than pain in my right foot, not all that bad."

"Broken?"

"Doctor says not. Bruise where the vest was hit. Nothing broken, thank God."

"Run that by again? I'm told you were shot in the foot. Bullet passed under the door. What was your vest doing down—?"

"Got stuck on the turn signal. When I broke it free it dropped to the ground. Saved my leg."

"Lucky you! Suppose you know the shooter's dead."

"I heard that? I didn't see my shot hit him."

"I'm turning on the recorder. You're going on record. Hopefully, this will be your only official statement since everything that happened out there was captured by video. At least ten bystanders had their cells running, not to mention dashboard cameras from six department cars. If there's an angle missed, I'd be surprised."

"What can I add then? And don't I get a union rep?"

"The rep is up to you. Only then, we must do this with Internal Affairs. Want to continue or—"

"Continue is fine. If you think that's best."

"As I said, what physically happened is all on tape. But only you know what you were thinking, what you saw. That's all that's missing. This was a clean kill. When you give your statement, we close the record. Simple as that."

"Okay."

"Good to go?"

"Good to go," Leslie repeated.

"Okay. Tape's on." Stetson proceeded to identify herself, then Leslie. She added the name of the hospital, date, and time. She then looked at Leslie, smiled, and said, "You're on, Leslie." In a voice as serious as Leslie had ever heard it, Captain Stetson said, "Please tell me what you saw, starting from when your car stopped in the Costco gas station lot at three-twenty-five on this day. Take your time. Think about it."

"The man—I'd put his height at six-one, weight, I'd say, two-ten—was standing next to a gas pump, holding what I believed to be a semi-automatic rifle in his right hand. He had his left hand around the neck of a white woman in her late forties, early fifties. We, my partner, Simeon Cox and I, spotted him by the pumps. I was driving. I positioned the car as close to him as I could."

"How close was that?"

"About twenty yards. Off to his right as he faced us. I positioned the car so the door would act as a shield so to speak. Almost immediately, rounds from his weapon began hitting the windshield. We both ducked down."

"Were you wearing your protective gear?"

"Cox was. Mine wasn't fastened."

"And why was that?"

"I had stopped to retrieve the protective gear from the trunk. Since I was driving, I thought it was more important that we get on scene than to take the time to tighten the vest. I put it on but didn't take the time to fasten it. I know it's not—"

"Go on, Detective Hodges," Stetson gently encouraged, trying to protect Leslie from admitting that the vest she was referring to was an older zip-up version. Knowing Leslie as she did, she assumed the vest had been her late husband's from the Tampa Police Department, maybe even the one he had been wearing when he was killed responding to a bank robbery. "What did you do when the shots hit your windshield?"

"Slouched down in my seat and worked the door open. That's when a vest strap caught on the turn signal lever and I couldn't slide out. More shots were fired. Another unit arrived and stopped behind and off a bit to my left. Perp fired at them once, maybe twice. During that time, I got the strap off the lever and managed to slide out of the car. The vest slid to the ground, apparently propped against the door. I'm guessing it made a barricade. Between the vest and the door my legs were protected. That's when I saw the perp shoot from beside the hostage. He leaned away from the woman when he raised the weapon. I instructed the deputy in the car behind me to call out on my command. I wanted to encourage the perp to shoot when I was in a position to take advantage of the open space he would present when he shot."

"Keep going. You're doing fine. What happened next?"

"Not much more to tell. When the perp leaned away from the hostage I fired. Didn't see what happened after that."

Stetson pointed out that video shot by a pedestrian showed Leslie being hit before she had fired. In response, Leslie simply replied, "I was concentrating on the shot, making certain I wouldn't hit the hostage. I wasn't aware of being hit myself."

"Anything more you care to add?"

"Can't think of a thing."

"Okay. Recorder's... off."

"Cap, can you tell me how many people were hit? Anyone die, I mean beside the shooter?"

"Five hit. No other deaths, thank God. Three of our cars ripped apart, yours included."

"Will I be put on—"

"Sheriff watched it live. Most of it anyway. He said, and I quote, 'Give that gal an atta-girl from me!' I won't repeat what he said about the shooter. But you know he likes to say, 'You come to Lee County with a gun and crime on your mind, you leave in a body bag!' You're now the sheriff's poster child. You proved the rule. He doesn't want you sitting on the bench, even though a man died at your hand. That means a hearing. There's nothing to discover. It's all on video. And your story matches perfectly. You need to see the counsellor, but that's a formality. You're back at work the moment the doctor okays it."

"Thank you."

"Don't thank me. Thank the sheriff. You've solved more capital cases in the relatively short time you've been in the department than anyone currently on the payroll. If the man played favorites, you'd be it."

"Just doing what I get paid to do. Mostly luck."

"Don't sell yourself short., Leslie. You even have Cox shaping up. He's turning out to be a good cop. All thanks to you. You're the one saw the good in him. Speaking of Cox, I see he's lead on your new one. The floater found in the lake over at Miromar. Should be easy to wrap that one up. I'm putting my money on suicide."

"Don't know what to make of that one. Suicide's a possibility. Either from a small plane or off the dock. Although ME thinks suicide off the dock isn't in the cards because of the damage to the man's head. Believes he fell from over a thousand feet, and most likely even higher."

"Didn't I read your note saying there was no plane in the vicinity?"

"You did. That's what puzzles me, to be honest."

"That's what you're being paid to find out. Run that angle to ground. FYI, I've instructed Cox that you're to be lead on this case. That is, when you're released. Other than Cox, is there anyone you want to see? Half the world's out there. Including two of your *special* friends. Allen Smith, and—"

"That's long over!"

"And... Pete Jakowski."

"Jak! What the devil's he doing down here? Thought he was at home in Pittsburgh."

"I thought you two...?" Stetson, seeing the look on Leslie's face, cut off her question.

"Cooling off stage," Leslie volunteered. "He needs to resolve his home life before we move on."

"I see," the captain replied, assimilating this bit of information with what she already knew. "Should I send him away?"

"No, I'll see him. You can, however, do me a favor and send everyone else home. And... and... thanks, Captain, for having my back."

Stetson threw a crisp salute, and without saying another word, left the room.

"Why the hell are you here? I thought we agreed that—"

"Agreements don't hold when you make national news—especially the way you did it."

"You flew down because of the Costco thing?"

Instead of answering, the big Pittsburgh cop flopped down in the only chair in the room, a smile slowly spreading across his rugged face.

"Or... or" Leslie added, the full picture dawning on her, "you never went north?"

"I plead the fifth."

"You think that's funny?" Leslie forced herself to sound angry with the man she had been, and could still be, in love with. The man sitting across from her, one of the few she would allow in the hospital room, had a wife. 'Estranged and about to become an ex,' as Jakowski had repeatedly reminded her. But he was married just the same.

"Wasn't meant to be funny," Jakowski chuckled, "just a fact. Okay, if I must confess, I never went north. Truthfully, there's nothing up there for me. Lawyer advised me to stay away. He says the more I interfere, the worse it'll be for me. Captain settled it when he forced me to take accumulated vacation."

Realizing that Jakowski's face had grown solemn as he spoke, Leslie decided not to press him for details. "So, Big Guy, what've you been doing since—how long's it been? Three months since we last spoke?"

"Five. But who's counting? You were clear about one thing. Until the divorce was final, I was not to call. You even said, and I quote, 'That if I even so much as drove by your house, I was in great danger of getting shot'. Just following your rules."

"So, what have you been doing? I can't believe you had five months' vacation."

"Lucky for me, I'm on loan to the Fed task force. For the most part, working with Agent Ghana on Seminal Society collector shenanigans."

The Seminal Society collectors, as Leslie had learned, are a group of billionaires who collect artifacts, usually First items, from Seminal Society geniuses who span the fourteenth to the twentieth centuries. The collectors believe that Oswald Von Wolkenstein, composer, 1376 to 1445; Leonardo da Vinci, artist, inventor, 1452 to 1519; Galileo Galilei, father of science; 1564 to 1642; Isaac Newton, laws of motion; 1643 to 1727; Ernst Chladni, father of acoustics; 1756 to 1827; and Thomas A Edison, sound recording,1847 to 1931; all share a common soul. Leslie had investigated four deaths relating to thefts of Seminal Society Firsts, so she knew all about the Seminal Society and the quirky billionaire collectors who would stop at nothing to possess an original creation from anyone of them.

"Leslie!" Jakowski exclaimed, suddenly concerned, "Your eyes went blank at the mention of Ghana. What's that about? Are you okay?"

"Just thinking of the Seminal Society is all."

"That was too much of a reaction for the Semin... Oh shit! You think maybe she and I are—"

"If you want her, then go for it! I'm not stopping you! That thought hadn't even crossed my mind. Are you telling me something?"

"Hell, no! It's just that—"

"The Seminal Society! That's all I think about. The Galileo Telescope Trial—that's what the papers call it—is about to start. And I don't know what to expect."

"That's another reason why I'm here. As you know, I'm a witness."

"So, they decided to call you? I understood they didn't need you."

"Plans change; I guess."

"Can't wait to get that one behind me," Leslie admitted. "Been thinking of little else for months now. Edison's phonograph. Chladni's euphon. Newton's manuscript. Galileo's telescope! It's not just that these billionaires acquire valuable art, but that because they are so determined to get what they want, crimes are usually committed."

"Billionaires can have anything they want," Jakowski agreed. "Yet they never seem to be happy, not even when they successfully acquire things that are forbidden to everyone else. The Firsts from the Seminal Society are perfect examples of this behavior."

"Isn't justification wonderful? Covers over a boatload of sins."

"Look at it this way, Leslie. It keeps them from destroying the planet."

"Jak, now you lost me."

"Unlimited wealth, coupled with boredom, make for a bad combination. These folks are just as capable of starting a war as they are of stealing a painting from a museum. For my money, I'd sooner have them concentrate on artifact collecting. What's the big harm if a museum has one less piece—or a forgery substituted for the real item—on display. Who really cares?"

"Cynical now, are we?"

"Tell me with a straight face I'm wrong. Bet you can't."

"If people didn't die in the process of their collection efforts, I might be in your camp, Jak. Unfortunately, we have at least four dead—that we know about. Keeps me up at night."

"Want a cure—to your sleepless nights?"

"Don't go there, Jakowski. Just don't go there. Keep replaying my quote."

The door closed behind the big Pittsburgh cop and immediately swung back open, this time with her partner framed in the doorway. "Boots says you're good to go. You don't know how happy I am to hear that. Got to say, you look better than I thought you would after seeing you lying crumpled on the ground. Never want to see that ever again!" Cox took a step in her direction and stopped, a puzzled expression on his face. "Can I at least hug you? A friendship hug. Nothing more."

"Of course."

Cox approached her and tentatively allowed his arms to encircle her, pulling her body close to his. In her ear he confessed, "Partner, you don't know how scared I was when I saw you go down. It felt as if my own life was over. Glad it was all superficial. Don't know what I would do if it was your turn to go."

When Cox pulled back, Leslie said, "I'm not giving you any time to find out. Be back tomorrow."

"Boots asked me to persuade you to take time off. She suggested a week. I told her she'd be lucky if you took a day."

"Not on your life. Perps have kicked me worse during an arrest. Bit sore. Nothing I can't handle."

"Maybe compromise and come in an hour or two late? You and Jak could—"

"Cox!"

"Okay! Okay! Got the message. What the hell's he doin' down here anyway?"

"How the hell should I know?"

"Then I take it you two aren't—"

Leslie took a step back, faking anger. Sitting on the side of the bed, she said, "Cox! How the hell many times need I tell you that my relationship with Jakowski—whatever the hell it is—is off limits to you?"

Cox held his ground. "You confuse me, is all. One minute you're travelling 'round the world with him. The next minute he's persona non grata. Then I see him in your hospital room. Tell me it isn't confusing."

"I'm not telling you anything!"

"Wouldn't be much of a detective if I didn't wonder what gives?" Cox pressed.

"If you must know," Leslie relented, "we're on hold until his divorce is final. Then we'll see how I feel." Privately, Leslie was thinking her time with Jakowski had been a mistake and it was time to move on with her life.

"Why's he down here then?"

"Says he's working with Ghana. More Seminal Society shit."

"Believe him?"

"No reason not to," Leslie responded, defensively. "No reason not to."

Cox's eyes closed for a moment, taking time to form his thoughts. "Les, this is interesting. Hadn't considered this before now. But in thinking of the Seminal Society, I think of thefts of Edison, Chladni, Newton, and Galileo."

"And in that exact order!" Leslie exclaimed, suddenly realizing what Cox was about to point out. "That's the exact order—actually, reverse order—of how the common soul is believed to have gone from one body to the next! Are you thinking—"

"Exactly!" Cox confirmed. "Not only are the collectors going for Firsts, but they're also playing a game! Doing it in reverse order!"

"And the next in that order is da Vinci." Leslie slid off the bed. "Come on, we—"

"Whoa! You're not going anywhere until you're released. Get back in that bed!"

Leslie stopped herself from going into the bathroom to change but didn't get back in bed. Instead, she turned to him. "We heard the name da Vinci earlier today" she said. "But I can't recall exactly—" She closed her eyes, forcing the conversations of the day to play back in her mind. "It's coming back now."

"That total recall of yours is sure something," Cox acknowledged, not for the first time. "What's the context?"

"You and I were interviewing one of the... women down on the beach over at Miromar. She and her friends were staying at her grandfather's house. I asked if her grandfather was home, thinking we'd go and interview him. She said he was, and I quote, 'off in Italy, or somewhere, chasing his latest itch.' You asked what that itch would be. Her answer, abbreviated a bit, was, and again I quote, 'he has this interest in art. Original art. Firsts, he calls them. He's right now chasing after Michelangelo—or da Vinci. One of them.' You think that's a coincidence? I don't."

"Eerie. If nothing else," Cox responded. "Now I recall that conversation. It was on the beach with the woman who found the floater, Jacobi."

"You would remember her."

"Now who's doing it?"

"Sorry," Leslie apologized, climbing fully back onto the bed, her legs dangling over the side. "If the ME secured the house, then tomorrow's soon enough. We didn't see much on the first go-around."

"We also didn't get into the private locked room," Cox reminded Leslie. "Need to do that. Sooner rather than later. I agree."

"We need to talk to the granddaughter as well."

"I'll get it set up," Cox assured Leslie. "How about noon tomorrow?"

Leslie nodded her assent, her mind replaying the full day's conversations.

"Hate to interrupt your concentration, Les, but I forgot. Boots gave me your phone. Told me to give it to you when you were ready for work." Handing it to her, Cox said, "Here, don't say I never gave you anything."

A moment later, Leslie said, "Got several messages. Not surprising. Always happens when you're in the news. Bunch of well-wishers." She began punching buttons.

Cox watched from across the room as she cleared message after message, barely listening to the content. Suddenly, she called, "Hey! Listen to this!"

Switching her phone to speaker mode, they both heard the caller say, "I'm Roo Pecking. I'm a pilot. Please call me back. It's important."

"Think it has something to do with the floater?" Cox asked.

"Can't imagine what else," Leslie answered, pressing the return call button.

"Detective," the male voice answered without an initial greeting, "my lawyer says I can't talk to you without him."

"Am I speaking with Mr. Pecking?" Leslie asked, not deterred.

"You are. I'm him."

"What's this about?"

"I've been told to say nothing."

"Then why did you call me?"

"I left that message before I called the lawyer."

"You answered my call, so—"

"Call my lawyer. Name's Bear Breaker."

"That Roo guy's shaking in his boots," Cox commented when the conversation ended. "What the hell'd he do? If this isn't related to Jacobi, I'll eat my hat."

"Lawyer Breaker has a reputation as a tough guy," Leslie informed her partner. "Bark worse than his bite. Word on him, as they say in Texas, all hat, no cattle."

"This is Detective Cox calling Attorney Breaker," Cox said into his phone a moment later. "I believe he's expecting a call from the Lee County Sheriff's Office. This is that call." Holding his hand over the phone, Cox turned to Leslie, "Got the secretary. Let's see how they handle this."

"Yes, I believe he is," the pleasant-sounding woman responded almost immediately. "I'm afraid he's busy for the remainder of the day. I can set up an appointment for you in his office at ten in the morning if you wish."

"See you at ten," Cox answered. "Please have your client present."

SIX

THE STENCILED NAME on the frosted glass door panel read:

BERNARD 'BEAR' BREAKER

ATTORNEY AT LAW

CRIMINAL DEFENSE
PERSONAL INJURY

WALK-INS WELCOME

Breaker's office was one block east of the Caloosahatchee River, on a street featuring several hairdressers, at least three nail and spa shops, a luncheonette, a cigar store, two coffee cafes, a used clothing store, and a bodega. The bodega was stuffed with a little bit of everything, with items spilling onto tables on the front sidewalk.

"Can't imagine not finding anything I'd ever want right here on this street," Cox commented, slowing his pace to match his partner's, who was not walking as fast as she usually did.

"Only thing missing," Leslie volunteered, "is a gun and ammo store."

"I believe I saw one over on the next block, near where we parked."

"That you did," Leslie acknowledged. "Along with several criminal law offices."

"Your leg doing okay? You're walking—"

"Fine. Just fine. Maybe a little bit stiff, but nothing I can't handle." She pushed open the door, expecting a lobby full of people waiting for the lawyer. Instead, the small room held six chairs, all empty. There was no receptionist, nor a desk for a receptionist. Leslie scanned the room for a bell to ring, or a button to push, to signal they were in the waiting room. The only thing she saw, other than a plaque proclaiming Bernard 'Bear' Breaker one of the Ten Best Criminal Lawyers in Fort Myers, was a small paper sign instructing visitors to TAKE A SEAT AND WAIT FOR THE LAWYER. The message was repeated in Spanish.

"How long you suppose we'll have to wait?" Cox said, pacing the room. "I have half a mind to—"

The only door in the room opened, revealing a man sporting a loosely fitted tie, no taller than five foot four, weighing well over two hundred pounds, with tufts of dark-brown hair hanging down almost to his eyes. "Welcome, detectives. I'm attorney Breaker. Glad you're on time. Got a very busy morning. Follow me inside." He abruptly turned and disappeared back through the doorway.

Leslie threw a glance at Cox, as if to say, "This'll be fun." They followed Breaker into what turned out to be a hallway leading to another set of offices. This time there was a proper receptionist. In a bull-pen area behind the receptionist sat about a dozen people, working at computer screens. It was impossible to know if they were lawyers, secretaries, paralegals, or possibly even clients filling out paperwork. Leslie figured it was a mix of people, with probably an investigator or two mixed in. The fireplug of a lawyer was waiting for them in a glass-enclosed office off to the side.

"I'm Leslie Hodges," she said, extending her hand, prepared to having it crushed. Breaker didn't disappoint. Forcing herself not to wince, she continued, "And this is my partner, Simeon Cox."

Now it was Cox's turn to not show weakness to the crushing handshake. He went a step further, returning the pressure to a draw.

"You're here on the—" The attorney caught himself, then said, "Why don't you just tell me why you're here? Oh, and please take seats, won 't you? I'd offer you coffee, but we're busy out there right now as you can see. Murder trial starting in the morning. First degree, no less."

Leslie wasn't aware of any homicide cases beginning soon in any Florida court close enough for him to still be in his office but let his boast stand unchallenged. She began, "I received a call, actually a message, from someone calling himself Roo Pecking. The message said to call back. When I did, he wouldn't talk. Said to call you. That's what brings us here. Your secretary set ten o'clock. So here we are."

"Woman of few words, I see."

"Need you to fill in around the edges here," Leslie answered, refusing to be pushed around. "Why are we here? Why did this Roo guy call in the first place?"

"Why do clients do anything?" Breaker replied. "Who the hell ever knows?"

"You—or he— set this meeting," Cox interrupted, "so stop playing cat and mouse! Why the hell did your client call Detective Hodges?"

"Ever hear of the fifth amendment, Detective? Bet you have. I don't—"

"What're you trying to tell us?" Leslie demanded. "He did something illegal? He's the one called us. Hope this is not a wild goose hunt."

"He called before he knew his rights."

"You, sir, are wasting our time," Leslie said, standing and turning toward the door. Cox right behind her.

"Sit! Both of you! I have information for you from an anonymous source. Information I believe you will want to have."

"Better be good," Leslie said, nodding to her partner to follow her lead.

"A pilot, small plane pilot, took a passenger up for a ride yesterday at daybreak. Didn't register his flight, said he didn't go over five thousand feet. But he did fly out near RSW during a TFR."

"Over Miromar Lakes by chance?" Cox asked.

Leslie threw Cox a threatening glance but said nothing.

"Over Miromar Lakes," Breaker conceded. "Yes."

"You know, that's—" Cox began but stopped when Leslie's knee hit his.

"I very well know being within the Temporary Flight Restricted area is a major problem, Detective. That's one reason why this is anonymous. You understand me?"

"Go on!" Leslie said, not allowing Cox time to respond. "What does your client want to tell us beside the fact he violated FAA rules?"

"Here's the thing. We want immunity from the FAA. Client can't afford to lose his license. Makes his living with his plane."

"You know of course," Leslie said, "we can't grant federal immunity, even if we wanted to."

"This is one of those situations where if it was up to me, I'd tell you absolutely nothing. Client waved me off. He insists. Please do your best to keep him from being grounded. Promise me that much."

"That much I can promise," Leslie nodded. "Do my best. Nothing more."

Attorney Breaker sat back in his chair, as if he had just won a major concession. "I'll accept your word, Detective. According to the news reports, a man by the name of Marino Jacobi was found in a lake out that way. The way my client tells it, his passenger jumped from the plane over one of those lakes. He knows the man only by the name Tac. Believes it's the same man."

"Jumped?" Cox exclaimed. "Just opened the door and jumped out?"

"This guy, Tac, or whatever his name is, was wearing some sort of pack. Rather large one I believe. Had wooden struts. He pushed the pack out and jumped behind it. Pilot believes he was strapped to the pack but isn't one hundred percent positive."

"Like a parachute?" Leslie asked.

"Like a parachute, yes."

"What's Roo's full name? Address?" Leslie pressed. "We need to speak with him ASAP."

"He's shaken up. Frightened out of his mind. Understand one thing here," Breaker responded, "I want no part in this. I've told you what I have at his insistence. Hopefully, your promise will mean something. You'll get nothing further from me. You won't see or hear from me again, unless... unless we go to court over this. And then you'll get the real me." Bear Breaker's eyes came alive for the first time since they were in his presence. "This today," he added, "this today is me playing Mr. Nice Guy. In court there'll be no hint of anything resembling nice. Trust me on that. Interview over."

Without a word both detectives got up to leave.

"One more thing," Attorney Breaker barked in their direction as they left his office, "FYI. Roo's a red head. Wears his hair in a mohawk. Can't miss him in a crowd."

No one looked up from their work as the two detectives retraced their steps through the office area heading toward the sign that said **EXIT**. Once in the hall, they stopped under another **EXIT** sign.

"Seems our floater may have jumped from a small plane," Leslie said, puzzled. "Why? According to the lawyer he had a parachute? If so, where'd it go?"

"I'm still wondering what his hair color has to do with anything," Cox answered. "And his haircut. That attorney's a piece of work."

"Caught him on a good day, I'm told."

"Allen tell you that?"

Cox was referring to Allen Smith, Leslie's former boyfriend, the first she had had since Junior, her late husband, was shot and killed while responding to a bank robbery in Tampa. "Among others," Leslie acknowledged. "Man has a reputat... Oh, what have we here?"

"You must be Roo!" Cox addressed the skinny red head who appeared in front of them, his head shaved to form a mohawk.

"Roo Pecking," the twenty-something responded, shoving his hand out in greeting. Turning to face Leslie, he added nervously, "Real name's Sylvan. Kids started calling me Rooster in fourth grade. Hair bunched up in back. Looked like feathers."

"We understand," Leslie began, "that a man you know as Tac jumped yesterday morning from a plane you were flying. Is that accurate?"

"Yes," Roo answered, his hands rapidly opening and closing. "I can't afford to be in trouble. I didn't do anything all that bad. Promise me I won't be in trouble."

"We can't make any promises, Roo, other than I can promise to listen carefully to what you have to say. If you're straight with us, we'll play straight with you."

"I'm finally graduating from FGCU. Got only one class left. I've been flying that stupid plane to pay tuition! Now this goes and happens!"

"This isn't the place to talk," Cox interrupted. "Let's go to the station and we can sort it out there."

"I've a better idea," Leslie said, realizing they were about to lose this nervous witness. "Let's go inside and see if they'll give us a room."

"Stay here," Cox said, "I'll see what I can work out."

Cox walked back to the receptionist desk and Leslie, trying to put the redhead at ease, asked, "So you're about to graduate. What're you majoring in?"

"Resort management," Roo replied, relieved to be talking about something other than his dead passenger. "I really like working with people on vacation, having fun. Been doing it for years with the plane." His face sagged, "Glad that's almost behind me. My parents'll be happy I'm out of the basement."

Before Leslie could respond, Cox called, "Got us a room. Over here."

"This young man," Leslie said to Cox when the door closed behind them, "is about to become a resort manager. Only one more class and he can give up flying lessons, or whatever." She turned to Roo, whose hands had stopped twitching, asking, "Exactly what did you do with that plane?"

"Taught people to sky-dive."

"I don't know much about skydiving," Leslie continued. "I assume you're licensed to teach."

"Yes, Ma'am. For six years now."

"Do skydivers need to be licensed?"

"To jump without supervision, you need at least an 'A' license."

"Did Tac have such a license?" Cox asked, breaking his silence.

"Oh, he was a good student. He was about to get his 'D' skydiving license. All he had left was the exam part."

"You taught him?" Leslie enquired.

"I did. Every one of his hours! He was the best student I ever had. Really into parachutes, how they worked, everything. I can't believe his chute didn't open. Not really possible since he packs them himself."

"Tell us about it. Was he wearing a chute on his back?"

"Typically, I pack all the chutes myself. For the real beginners, I even supervise the chute being strapped to their backs."

"Did you do that for Tac?"

"Oh, no! Once they hold an 'A' they can strap their own on."

"By, 'their own', do you mean they bring their own chute or—"

"No! They still use mine. The chutes I pack. At the 'C' level they can pack their own if they wish, but they still use my equipment."

"I take it then at the 'D' level they can—"

"Bring their own chutes. They need to tell me they packed it themselves, is all."

"Did Tac bring his own?"

"Two. One he put on normal like. It had wooden struts that folded. Almost too long for the plane, but somehow we managed. The other one was in a bag strapped to his chest. The first one was connected to his body with a harness contraption I'd never seen before."

Cox opened his phone, sorted through several photos, found the one he wanted, cropped it so that just the chest area was visible, then turned the screen to face the lanky, nervous kid siting across the table from him. "Is that the harness Tac was wearing when he left your plane?"

"It certainly was. But attached to another bag as I said."

"This other bag? Canvas? Leather?"

"Looked to be chute material. Mostly orange with some yellow. I can't say for certain."

"Can you describe the first chute?"

"It was folded of course. Looked to be in a triangular form. I couldn't tell you if it had anything written on it. Hard to say."

"Time he went out?"

"Seven-ten."

"Exactly?"

"Eight seconds."

"Seven-ten and eight seconds?"

"That's as exact as I have it."

"Did you log it at the time?"

"Always do," Roo responded, smiling.

"Altitude?"

Roo's hands twitched rapidly, as did his chin, the smile instantly gone. His eyes darted around the room as if looking for a way out. "I... I don't think I should answer that question because—"

"Because why?" Leslie gently coaxed.

"My rights," he blurted. "I take the fifth."

"I think we're long beyond that now Roo."

Pecking stood, knocking over the chair as he did so. "I'm out of here!"

Before he reached the door, Leslie said, "Were you too low? The airport is just a few miles north of Miromar Lakes where Tac landed. Is that what happened? He jumped too low; his chute didn't have time to open?"

Roo pulled the door open and at the same time, mumbled, "Too high for the—" His voice was so low that the creak of the hinge muffled what he said.

SEVEN

—Preliminary Cause of Death—
+Marino Taccola Jacobi AKA Tac
+Drowning after being rendered unconscious by blunt force trauma to the head
+ Body estimated to have fallen a minimum of 10K feet
+Parachutes (2) on body-No evidence of parachute use

LESLIE STUDIED HER SCREEN, digesting the information provided by Bratton Goodrich, the Medical Examiner's assistant assigned to the Jacobi case. The blunt force trauma to the crown of the head extending to the neck (broken C4) and upper back (broken T2), is consistent with a fall from a height of ten thousand feet. Deceased was rendered unconscious upon impact, and drowned face down in the water. Other than the impact wounds, no other trauma was found.

"Cox," Leslie said into her phone when her partner answered, "see the ME report?"

"Preliminary report," Cox corrected. "Poor soul was alive when he hit the water. I can't imagine what he was thinking?"

Not one to normally make light of death, Leslie quipped, "Probably, something to the effect of, 'Where the hell's my parachute?'"

"Speaking of parachutes, I was reading the logs from where the uniforms talked with possible witnesses. The main restaurant overlooks the lake. A woman by the name of Jessica was in early making sure everything was in order for a luncheon later in the day. She claims she saw something hit the water."

"Time?" Leslie asked, mentally berating herself for not reading the canvasing reports, even though she had been preoccupied with polishing her account of the Costco shooting. "By chance did this Jessica person note the time she saw that something hit the water?"

"As a matter of fact, she did. In fact, it was two objects a few seconds apart. First one hit at seven-twelve. Second, about three to five seconds later."

"Did she report it?"

"That's just it. She wasn't certain of what it was, if anything."

"Okay. I see her report. Looks like one of the objects appeared to be elongated like a ski. No color identified."

"We're set to speak with her at two today. FYI, I've asked Brat to search the bottom, see what we get."

"Good. But I'm still troubled by one thing. Roo clammed up when asked about how high he was when Tac jumped. Up to now I've been thinking that's because he was too low. The parachute didn't have time to open kind of thing. But—"

"That's exactly what I thought," Cox affirmed. "Like you, I thought he was blaming himself. But he did insist he wasn't too low."

"Maybe he was up in some restricted airspace or something? That's what the controller audio sounded like to me."

"Could lose his license."

"Either way, he's in trouble. So, what is it? Too high? Or too low?"

"Les, my money's on too high."

Leslie was silent long enough for Cox to ask, "So, what's bothering you, partner?"

"I'm thinking of that professor dude, the one up on the fire engine platform. Remember him? The one who dropped the bowling ball and the apple. Remember that case? Had to do with Newton."

"Never forget it," Cox said. "Both the heavy bowling ball and the apple hit the ground at the same time! Seems impossible. Even after you see it. Feels like a magic trick of some sort."

"I was taken by how fast they fell. Jessica said she saw something hit the water about seven-twelve. Yesterday, Roo said Tac jumped at... at seven-ten. Seven-ten and eight seconds to be exact. Well, if Jessica is right, Tac was out of the plane for approximately two minutes before he hit the water."

"Meaning, the plane was certainly not very low," Cox filled in.

"Or Jessica's wrong on the time. My money's on the plane being up closer to ten thousand feet. Maybe even higher."

"So where does that leave us?"

"This is shaping up to be an accidental fatality," Leslie answered. "If Roo did anything wrong, it's going to be with the FAA's jurisdiction, not ours."

"Maybe he was too low when Tac jumped."

"You thinking involuntary manslaughter?"

"Sure as hell am," Cox confirmed. "Classic acting without regard for human life while engaging in wanton or reckless behavior."

"I think you're out in front of your headlights. How the hell we going to prove the plane was dangerously low when he allowed Tac to jump? In fact, maybe Tac jumped without his permission. Don't rule out suicide."

Cox was silent a long moment. "If there was a plane over the lake, which by all accounts there seems to have been, then RSW knows all about it. From what I know, a pelican can't fly near the runway without calling the tower for... Hey, who're you calling?"

"Lizbeth Hillard. My favorite Criminal Investigative Assistant. As far as I'm concerned, she's the best in the business."

"I agree with you on that. She'll get to the bottom of who and what was flying over the lake. Don't believe we have that nailed down yet."

"Unless some passenger fell from a commercial plane. If the military lost someone they'll classify it for five generations and never fess up. I suppose anything's possible." When CIA Hillard didn't answer, Leslie left a message and hung up. Her phone rang almost immediately. "Beth! I just left a—"

"I know. I was on another line. I have what you just asked. One better. The tape of the conversation between air traffic control and the pilot. He identifies as NAZ. Assume that's the first and last letters of his tail number."

"Roger that," Cox replied, jumping into the conversation. "Thank you."

"You're welcome. FYI, I had them add a time stamp to the recording. The number you hear first is the time. And I removed all radio traffic but NAZ. The full original is in the file if you need it."

Cox brought up the audio file labeled NAZ Only and put his cell's sound on speaker.

"SIX-FORTY-TWO AND THIRTY-SEVEN SECONDS: RSW Control this is NAZ. Heading one-seventy-five at three thousand. Permission to cross airport."

"SIX-FORTY-TWO AND FORTY-FIVE SECONDS: NAZ. Climb and maintain five thousand. Permission granted.

"SIX-FORTY-TWO AND FIFTY SECONDS: NAZ. Climb and maintain five thousand."

"SIX-FIFTY-EIGHT AND THIRTY-SEVEN SECONDS: NAZ to RSW Control. Permission to climb to thirteen thousand feet."

"SIX-FIFTY-EIGHT AND FORTY-ONE SECONDS: RSW. Permission denied. Climb and maintain eight thousand feet."

"SIX-FIFTY-EIGHT AND FORTY-EIGHT SECONDS: NAZ. Roger that."

"SEVEN-ZERO-THREE AND FIVE SECONDS: NAZ to RSW. Passing through eight thousand."

"SEVEN-ZERO-THREE AND TEN SECONDS: RSW Control to NAZ. Hold at eight thousand."

"SEVEN-ZERO-FOUR: RSW Control to NAZ. Acknowledge eight thousand hold."

"SEVEN-ZERO-FIVE: RSW Control to NAZ. Return to eight thousand and hold."

"SEVEN-ZERO-SIX: RSW Control to NAZ. Repeat! Return to eight thousand and hold."

"SEVEN-ZERO-SEVEN: RSW Control to NAZ. Is that you at twelve thousand feet? Immediately return to eight thousand and hold!'

"SEVEN-ZERO-EIGHT: RSW Control to NAZ. Be advised that you are unauthorized for thirteen thousand! Return to eight thousand immediately!"

The file ended. Leslie was the first to speak. "According to that, Roo was up at thirteen thousand feet when Tac jumped."

"Not necessarily," Cox demurred, playing devil's advocate. "He could have come down somewhat."

"Two minutes later, roughly, Tac hit the water. Roo said he jumped. How the hell long does it take a body to fall that far?"

"I suppose it depends on whether or not he was wearing a parachute," Cox reminded Leslie. "We have every reason to believe he was. There's one missing from the garage. Roo said he was. But Roo may be covering his ass!"

"He certainly wasn't when he hit the water. That much we know for certain. If he was wearing a parachute, it sure didn't slow him down very much."

"That seems to be about all we know for certain," Cox reminded his partner. "Not much at all, I'd say."

EIGHT

COX AND LESLIE WERE ON their way to Miromar Lakes to interview the restaurant worker Jessica who, so far, was the only person who reported seeing anything hit the water the previous morning. Cox was driving, their conversation had run its course, and Leslie was mentally replaying everything she had heard about the deceased, Marino Jacobi, AKA Tac.

"Hey, Partner," Cox began, his voice upbeat, "how the hell's Jak doing? You haven't said much—"

"Cox! Knock it off! We've had this discussion enough times already! Stay the hell out of my personal space!"

"Wait a minute," Cox complained, "he's fair game. After what we went through with the Galileo telescope, it's only right you fill me in. His divorce go through? What?"

None of your business! is what she wanted to say about Pete Jakowski, the Oakmont, PA detective she had built a relationship with. They had met on an earlier case, her very first homicide investigation, when an Edison First phonograph went missing around the time an elderly woman ran off the road, hit a tree and died. Leslie had uncovered the Seminal Society collectors at that time. Jak moonlighted for Morris Dexter Stratis, one of the billionaire Society collectors, who was desperate to own Firsts from the hands of the Seminal Society. Jakowski had been assigned by his commander to work with a federal task force, run out of the IRS, by a somewhat shady agent, at least to Leslie's way of thinking, named Maxine Ghana. "As a matter of fact, I spoke to Jak just last night," Leslie confessed, not wanting to play up the conversation by denying its existence. "Divorce should be final any day now is why he called."

"I take it that's good news. I mean for you."

"Enough!" In fact, that was the exact question she had been debating. It wasn't the eighteen years between them, although that did enter her mind from time to time. But he was an active cop, as had been her husband, Junior, who had taken a bullet responding to a bank robbery a few very painful years back. On the other hand, she had broken up with Allen Smith, a Lee County prosecutor, mostly because every morning when she strapped on her weapon she didn't know if she would return home. Subjecting Allen to such uncertainty was no way to return his love. "Cox, we're not discussing my private life! How many times—"

"Touchy, touchy. Have it your way. But there's not much that's private between you and Jak."

"I don't know what that means. And frankly, I don't want to find out."

"As I said, have it your way. Change of subject. How long you been with Lee County now? Four years?"

"Three and several months. But who's counting?"

"Brass. That's who."

"You telling me something?"

"There's talk, is all."

"About?"

"You."

"What about me?"

"See, now you want to talk personal. Make up your mind."

"Cox!" Leslie glared at him, her deep green eyes going dark.

"How many homicides you work on?"

"Four. No five, including the one, Chase Montrose, you headed up."

"Bakery man. Pleaded guilty. Saved me from the trial prep. I had half a mind to take him a freshly baked pie as a thank you. Those four, all Seminal Society related. Edison, Chladni, Newton, Galileo."

"What's that have to do with—"

"Got lots of coverage, they did. Good PR for you. That Costco take down didn't hurt one bit. No pun intended. I mean with your leg and all. By the way, how's it doing?"

"If you're asking about my leg trauma, it's healing just fine. A little sore from time to time, nothing to slow me down. Goes with the territory."

"That's just it, Les. Nothing slows you down. You need something. You go get it. You know what they say about all work and no play."

"You calling me dull?"

"If the shoe fits! FYI, IRS been sniffing around."

"What're you telling me?"

"Watch your ass!" Cox answered, slowing to allow the Miromar Lakes guard to open the gate. "Light's focused on you good and bright."

The interview with Jessica went about as expected. She reiterated the times she saw something hit the water. She was now certain that there had been two somethings, both about the same size, hitting the water seconds apart. She remained unable to specify exactly what she had seen.

In answer to Cox's question as to whether this was the first time she had seen something falling from the sky, Jessica responded, "This is going to make me sound a bit off, but truthfully this was the second. The first time was about a week earlier. I came in early to do a few things and out of the corner of my eye I saw something, or I thought I saw something, fall into the water. I wasn't certain what it was and I didn't see anything floating, although my vision of the surface of the water was limited. A little while later I saw what I thought was a man swimming. He was wearing something yellow. As you can see, it's a long way down there and I was working, so I can't be certain."

"Any boat around?"

"Didn't see any. If there was, it would have to have been a private boat. Our boathouse wasn't open yet."

"What do you make of that?" Cox asked Leslie when they were back in the car. "That young woman seems reliable enough. Yet she can't say if the earlier *something* she saw was a swimmer or not. Nor can she say where he—or I suppose she—came from. Could have been from the shore, a boat, or an airplane."

"She's being truthful, is all. As she pointed out, it is a long way across the lake. And she did say it was possible that it was a swimmer heading to a house on the south shore. She doesn't realize it, but she pointed to Tac's house." Leslie fell quiet for a few minutes, then said, "Let's check with the pilot Roo. He's hiding something. Lean on him a bit, see what pops out. Hey, speaking of Tac's house, now that we're here, let's go over and see what turns up. You got the key?"

"Got the key. Didn't find much the first time. Don't expect much more now."

"We didn't spend much time either, as I recall. Had no idea what to look for."

"I'm not sure we yet know any more. But it doesn't hurt. We can check his dock, see if it's set up for getting in or out of the lake.

Marino Jacobi's house was just as they had left it. From all appearances, Tac had lived alone and was extremely neat. His office faced the front and held a single desk positioned between the front two windows, floor to ceiling bookshelves covered the side walls. There was an alcove across from the windows with file drawers lining each side. A printer sat on a credenza spanning the back wall of the alcove, which Leslie believed originally had been a closet. Nothing was out of place based on how she remembered the house from their original inspection.

Leslie had been thinking about the books she recalled from their original visit. Strange choice of reading, she had concluded. The shelves to the right were all paperbacks, mysteries mostly, with a few woodworking texts and one illustrated book titled: HOW TO SEW ANYTHING.

But it had been the opposite shelves holding what appeared to be old leather-bound volumes that had captured her interest. On close inspection, she noted that only the books on the top shelf were leather. The others were traditionally covered but appeared old. There was a full shelf having da Vinci in their titles. The top row, the leather-covered books, all appeared to be lab notebooks. Moving closer, Leslie expected them to also bear the name of da Vinci. She was surprised, and puzzled, to see the name; Mariano di Jacopo Taccola on each of the volumes, many of which appeared to be laboratory notebooks. "I assume," Leslie commented to Cox, "all of these books are listed in the inventory log?"

"Pictures as well as log entries, book by book, are in the file," Cox confirmed a moment later. "There were also three books in the main bedroom, labeled, LAST SUPPER, PORTRAITS, and CODEX."

"For now we're done in the office. Let's see what else the house yields."

"There's a note that the floor of the second bedroom is some kind of hard material. What's that about?"

"The file calls that room the sewing room." Opening the door to the bedroom, Leslie exclaimed. "I see why someone called this a sewing room. That sewing machine is much too large for sewing clothes. That's a—"

"Sail loft! This looks like a sail loft," Cox exclaimed. "I used to sail with a friend, and we went several times to have the sails cleaned, that sort of thing. Anyway, the floor of the loft looked just like this one. So did the sewing machine."

"Those bolts of material over there. Same colors as Jessica saw. Yellow and orange. Parachute loft, I'd say. Folding and packing table over there by the window."

"Cut the chutes on the floor. Table wouldn't be large enough," Cox pointed out, adding, "We saw the mechanical parts, harnesses, snaps, etcetera, etcetera, out in the garage. Let's check that out again."

"I'll follow," Leslie said, nodding her head in the direction of the garage. "Lead the way."

On further inspection, the garage floor was heavily sealed in what appeared to be epoxy and, as earlier noted, spotless. An air conditioner was doing its job of keeping the space workable, despite the outside temperature in the low nineties and the humidity feeling as if it matched the temperature. A professional-appearing work surface spanned a corner forming an 'L'. A peg board was positioned above each surface, holding recognizable tools, such as pliers, screwdrivers, saws, as well as tools that neither Cox nor Leslie could identify.

"Judging from the cutting board in the center, that corner table," Cox said, pointing to the leftmost table under the pegboard, "appears to be used for cutting. Doesn't take a genius to know that."

"I'm thinking Tac made his own parachutes," Leslie commented. "Don't know why else he would have so many parachute books. Not to mention all this."

"My guess, that open slot up there on the loft platform, the one with the lock, held the parachute he jumped out of the plane with. Must have been valuable."

"I think we're done out here," Leslie commented. "Let's finish the inside."

Cox followed Leslie to the bedroom overlooking a pool, at the back of the house. Beyond the pool was a grassy backyard sloping down to the lake where Tac had landed. While Cox was studying the yard, Leslie, her gloves in place, opened a rather thin PORTRAITS book that she found lying on a dresser. She flipped the pages, reading the portrait names as she went: MONA LISA, LABELLE FERRONNIERE, LA SCAPIGLIATA, WOMAN'S HEAD; LADY WITH ERMINE, PORTRAIT OF ISABELLA D'ESTE, PORTRAIT OF GINEVRA DE' BENCI.

Ginevra de' Benci! It took Leslie several seconds before her mind replayed a conversation she had had with William Packard Blair, managing director of the Edison Museum, during her very first homicide investigation. The *de' Benci* was an oil on wood and painted around 1475 by da Vinci. It was housed at the National Gallery of Art in Washington, D.C. and is the only painting by Leonardo on public view in the Americas. "Cox, hate to break it to you. Looks like we have another Seminal Society case on our hands. If previous experience is a teacher, this one will turn out to be a homicide as well."

NINE

COME SEE ME—ALONE the folded note on Leslie's desk read when she arrived back at the Pit. It was signed with a sprawling, S. Unusual for Captain Stetson to even be in the Pit area, let alone doing her own fetching. What the hell did I do now? Leslie asked herself, mentally cycling through the files she had recently worked on. Probably has something to do with the Costco shooting, she decided, taking a deep breath and blowing it out slowly just before knocking once on the closed door. Stetson's assistant was nowhere to be seen.

"Enter!" came the immediate reply.

To which Leslie silently added, *At your own peril!*

"Oh, Hodges. Glad it's you. So, how's your leg?"

"No, problems, Cap. Little twinge from time to time. Nothing to be concerned over."

"That's good to hear. That drowning's a strange one over at Miromar. Why's Cox's the lead?"

"Got there first."

"That a problem for you?"

"I don't know why it should be, Cap. He's settled down since I came on."

"Thanks to your guidance. Truth is, I don't like that formula. Not with your record. I want you in the lead. Any problem for you?"

"Not in the least."

"I'll let Cox know. Looks to me to be an accident. Or possibly a suicide."

"No suicide note. No evidence of depression. Not yet anyway. Something you know that I don't?"

"Nothing. Hunch."

"We just came from the deceased's house. He turned one of the bedrooms into a parachute loft. Several bolts of parachute material are in the garage. Looks to me as though he meant to return. Build more chutes. From all that we saw, guy's too good for accidents."

"So, suicide and accident are off the table?"

"For now, yes."

"Homicide, then?"

"The only thing pointing to a third party is... well I hate to put it out there with what we have, which isn't much, but—"

"You saw something that triggered a hunch?"

"How'd you know?"

"That's what separates the great detectives from the run of the mill. Instinct. What is it?"

"Bedside books about Leonardo da Vinci, including a portrait book showing the relatively few surviving pieces da Vinci created. Office bookshelves jammed with books and other information on da Vinci's life. He has what looks to be original volumes of da Vinci's notebooks. Those are in a locked cabinet."

"And?"

"And one of the portraits is that of Ginevra de' Benci."

"Should that mean something to me? I don't understand."

"As you said, it's only a hunch. But... but the de' Benci is the only da Vinci painting on public display in the United States."

"And you know this how?"

"From the Edison investigation. The acting director had come from the Washington National Gallery where—"

"Oh, now I recall! Rumors were that the de' Benci portrait had been stolen and a counterfeit substituted. Are you thinking this death is—"

"Maybe it's nothing. But seeing the de' Benci triggered me to think that the de' Benci would be a natural target for the Seminal Society. I know this is a stretch, that's why it's not in the file."

"A word of advice: Those billionaire collectors are not behind every death. Or to say that another way. Not every death is a homicide."

"Roger, Cap. That's what I keep telling myself. We're at the early stages on this one. But I can't help feeling the signs are there."

"What signs?"

"To start with, we found dead people in conjunction with Edison, Chladni, Newton and Galileo. Now da Vinci surfaces and we have a body! Got me thinking's all I can say. Maybe it was an accident. Gut tells me otherwise."

"Okay. But I have another assignment for you. Really, two assignments."

"And they are?"

"You been following the Popeye robberies? The ones Detective Rodriguez has been working?"

"Guy—or woman I suppose—wearing a Popeye disguise, housebreaking. No deaths so far. That's all I know about it. Should I know more?"

"Graduated to robbing liquor stores and service stations. Hit a bank yesterday. Sheriff's had enough. Asked for you—by name. Highly unusual, I might add. So here you are."

"What about—" Leslie began, thinking about the floater Tac.

"Stay on that, but you can slow roll it. No next of kin to worry about far's I can see. Use Cox for Popeye, if you want. Or select anyone else. Just, and I quote the boss, 'Get that deformed cartoon bastard off our f'n streets! And do it yesterday!' That clear enough?"

"Aye, aye, Cap." The thought of clicking her heels crossed Leslie's mind, but she thought better of it. "Will that be all?"

"Oh, I almost forgot. The second request. Put in to take the sergeant's exam. Department is counting your time with Gulfport and Tampa. And in your spare time enroll in FGCU, at Department expense, to finish up your degree. That'll be all."

Leslie had just been given more rope than she knew what to do with. For her, the exam would be trivia, having graduated from the academy with straight A's and passing the exams with the highest score in recent memory. But finishing her degree was another thing. Being in a classroom was bad enough. She couldn't imagine anything worse than being confined to an office. And that's exactly what Stetson had just told her with the comment about her degree. She was on her way to captain and perhaps deputy chief. But in her heart, she belonged on the street doing exactly what she was now doing. Solving puzzles. Nothing else made sense to her.

I'm Popeye the Sailor Man. The song played over and over in her head as she studied the extensive file that had been created by Lewis Rodriguez, the newbie detective she had been introduced to at her former partner's retirement party, but they hadn't spent much time talking. "Smart, but timid," is how Cox had characterized him. "Kid needs someone to show him the ropes."

Cox had been on the mark with timid. It came through in Rodriguez's reports, and in his follow up questioning of a suspect. "Lewis," she said to him when he answered his cell, "this is Leslie Hodges, I've been assigned to work with you on the Popeye cases."

"Detective Hodges. Sarge said to expect you. My base is Forty-One. No need for you to drive over here. I'll come to you. I hear you're located in the Pit."

"Don't mind the drive. I'm out and about. See you in twenty."

"If you insist. I'll have the file ready. I can sure use help on this."

Leslie spotted the stocky Rodriguez the moment she opened the front door to the Forty-One substation. The room held a dozen desks, but only his was occupied. "Where's everyone?" she asked when the young man, whose age she had noted from the file was thirty-one, quickly jumped up and came to greet her. "You can't be the only one here."

"All the detectives are out. We only have two assistants, and they're both in the back on break. I remember meeting you at Fischer's retirement. I didn't know him, but I've heard a lot of stories."

"All good, I trust," Leslie said, sizing up her new temporary partner.

"All good. Someone for you to look up to, learn the ropes from."

Leslie liked this kid. He indeed was timid, but smart as well. By talking about Fischer, he had subtly communicated that he had looked her up as well and was willing to learn from her. The direct opposite of Cox. She wasn't certain which she preferred. "I've read the file. Now tell me what is really going on here."

"What do you mean?"

"I mean, give it to me straight. Not that pablum you fed to the file."

"I'm sorry if that—"

"Hold that sorry stuff. I'm not grading you. If we're to have any chance of catching this... this cartoon character, then I want it straight, unbleached. Throw it out there, theory, speculation, hunch. All of it. You hear me?"

"Loud and clear."

"Go!" Leslie commanded.

"The first Popeye case was a home intrusion. Caught on Ring Doorbell. Why the woman opened the door knowing a Popeye character was out there makes me wonder. Once the door was opened, he pushed past her without saying a word. They went off camera and the sound ended. Ten minutes later Popeye again appeared on the Ring camera, this time carrying two pillowcases full of what the woman said was 'her good silver'. She set a twenty-thousand-dollar value on the silver."

"And?"

"And, well I'm not buying it."

"Why?"

"Hunch, I suppose. Looked staged to me. Why open the door for Popeye? Why not run out of the house when he pushed his way inside? Instead, she follows him around! If I was her, I'd be thinking rape, not logging the cost of what he took. In any case I'd grab my cell phone and get my butt out of the house. Call 9-1-1."

"Good observation. What did you do to follow up?"

"Took her statement. It's in the file."

"And?"

"And nothing more. What should I have done?"

"There are no magic steps. But how about insurance?"

"Oh, she said she would file a claim with her insurance company."

"How about finding out exactly when she took out that policy? What was taken—and the value of the items. And what about the Ring camera? When was it installed?"

"What's that have to do with anything?"

"Following up on your concerns that it was staged, suppose Ring was installed, say, within the week. Then—"

"I never thought of that! Then it could be evidence of collusion."

"Is the woman married? Have children? If so, where were they at the time? Does anyone she know match the physical description of this Popeye character?"

"Married. Don't know about kids. Didn't think to ask about the husband. Shit! I screwed up!"

"Nothing that can't be recovered. Tell me about each of the other Popeye events. We'll make a list of possibilities and then go track them down. One by one. Also, as you're talking, I want you to be generating in your mind a physical description of this Popeye character as to height, weight, build, possibly gender. We might not have his or her face and arms, but we have everything else."

"Height, I know to be five-foot-five. Slender build."

"And just how..."

The young cop broke his first smile. "From the Ring camera. Counted the bricks on the wall beside him," he said confidently.

"How do you know Popeye's a he?"

Deflated, Rodriguez admitted, "Just assumed, I guess."

"Always dangerous. You know that. Hold a moment," Leslie reached for her vibrating phone. Seeing Cox's name, she informed Rodriguez, "I gotta take this. Sorry." A moment later, she said to the detective, "I'm working a death case with Simeon Cox. Dead guy lived in Miromar Lakes. He's about to meet with some folks—neighbors, I understand—who reported a missing person. Got time to go with me? You're welcome to join. This missing person may or may not be related to our current homicide investigation."

"Love to!" Rodriguez said, jumping to his feet. "My car or yours?"

"Follow me. I'm not planning on coming back this way. Better yet. We're meeting over at Haney's on Route 41. Know where that is?"

"Never ate there myself, but hear it's a great place for breakfast. North of here about five miles or so."

"Seems these neighbors are the missing guy's bocce buddies. Guy's name's Andy. This is the second Friday Andy hasn't shown up for bocce. The group is having breakfast—or brunch—in Haney's back room. Told there'd be a dozen or so. Meet you there."

On the way to meeting Cox, Leslie called Lizbeth Hillard, her Criminal Investigative Assistant. "Beth," she asked when the CIA answered, "what do we know about this friend of the deceased out at Miromar? Guy by the name of—"

"Donatello Andino. Goes by Andy. Working it for Cox."

"Yeah, that one."

"Nothing much yet. Moved in about five years back. Wife died a year after they got down here. He was a private investigator. Albany police have nothing official on him. Off the record, he hit it big time."

"How big time? They have any idea?"

"Very big! Again, off the record?"

"If that's how you got the info, Beth, I'll honor it."

"It's a long story. Short version, the painting, Salvator Mundi, was auctioned last year for $450.3 million."

"I recall that. Some art dealer bought it for $10 grand. It was later authenticated as a da Vinci original. One of only a very few. What was this guy Andy's role?"

"That's where the story goes into the weeds. He was a middleman, hired to transport it from the auction house to the unknown buyer. Along the way rumor has it that the original was delivered to somebody other than the actual buyer who received a forgery."

"You know who received the true original?"

"Your Texas buddy, William Bishop the second. Or so the story goes."

"Little Billy Bob!"

"He of Seminal Society collector fame. Yes, LBB's the purported recipient of the Mundi."

"So, what was this Andy guy paid?"

"Fifty-five million. Again, as the story goes."

"Beth, you sound skeptical."

"Too many loose ends for me. Timing for one. Nothing official for another."

"What does the new owner claim?"

"Silence on that front. See what I mean?"

"I hear you, Beth. I hear you."

"Also, remember a few years back we did work on Edison's Phonograph?"

"How can I forget? Getting ready for trial."

"That's just it. Like you, I'm preparing our files for that trial and just yesterday I was reading about another art forgery substitution. Da Vinci's Ginevra de' Benci. A forgery was said to have been substituted for the original. This guy, Andy, is rumored to have been the PI who had last custody of the original until it was delivered also to your friend LBB. All rumors I know. But where there's smoke..."

"And what have you learned about Andy's recent contacts?"

"Guy by the name of Gino called it in several hours ago," Beth reported, her tone reverting to pure business. "Last he heard from Donatello Andino was last Friday morning when he received a text acknowledging he'd be at bocce at nine. No show that day. No other communication on his cell since then."

"I have to ask. Any suggestion this guy Gino has anything to do with the de' Benci? Or any other dealings with Andy?"

"Nothing at all," Beth quickly responded. "From every source I have, Gino runs bocci. That's it. Checked him out six ways to Sunday. Straight-up guy if ever there was one. You think Andy going missing is connected to Tac falling out of the sky?"

"Don't see how—or why. But truthfully, we're just beginning to piece it together. But it just might be connected to da Vinci. Schools out on that."

TEN

COX WASN'T HAPPY THAT his partner had invited Rodriguez to the bocce group interview. But he hid it well, greeting Rodriguez with a smile usually reserved for females. Shaking the young detective's hand, he said, "Glad you could make it to interview these guys. To tell the truth, I can't imagine there's much here. But in this business you never know." He held his iPad so Leslie could see the three neat columns containing men's names. "While I was waiting for you, I gathered their names."

ED	GINO*	RICHARD
TONY	JIM	ANTHONY
BRAD	GREG	BARRY
JOHN	CHRIS	GILL
BILL	PETER	DR. STEVE
KURT	TOM	DAVID
DAVE	GENE	GARY
LOU	PHIL	WALLY

"What's the star for next to Gino?" Leslie asked. "And since when do we deal only in first names?"

"Full name's there. Just hidden to make it easy. That's how they're sitting around the table. Left to right. Star's the guy who reported Donatello Andino missing."

"Okay, Cox, you take the lead," Leslie instructed. "This is your show. Rodriguez and I'll observe."

Instead of turning left into the main dining room area, Cox opened a door on his right and ushered the detectives into a private room where a group of men were talking softly among themselves, empty breakfast plates in front of them. The room fell silent as introductions were made.

"I'm Gino," a tall man sitting near the center of the group said. "I suppose I'm the cause of your being here. I hope it's just nothing. But thing is, we're worried about Andy. He doesn't miss Friday's without calling. Hey! Where's my manners? You want to sit? We can pull up three chairs. Get you coffee? Something to eat maybe?"

Cox, not sensing a desire on the part of Leslie or Rodriguez to sit, responded, "No thanks. We'll stand. Start at the beginning. Your call indicated Andy..." Cox checked his notes. "... Donatello Andino, plays bocce with you gentlemen on Friday mornings. This week, as well as last, he didn't show up. Do I have that right?"

"That's right," Gino answered. "And he didn't call me—or tell anyone else—he wasn't coming. That's not normal for him."

"He always tells you when he's not coming? That's what's troubling you? Could he have just forgotten? Maybe left town and forgot about bocce? Maybe overslept?" Cox looked directly at Gino. "I don't suppose you call the sheriff's office every time someone misses bocce."

"Andy's been playing with us for three, four years now. When he misses, he calls either me or Ed over there. That's why we're worried about him. That, and... and his car's in his driveway. When he leaves town his car's always in the garage. Or at the airport. Fact is, none of us has ever seen his car outside overnight." Gino looked around the table for support. Several men nodded in agreement.

A man sitting two down from Gino said, "I should have said something sooner, but... but there was no reason to. Until now. I saw..."

"And you're Richard," Cox interrupted, matching the speaker's position at the table to the names on his list. "Go on."

"I'm Richard. I saw Andy late Thursday afternoon. Last Thursday. He was a passenger in a car leaving Miromar Lakes."

"Where exactly?" Cox pressed.

"At the north exit gate. I was in the middle lane waiting to go over to Costco. Andy was in a car waiting to turn right toward Alico."

"Did you recognize the driver as well?"

"Not at the time, no."

"What do you mean by *not at the time*?"

"That guy, Tag. The one they found in the lake. When I saw his picture on TV, I thought I knew him. Couldn't place it until... until Gino mentioned Andy's name just this morning. Then I remembered seeing Andy in the car with Tag driving."

"Do you mean Tag—or Tac?"

"Yes, Tac. The dead guy in the lake. Didn't directly know him."

"You recall the make and color of the car Tac was driving?"

"Blue Honda Accord."

"That's his car!" Anthony called out. "Tac drives a Blue Honda Accord."

"Let me be certain I have this right. Thursday, a week ago yesterday, Richard, you saw Tac—full name, Marino Jacobi—driving a Blue Honda Accord leaving Miromar Lakes, heading north on Ben Hill Griffin. Donatello Andino, who you know as Andy, was a passenger in the car."

"That's what I saw," Richard replied.

"And what time would that have been?"

"Noon, or so. I was going over for a hotdog."

Cox pressed the group for further details, but all they had to offer, other than a million questions about Tac's death, was speculation.

A search warrant having been issued, Cox, followed by Leslie and Rodriguez, entered the Andino residence. A preliminary inspection revealed that the house, as expected, was vacant.

Turning to Rodriguez, she asked, "Note anything of interest?"

"Only that there's no women's clothing. And not all that much men's either, now that I think about it."

"Wife died a while back," Cox announced. "Let's see." He opened his electronic pad and started entering information.

"Wife's name was Marcy," Leslie began, not relying on notes. "Died about six months after they moved to Miromar Lakes. Leukemia if I recall right."

"How'd you know all that?" Rodriguez inquired. "You didn't even—"

"A gift she has," Cox responded. "Total recall. Comes in handy for her. But I gotta tell you, drives me crazy at times."

"I'd love to have that gift," the young detective replied. "Bet it really helps."

"I suppose so," Leslie confessed, her mind replaying what Beth had told her about Andy and the art heist. Deciding to play it straight with the team, she added, "Beth told me a story, maybe I should call it a rumor, about an art heist. Correction, a rumored art heist. Promised to keep it quiet, so do I have your respective words?"

"Yes! Of course," Rodriguez instantly replied.

"Depends," Cox said. "If I get the same info on my own then—"

"Then you're free to do with it what you will."

"Agreed."

"This part of the story is known fact. For any number of reasons there are very few paintings available today that were actually done by Leonardo da Vinci. For one thing, he seldom finished what he started. For another, his paintings were done directly onto walls and monuments. A painting, the Salvator Mundi, had hung in a private home for generations without anyone realizing it had been painted by da Vinci. It was purchased from the estate for ten grand by two art dealers. Believe it or not, it was then authenticated as a da Vinci original. That painting was auctioned last year for four hundred fifty million dollars. Andy, in his capacity as a private detective, drove the painting from the auction house to the buyer."

"I suppose you're about to tell us it was substituted during the delivery," Cox said.

"That's exactly what I'm about to say. Only that for our purposes the substitution is only a rumor."

"Substitution sounds bogus to me," Cox said, shaking his head in disbelief. "Much too large an operation for one man."

"Who says it was one man?" Leslie injected. "Besides, how else do you explain fifty-five million in an offshore account for our friend Andy here? Money showed up two days later."

"So where is the original painting now?" Rodriguez tentatively asked.

"Speculation has it that a guy, actually a guy that I know fairly well, a guy named William Bishop, is rumored to have it."

"Little Billy Bob! Your friend no less!" Cox thought for a moment before turning back to his partner. "What am I missing here? If LBB had wanted it, why not just bid directly for it? He has more money than God!"

"Been thinking about that. Seems that the Seminal Society collectors got themselves into a pre-bidding war. Price would still be going up if Billy Bob hadn't dropped out about a month before the actual auction."

"Four hundred fifty million dollars is still a lot of money for the auction. Who the hell... Oh, shit! If the Seminal Society collectors got themselves into a bidding war, there's no upper limit! That's what happened, isn't it?"

"That's what Beth believes. LBB dropped out and decided on going the forgery route and the others continued."

"So, who do you think bid the big bucks and got himself a forgery for his efforts?"

"Not a *him* according to Beth. An 86-year-old woman whose real name is Queen Baribah. She came to the U. S. in 1978, a year before the fall of the Shah, and took the name, Pearl Aribah. Beth pegs her wealth at between four and five billion dollars. In her close world she's known as Queen B."

"Are you saying this Queen B paid nearly a half billion and ended up with a forgery?"

"If you believe the rumors."

"Do you?"

"Beth's found nothing to contradict the story."

"And this Little Billy Bob character has the priceless da Vinci?" Rodriguez ventured.

"What's your take on all this?" Cox directed his question to the young detective.

"All I know, is that when giants fight it's best to keep your head down."

ELEVEN

THE CAUSEWAY TO SANIBEL was jammed, causing Leslie to be late by over fifteen minutes for her appointment with Pearl Aribah, the former Iranian Queen Baribah, who reportedly had bought da Vinci's Salvator Mundi at auction. Leslie was alone because Cox had demurred on the ground that they were investigating a suspicious death by drowning and that there was no connection whatsoever with The Seminal Society in general, or with the Mundi in particular. "Leslie," Cox had declared, "I don't know why you're so possessed over that Seminal Society BS. I suggest you get them out of your system. Those folks are so far out of our league that we'd need a Galileo telescope to see them from where we're positioned."

"Just cleaning up loose ends," she had replied. "That guy, Richard, said he saw our dead guy driving Andy, a person of interest with respect to a possible forgery of a coveted art artifact. Aribah is the person of record who purchased the artifact. Who the hell knows at this point what's related and what's not? I'm just closing the loop."

"Go for it if that calms your obsession with those billionaires. We found nothing at Andy's to suggest he was involved in any way with anything to do with the Society. But, hey, chase after what you think important."

"What are you doing?"

"Remember at Haney's that guy Gill stuck a note in my pocket with his name and phone number? Well, I'm on my way over to see Gill now. Probably nothing. But I'll close it out."

Leslie played that last conversation with Cox in her head several times, becoming increasingly more upset with herself. Cox was right about one thing; the Seminal Society, and particularly that Texas Billionaire Little Billy Bob, was on her mind more than it should have been, even when they were not working a case. Something was troubling her, but she couldn't put her finger on it. Not yet anyway.

The door to the Aribah house opened and Leslie came face to face with the most beautiful woman she had ever seen. Young and magnificent were the first thoughts that came to mind. Early thirties with ageless dark eyes, matching her ebony hair. The file put her age at forty-nine.

"I'm Lee Coun—"

"I know exactly who you are," the young woman announced. "Leslie Hodges, Lee County's star detective. Bibi said to expect you. She's napping. I'm appointed to answer your questions."

"And just who are you?" Leslie asked, knowing full well who she was talking with.

"I'm Bates, Bibi's granddaughter. And keeper of her estate. I'm the one you need to speak with. I handle her financial world." Bates turned abruptly and walked across the large foyer toward the back of the sprawling house, leaving the door open behind her.

Leslie followed, eventually stopping on the back deck overlooking the Gulf of Mexico. "So," Leslie began when they were seated beside a pool that appeared to flow directly into the waters of the Gulf, "your grandmother delegated you to speak with me about your recent artwork purchase. Is that what I'm to understand?"

"Not exactly."

"And just what does *not exactly* mean in this instance?"

"Bibi asked me to sit in for her. She knows nothing of the financial arrangements pertaining to art of any nature. She's not in the least interested."

"Who then?"

"Texan named Bishop. William Bishop. I believe you've had dinner with him on two occasions."

"How do you—"

"There's not much I don't know about Lil Bob. That's what I call him, Lil Bob. He and I are... shall we just say... good friends. Just love that key lime pie of his. Just to die for. Wouldn't you agree?"

"I wouldn't go that far."

"How far would you go? Sleep with him?"

"That's a rude question that doesn't deserve an—"

"You came here to ask questions that are none of your business. You expect me to answer. I'd call that rude, wouldn't you? Don't I have the same right? Turn about's fair game, I'd say."

"I'm investigating..." Leslie paused. *Just what am I investigating? A man found drowned in a lake with perhaps some remote connection to da Vinci.* "Is it true your grandmother—or you—bought a da Vinci at auction?"

"See what I mean! What Bibi—or I—bought, or didn't buy, is none of your business. So, as I said, that's rude. You want me to answer your questions, then answer mine. Did you sleep with him?"

"No!" Leslie answered, surprising herself with the force of her answer.

"Did you have the opportunity?"

"We had two business dinners. That's all."

"You talk about the Seminal Society? His artifact collection?"

"We did. Yes."

"He tell you about—or better yet, show you—his Newton? Or his Edison?"

Leslie had not even considered that LBB had even one Seminal Society First, let alone two of the artifacts she had worked cases on. "That's enough. I can't discuss what we spoke about. And quite frankly, it's none of your business!"

"That's where you, Miss Detective, are wrong! I plan to marry the man! So it's pretty much my concern who he sleeps with."

The first thought that flashed through Leslie's mind was: *Does Little Billy Bob know that?* Leslie surprised herself with her second thought. *Over my dead body!* Forcing herself to focus on the business at hand, Leslie said, "I'm here to talk about *your* art. Not *his*. Is that clear?"

"So just what is it you want from Queen B—or from me?"

"Rumor has it your grandmother—or someone operating on behalf of her—bought a da Vinci—the Salvator Mundi to be exact, at auction. Is that true?"

"That is a correct fact. Yes."

"You bought it for your grandmother?"

"I told you. I manage the estate. Grandmother is way beyond managing anything, including, if you must know, herself. Now, please leave!"

"Is the painting here? In this house?"

"Take the fifth."

Leslie refrained from pointing out that not answering a question under protection of the Fifth Amendment to the U.S. Constitution would only be appropriate had a crime been committed. Instead, she smiled as if Bates had not answered. "Mind showing me the da Vinci? I'd love to see it."

"It's not in this house. Not going to happen," the young woman insisted. Quickly adding, "Even if I had it, I wouldn't show you where it was!"

"Unless you've done something improper, what's the harm?"

"I'm tired of answering questions. You gave me a headache! Please leave now."

"I'd like to speak with your grandmother. If this is not a good time I can come back when—"

"Not going to happen. Now please—"

Leslie turned toward the front door, taking in the art on the walls and the objects on display. "Quite a nice collection. I assume you had a hand in putting this all together."

"Some of it, yes. Bibi, in her day, had a good eye."

"That's where you get it from, I suppose."

"Get what from?" Bates responded, smiling as she held the door open for Leslie.

"Your appreciation of art."

"I suppose."

"Well, it was nice meeting you Bates," Leslie said, stepping out onto the front landing and turning to face Bates. "By any chance do you know a man named Andino? Andy Andino?"

"Never heard of him. Why do you ask?"

"He was the man you hired to bring the Mundi to you."

"I said, I never heard of him. Now if you don't mind, please leave me alone."

Before Leslie could respond, the door closed.

Cox found Gil washing his car in his wide driveway and pulled to a stop behind the gleaming SUV.

"Be with you in a sec," the big man said. "Dry my hands and put this hose away. Don't want anyone tripping."

"Take your time," Cox called. "I'm not going anywhere."

Within a minute Gill was back, his hand outstretched in greeting. "How're you? I'm Gill."

"I'm Detective Cox. I'm the guy called you earlier. Thanks for agreeing to talk with me."

"Just doin' my duty is all. Yinz have a tough job with all that's going on in the world."

"We're holding our own. My notes say you were in the Army. That right?"

"Sergeant. That's why I gave you the note. I served a tour with that Tac guy. The one who went an' drowned himself."

"Why do you think he drowned himself? Could've been accidental."

"He and I were drill instructor's together over in Fort Moore. Guy was an expert swimmer. He was also a jumper. Spent more time in the air than on land, he did. No sir. That wasn't any accident. He went and killed himself. Put money on it."

"You said he was a jumper. Paratrooper?"

"I don't know if he was official. But he sure looked good. I've seen them come and I've seen them go. Tac was the best jumper I ever saw."

Cox studied Gill a moment, thinking about his next question. Making up his mind, he asked, "Were you friends with him?"

"Not down here I wasn't. Fact is, I didn't even know he had moved into Miromar Lakes. We were friends back then. He was from up in Pittsburgh like I was. Just a couple a yinzers."

"What more can you tell me about Tac? What kind of person was he?"

"Serious is the best word for it. Serious. He made his mind up to something, better get outta his way. He damn near killed a whole squad when they showed up for drill a minute late. Marched them, non-stop for six hours in the beating sun. No stops, no water. If I hadn't intervened, they'd all be dead—or still marching. Guy made up his mind to something, there'd be no stopping him."

"Bad temper, you'd say?"

"Not so much temper. Just pure stubborn. He wanted what he wanted when he wanted it. No reasoning with him when he got in that mood. He was mellow as could be, until he focused on something. Fun guy. Just don't cross him, all's I can say. With him, nothing was off the table if it meant he could get what he wanted."

"Anything more I should know?"

"Heard he was in the police up in Pittsburgh. But that's only rumor far's I know. Oh, and for what it's worth, he was a rabid Stiller fan. Hey, good luck solving whatever you're trying to solve."

"Was he into da Vinci you know?"

"da Vinci? You mean the painter da Vinci?"

"Leonardo da Vinci. Yes."

"As I said, hadn't seen him for decades. He was into jumping from airplanes, flying gliders, that type of thing. I don't put him down as a painting kind of guy. Not Tac. After that forced march, he and I didn't see eye to eye. Fact is, I wanted nothing to do with him. Feeling was mutual, I'm sure of that."

TWELVE

"SO, COX," LESLIE BEGAN when the two of them relinked back at the Pit, "I see you interviewed bocce Gill. Find anything interesting on Tac?"

"Don't yet know what to make of it. In my mind, the guy had a bad temper. But Gil corrected me. Said Tac was focused on what he wanted. When he set his mind on a goal there was no stopping him. To quote Gil, 'Nothing was off the table if it meant he could get what he wanted'. Into parachutes big time."

"That's good to know. Did he know if Tac was into da Vinci?"

"Knew nothing about da Vinci. Only other thing I got was that Tac was a retired City of Pittsburgh cop—oh, and he liked to jump from planes. But that we already knew. May have been a paratrooper."

"His military record shows his instructor time, but there's nothing about jumping. He retired from Pittsburgh as a Lieutenant. Gill was right about that. That was seven years back. He moved down here two years ago."

"Do we have anything on those missing five years? I didn't see anything in the file."

"Beth sent over her findings this morning. Just going through it all. From what I gather, he did odd jobs, mostly security work, after his retirement. Beth also mentioned Tac working with Andy on several security jobs. Of particular note, he worked with Andy on the Salvator Mundi painting delivery. She also noted that any involvement of Tac in a forgery substitution is, in her words, "pure scuttlebutt" so far as she could determine. But here's what's interesting. Just before Tac moved down here, several million was deposited into his account. Beth is trying, so far with no success, to find the source of that money. She says it was professionally done and thinks that'll be a dead end."

"You interviewed that woman out on Sanibel. Queen something?"

"Queen Baribah. That was her name in Iran. She changed it to Pearl Aribah when the royal family was forced into exile. Her close friends apparently call her Queen B. Never got to speak directly to her. Intercepted by a young woman, going by the name of Bates Aribah, who claims to be her granddaughter. Bates also claims to be guardian of the old woman's substantial estate and the real purchaser of the da Vinci."

"I was reading up on da Vinci. The one you're talking about, I believe, is the Salvator Mundi, and depicts Christ in the Renaissance Theme."

"That's the one."

"It's supposed to be the last one by da Vinci."

"And, according to the Louvre, it was essentially destroyed," Leslie added, not to be outdone by her partner.

"I see you've also done your homework."

"Would you expect otherwise?"

"Suppose not," Cox conceded. "Suppose not."

"If the Louvre's correct, the one sold at auction was a fake," Leslie added.

"Yet it went for almost a half a billion dollars! What am I missing?"

"Someone, a lot of someone's I suppose, believed it was genuine. The appraisal consensus was that it was genuine. It's the only da Vinci in private hands today. The Mona Lisa is owned by the French Government and is on permanent loan to the Louvre."

"Bingo!" Cox exclaimed. "Reason enough for the Louvre to bad mouth the Mundi. Keeps up the value of their prize possession."

"I think it's more than that. A documentary's been made, and it appears that the latest belief is that it's a forgery. It's said to be owned by Saudi Arabia and will go on display when a new museum opens."

"You know, Les, if the Saudis prevent examination, then they can claim anything they like. Tourism is the thing and it'll sure draw a crowd. The bigger the dispute, the higher the audience."

"If a Seminal Society collector has the original and the Saudis have the fake, then we know their secret is safe because the original will never surface. Hey, a thought just occurred to me. By any chance could this Queen B be friends with the Saudi's?"

"I don't know much about Middle East history," Cox confessed. "But I do believe that before the revolution when she and her family were expelled, they were close."

"Maybe then Queenie is acting as a front for the Saudis? Just a thought. No that can't be right because the granddaughter says she, the granddaughter, is in charge. Not Queen B."

"There it is again, Les. Your eyes do a funny thing when you mention Bates. Fess up. What's got you so worked up?"

"I don't know what the hell you're talking about!" In fact, Leslie knew full well what Cox was picking up on; Bates' statement of her potential marriage to Little Billy Bob. In point of fact, Leslie had fantasized such thoughts herself. How wonderful it would be if she could do anything she wanted, whenever she wanted, and never have to think about money. Pure fantasy. But that had not stopped her from thinking about, then actually dreaming about, what it would be like to be married to someone as charming and comfortable to be with as LBB. Being one of the wealthiest men in the world added to the allure. She knew it was not healthy, but the thoughts and dreams still came despite otherwise rational behavior.

"Leslie, there's no doubt in my mind Bates troubles you. What is it?"

"I suppose the way she took charge. She wouldn't show me the painting or let me speak with grandma. I suppose I took an instant dislike."

Cox started to respond. Thought better of it and said nothing.

"I'm thinking," Leslie began when she realized Cox was remaining quiet, "it wouldn't do any harm if we again visited Tac's house. Maybe something will pop into our minds."

"We can do Andy's as well. I can't help but thinking those two are related. How, I don't know, other than Andy and Tac were seen driving together. And that was the last time that we know of that anyone saw Andy alive."

Leslie thought for a moment before adding, "You're right. From Beth's canvas of the neighborhood, that *was* the last time anybody saw Andy."

"I hate to say it, but other than the possible da Vinci connection, tenuous as it is, we seem to be at a dead end."

"It appears that way," Leslie agreed.

"Maybe it's time you called your Great Southern Insurance friend. Or possibly Billy Bob. If anything's tied to the Mundi, that guy'll know. That's for certain."

"That actually a good idea," Leslie admitted, forcing excitement from her voice. "That is, assuming he's in Florida."

"You have time coming to you. Go on down to Texas. The vacation would do you good."

Leslie, guessing this was Cox's not so subtle way of telling her he knew her secret, didn't respond. She knew her voice would betray her.

THIRTEEN

LESLIE WAS TEMPTED TO IGNORE her gently buzzing phone. But habit dictated that she at least read the screen. The words Silver— Great Southern were clearly displayed. *How the hell did he know I was about to call?* "Detective Leslie Hodges speaking. Mr. Silver, just who I was going to—"

"Please call me Jack," the smooth voice responded. "We haven't spoken in a while. I have been meaning to call and congratulate you on your splendid resolution of the Galileo telescope situation. You certainly have made a name for yourself. Scuttlebutt has it you're in for a promotion there in Lee County."

Just how Jack Silver, the CEO of Great Southern Insurance Company, a man who lives on, and works from, a custom designed private jet, knows about the inner workings of a county sheriff's office in southwestern Florida was beyond Leslie. "Thank you for the kind words. I certainly wouldn't know anything about a promotion."

"Your work has also caught the attention of both the IRS and Homeland Security. If I were a betting man, I would put my money on one of the federal agencies offering you a position. That's how impressed they are."

"You flatter me, Jack. But I'm content where I am." In fact, Leslie had heard the same rumors, but nothing had materialized, saving her from making a difficult decision. On the one hand, her life was working the streets, solving crimes, putting law breakers in jail. On the other, she wasn't getting any younger. Other than the house she bought with her late husband's payout money, she had no savings, and not likely to build up anything. A family didn't appear to be a viable option.

"Leslie, please don't dismiss the feds that fast. Bet they quadruple your salary."

Realizing that Jack Silver, the man who insured artifacts for hundreds of millions of dollars, wasn't calling her to chat about her salary, Leslie asked, "Jack, thanks for the heads up. Now what can I do for you?"

"Right to the point as always. That's what I like about you Leslie, no beating around the bush. What you see is what you get.

I like that. Two things are on my mind. First, and this is very confidential, Great Southern insured the Mundi when it was sold at auction. Rumors, with no credible proof, have been circulating for years of it having been substituted. Up until recently, as I said, nothing was credible. That all changed a few months back when a resident of Miromar Lakes, a man by the name of Donatello Andino, was identified by a notorious art forger as the middleman in a substitution involving the Mundi."

"And your question is?" Leslie asked, playing dumb.

"Andino apparently went missing. What can you tell me about his disappearance?"

Normally, Leslie would lock tight and reveal nothing. However, Jack Silver had pointed her in the right direction when she had reached a dead end in the Edison Phonograph investigation. And he had been invaluable for Chladni, as well as Galileo. "The best I can do for you is say that Andino was last seen in a car with a guy named Marino Jacobi. Hasn't been seen since."

"Tac! That's interesting. Tac's name also surfaced as working with Andino with respect to da Vinci artifacts. As I understand the relationship, Tac was focused on parachutes, not paintings. It is my belief that Tac assisted Andy with the Mundi."

"How does that all work?"

"This is all speculation and conjecture mind you, pieced together from several unnamed sources. And from knowing the buyers and the sellers."

"Understand."

"Apparently Andy required assistance with the Mundi forgery and Tac wanted parachute material from da Vinci. Andy either had, or knew where to find, a trove of da Vinci material. The logistics of the Mundi art substitution, if, in fact, there even was a substitution, were complex. Timing was critical. That's what Andino specialized in. He was a master—or so I'm to believe—of creating situations that allowed for substitutions. Tac provided the diversion. They were both ex-cops and were masters of confusion."

"How serious is the Andino connection to Mundi?"

"Enough that the Fed Task force was about to interview him."

"Why haven't they?"

"Can't find him."

"What role did Tac play in all this?"

"Pure speculation on my part. Tac was the weak link. He would know, and possibly have proof, that Andino made the substitution. Again, assuming that there was a substitution. With the Feds closing in on Andino, I'm not surprised Tac's dead. He presented a danger to Andino."

Leslie took a moment to digest what she had just heard. Knowing Silver had given her more information than usual. Not wanting to overstep her welcome, she changed the subject. "I assume you're insuring the Mundi. But, according to what little I could find, the Saudis have the original."

"That's what the Saudi's want the world to believe. I can assure you theirs is a clone. The original authenticated piece is in private hands. And yes, we have coverage liability on it."

"And what about the one Queen B bought from auction? You're saying its not authentic."

"That's the one the Saudi's have. Baribah sold it to them for an undisclosed amount."

"Can I assume then a substitution has been made?"

"Neither confirming nor denying."

"The granddaughter, Bates, says she bought the Mundi and sold it."

"Piece of work that young woman. Let's just say Great Southern wouldn't insure anything she owned—or ever touched for that matter."

"May I ask why not?"

"Let me just say, from my perspective, she's somewhere between delusional and an outright liar. Can't decide which."

"Sorry I can't be of more help."

"Just keep me in mind when you hear anything I might need to know."

"Will do," Leslie committed, not knowing if she could comply even if she wanted to.

"Oh, I almost forgot," the insurance man said, making it sound to Leslie as an afterthought, "the Kumars, correct that, Riya Kumar, is on her way to Fort Myers. Believe she's after a da Vinci."

"How credible?"

"Highly credible that she's coming. I wouldn't go to the bank on it, but Thunder's flying in as well. That can only mean someone of high net worth is—or will be—in town as well. My best guess is that she's meeting with Thunder. Although, I might add, LBB is also in town."

"Thunder? Who is that?"

"Sorry. Thunder's the managing partner of the law firm of Showers and Moore. Guy by the name of Hugh Showers. He's known as Thunder. Firm specializes in offshore protection of assets. Showers handles the trust setup aspect of asset protection while his partner, Jonathan Moore, handles the actual banking and asset movement details. Nothing of any great value moves anywhere in the world without their help—and blessing."

"Are you talking tax evasion? Money laundering? Just what does this Thunder actually do?"

"There may be some incidental tax evasion—I prefer to think of it as minimalization—going on. I couldn't speak to that. But minimalization and money laundering are far down their priority chain. The firm's not known for hiding the assets from the government, just for keeping those assets away from hostile hands. In that respect, Showers and Moore are the gold standard. Thunder is as tough as they come. Texas boy through and through."

"I suppose this hiding is done outside the United States."

"You suppose correctly. Nevis is one location. But for their really serious clients, they use the Cook Islands."

"Never heard of the Cook Islands. Where are they?"

"South Pacific. Near New Zealand. Population roughly fifteen thousand. And truthfully, I don't know Kumar's connection with Thunder. The fact she'll be alone tells me she doesn't expect to view, or take possession, of an original."

"Then why—"

"Think of it as three-card monte. The mark convinces himself he can follow the queen, but in the hands of a professional its simply impossible. Same with these art thieves. Andy and Tac were at the top of their game. My guess, they paired up with a third player, making it impossible to follow the original."

"Are you telling me Kumar is that third player?"

"That would be a stretch indeed. However, when the stakes are as high as they are with the Seminal Society, anything is possible and anyone could be a player. With that, you have exhausted my knowledge."

"Hey, Popeye," Leslie called to Lewis Rodriguez, "how you coming with that investigation?" Leslie was at her desk in the Pit when the young detective who she was now mentoring, stopped by. "I haven't seen any arrests. Any leads?"

"Might be getting close. I did what you suggested and canvassed the stores that sell masks. That was a dead end. But I had Beth's team work on the manufacturers. Got a list of who they sell to. Amazon sells the most, by far."

"That's country wide. How about—"

"Getting to that. Locally—Lee, Charlotte, Okeechobee, Collier—got almost a hundred. Good news, ninety-two of them are kids and are accounted for."

"And the other eight?" Leslie asked, impatient to get back to working on the da Vinci angle to Tac's death.

"All but three are accounted for. One was delivered to a postal box in a UPS store. But here's the thing. The driver's license used to rent the box turned out to be lost—or possibly stolen. The license actually belongs to a guy in a wheelchair. The other two masks were delivered to people who were up north when the incident occurred."

"Any surveillance video?"

"Yes and no. There's video, but his head was down. Guy's slender, about five-nine. Blue ball cap."

"That all you got?"

"That's it."

"Not possible! Think about it. Bet you can determine if he's right-handed or left? What about age? Any limps? How he holds his head? Are his hands steady or does he fumble with the key when he opens the box? You know more about the perp than you believe. Think is what a detective does. Think!"

Leslie was about to dismiss Rodriguez when Cox appeared. "Hey Rook," he called, "aren't you lead on that Popeye robbery?"

"Working with Les I am. Why's that important?"

"Your beeper's about to go off. Heard it live on the dispatch radio a moment ago. Bank robbery in progress. Fifth Third Bank. Not all that far from here over at Metro Parkway and Daniels. Man in a Popeye costume. They've called for All Available."

As Cox was talking, both Leslie's and Rodriguez's comms went off simultaneously. Each with the same 10-74, armed robbery code. Immediately following the 10-74 came 10-43, meaning the request was urgent—and they were to use lights and sirens. The address was consistent with what Cox had just communicated.

"It's going to be congested over there. No need for two or three cars. I'll drive," Cox announced, turning toward the door and breaking into a fast walk.

Leslie, with her long legs was no slouch in the hustle department and had no trouble keeping up. Neither did the much younger Rodriguez. The three of them jumped into Cox's car and slammed their respective doors closed almost simultaneously. Leslie activated the lights, then the siren, as the unmarked car sped from the lot, bouncing onto the roadway. The traffic was heavy, but thankfully people were able to pull to the inner and outer berms just enough so that Cox, except for a major congestion point when they turned north on Metro Parkway, was able to maintain good speed toward the bank.

The radio crackled alive with a dispatcher's voice announcing, "All cars! All cars! Perps cleared the bank—on foot going west."

Thirty seconds later the dispatcher announced, "Pursuing Officer reports he lost the perp. Last seen on the west side of John Yarbourgh Linear Park. Officer believes the perp was heading south, but not certain. BOLO for a man on foot in costume in or near John Yarbourgh Linear Park."

"Stop!" Rodriguez yelled. "Don't go through that light! Turn left."

"What the hell?" Cox replied, the brakes screeching as the car skidded and started to spin out of control before Cox got it slowed down enough to make the left turn. "Rook, I hope to hell you know what you're doing! Damn near turned the car over!"

"I know where he's going!" Rodriguez replied. "We tracked one of the Popeye costume's over here. On Morgan La Fee Lane. No one ever answers the phone. That address was on my list for follow-up. The park trail runs down this way. Too much of a coincidence."

Again, Cox jammed on the brakes. This time bringing the car to a stop at the side of the road. Ahead there were several homes scattered among the trees. Nothing seemed to be moving. "We don't know if The Sailor Man is armed or not. Need to assume he is. Need to get vests on. Let's go!"

Both Leslie's and Rodriguez's doors opened simultaneously, causing Cox to yell, "Hold! Not safe for all of us out there at once. Leslie, you go first. Rook'll follow. I'll cover you from in here."

"Roger that," Leslie acknowledged, darting from the driver's side to the trunk, her weapon drawn. Within a minute she was back, wearing a vest and carrying another. "I thought you had four," she declared, "but could only see two."

"Rook, put that on," Cox commanded. "The other two are under the blanket, along with my M4. Cover me while I get it."

Leslie rolled down her window and focused on the tree line nearest where the trail Popeye was on was situated. Rodriguez slid to the other side of the car, opened the window and balanced his firearm on the window ledge, ready to fire on anything that moved.

"Something's moving over here!" Leslie shouted. "Somebody's running this way! Cox," she yelled, "movement to your right! Get down!"

Cox grabbed his vest with his right hand and reached for the Colt Carbine with his left. He started to duck beside the driver's side of the car to put on the vest. He never had a chance. The bullet nicked his upper left arm and entered his chest just above his heart. He fell against the car and slid to the ground.

Instantly, Rodriguez slid across the back seat and opened the door. Several bullets hit the car: one a half-inch above the door opening, just missing the rookie's head. Another hit behind the door. A third directly in the middle of the now closed door just below the window.

Leslie tried to focus on anything moving but saw nothing. "You okay?" she called to Rodriguez.

"Wasn't hit," came the shaky answer. "But Cox is down!"

"Get to the other side and see what's over there. Use the car as a shield. But for goodness sake, be careful. I've got this side covered. I think the shooter's in those trees on this side of the car."

The sound of gunshots again filled the air. This time the bullets didn't strike the car. A moment later, Leslie heard, "Police! Put your gun down!" The sound came from the tree line on Leslie's side of the car.

Rodriguez worked his way to the back of the car. "Les," he yelled, "Cox is down! Not moving!"

Leslie immediately pushed her mic button. "This is Detective Hodges. I'm on Morgan La Fee Lane. Detective Rodriguez is with me. My partner, Detective Cox, is down. Hit by gunfire from one or more unknown persons. Please dispatch medical emergency team ASAP."

The communication link crackled almost immediately. "This is Officer Rodgers with Officer Pasqual. We are on the pathway inside the tree line east of the black Ford. Have the perp in our sights. Ordered him to put his weapon down. No response. Request backup."

"Detective Hodges. Don't see you or the perp. We can—"

Leslie's communication was interrupted by Dispatch. "Do nothing," came the command. "Tac Team's less than a minute out. We have your location pinpointed. Helo will be on scene in ninety seconds. EMS two minutes."

Carefully, Leslie opened the car door, waiting a few seconds to see if she would draw gunfire. Nothing. She eased herself to the ground and crawled to the back of the car where Rodriguez was lying overtop of Cox. "Cox," she called. "Are you okay?"

Hearing no answer, she repeated, "Cox, talk to me! It's Leslie!"

Still nothing.

A bullet slammed into the car behind her head, hitting the gas cap.

Several shots rang out, followed by silence.

"Cox, can you hear me?" Leslie again called, motioning Rodriquez to move off her partner. Cox's shirt was soaked in blood, as was the ground around him. Despite her training, and her years of tending to gunshot and stabbing victims, Leslie's heart raced. *There's too much blood! He'll die if I don't stop this bleeding right now!* She ripped his shirt open to expose the wound. Kneeling over his body, she applied pressure directly to the hole in his chest even though deep down she knew the truth. The wound was dry. Her partner's heart had already stopped. Only a miracle could save Cox now.

FOURTEEN

THE MEMORIAL SERVICE FOR COX had come to an end. His brother had spoken eloquently about growing up with an older brother who poked into everyone's business, but who never allowed anyone near his. The brother had chided about all the females Cox had in his life but confessed that there had never been one that was special. Leslie learned something she hadn't known about her partner. Speaker after speaker repeated the same theme. That if you were in need of anything, from tangible items to emotional support, Cox would see to it that you got what you needed.

The sheriff spoke. As did Captain Stetson. And even Sergeant Oakmore. Leslie had been asked, but politely declined, saying, "It's still too raw. He died just as my husband did, protecting the public. I'm just not ready." However, the true reason Leslie held back is because she didn't trust herself. Guilt had overwhelmed her. Cox died because she hadn't brought him his vest. Had she done so, he would be alive today.

The overflow crowd had dispersed, leaving his mother and her two sisters alone with her son's urn, the brother standing off to the side. A limo waited patiently outside the gigantic church to whisk the family to their homes. Looking around, Leslie realized the reporters and their cameras were gone and the endless interviews were thankfully over, leaving Leslie to her tangled private thoughts.

She was about to open her car door when a tap on the shoulder startled her. She hadn't been aware of the presence of the solidly built, five foot nine, IRS Agent Maxine Ghana, she with wideset eyes, high cheekbones, and short curly hair. Ghana had been born in Trinidad and immigrated to America at the age of twelve when her father got caught up in the Jamaat al Muslimeen coup d'état attempt in 1990. "I didn't realize you'd be here. Thanks for coming, Agent Ghana."

"You are my contact with Lee County. You, and to some extent, Boots who I've known for a long time. Didn't have much contact with your partner, Simeon. Heard the other side of him today. He hid that well. Wanted to be a cop all his life, so it appears."

"He was good at what he did, that's for certain."

"I thought you two were at odds."

"At times, he and I got at cross-purposes. Usually that had to do with his constant poking at my private life. But he was good at what he did."

"According to what his brother said, that was his way. Possibly covering for something missing in his life. Who the hell ever knows. People are far more complex than we give them credit for, that much I know. For what it's worth, I have to say you and Cox did well together. From what I've learned, you saved his career."

Leslie stopped walking and confronted Ghana. "For what purpose? He's dead! In the end, I didn't have his back! I'll go to my grave with that on my conscience. I failed him!"

"Leslie, listen to me. I've seen the preliminary investigation. You did nothing wrong. There was no way for you to know where the perp was. You were over a mile from the last sighting. How could you have known he wasn't on foot, had stashed an electric bike?"

"All I know is that I failed my partner."

"I understand your frustration, Leslie. Honestly, I do. But you're being way too hard on yourself. Come, my hotel's just a few blocks from here. A drink'll do you good. Besides, I want to pick your brain."

"What'll do me good is being left alone!"

"That's the last thing you need. Believe me. Besides, I have a few things to talk over with you."

"Like what?" Leslie demanded. "I'm not in the mood to be double-talked."

"I've always been straight with you. When I was not at liberty to tell you something I told you so. Hey, speaking of not telling things, didn't see Jak here today. I thought he'd be working the Tac case with you?"

"Why would you think that?"

"Tac was into da Vinci. So is Queen B. There have been several transactions—and rumors. Mostly rumors, I must admit."

"Told him to stay away. His divorce isn't final, keeps getting pushed back. I don't want to deal with him around until then. Simple as that."

"Look, I know about your relationship and it's anything but simple. Come on, let's have that drink. Got a few things to discuss with you."

"If it's about Jak, I'm not interested."

"I can't promise anything about him, but we have other business. For starters, I'd like whatever you can tell me about Tac Jacobi. Rumor has it that it was a failed parachute."

That caught Leslie's interest. "Lead on," Leslie reluctantly consented, thinking that Ghana was right, focusing on work would ease the pain of her partner's death—at least for the moment.

They walked in silence for several blocks before Ghana said, "It took me a while to link Tac's unfortunate demise with the Seminal Society collectors. But the more I think about it the more I believe I'm right. But truthfully, for the life of me I'm perplexed as to what it is."

"Ground rules!" Leslie said, suddenly stopping. "Promise me, no Jakowski talk. I can't deal with it. And no more counselling on Cox. That's my issue to work out."

"No Jak. And no Cox. Got it. I promise."

Ghana led the way to the hotel bar and remained quiet until their drinks came. "Let me give you some information you may or may not already know. There's a guy by the name of William Paxter Skyler. He first came to the attention of the IRS when his tax returns didn't match his lifestyle. He built up a nice business selling shoes. Actually, he created a national string of upscale shoe stores. When his wife came down with breast cancer, he sold the chain. He then bought several homes, one in Sag Harbor, New York; one over in Miromar Lakes and one in the hills of Italy. Wife lived there for five years before passing."

"His granddaughter is the one who found Tac," Leslie injected. "Name's Orion. "Everyone calls her Star," Leslie added, quoting from her interview with the granddaughter. Trouble with that; Orion's a constellation, not a star."

"Another case where the nickname makes no sense. Someone starts it and it sticks. Careful what you wish for I suppose."

"Orion did say her grandfather was off in the hills of Italy visiting friends."

"Would it surprise you to learn that Skyler collects Seminal Society Firsts? And is, indeed, at this very moment, in Italy. Only he's not visiting friends. As of a month ago, he's thought to be hard on the trail of a da Vinci parachute sailcloth. In fact, we have good reason to believe he found what he was seeking and it's now in the states."

"He was in Italy at the time Tac drowned. Had been for weeks. He's far down on the suspect list."

"And rightly so. If our information is right—and I think it is—Skyler found what he was after and it is now in the possession of the man, Mr. Donatello Andino, who, as you know, went missing."

"Andy! His name's been linked to the deceased! What a small world!"

"Not so small, my dear. Not so small. It's no coincidence they're all in the same area. Allows them to keep a close eye on their pet projects—and on each other. They come and go at each other's houses without notice. It all fits."

"Any other connections you want to impart?" Leslie asked, focusing on the IRS Agent across the table who clearly was working an agenda that Leslie didn't yet understand.

"That's enough for tonight. My suite has two bedrooms. You take the other one and we'll finish this in the morning. Oh, I almost forgot, I was asked to pass a message to you from a big time admirer of yours. He's here in town and would love to have a meal with you. He's also very much interested in da Vinci's parachute as well."

"And who might that be?"

"Little Billy Bob."

FIFTEEN

"JUDGING FROM YOUR REACTION," Ghana commented, after studying Leslie's reaction to Billy Bob's invitation, "I'd say you're just as interested in spending time with him as he is with you."

"I suppose I should deny that, but you're too good at what you do. The man does intrigue me. But I thought he's tight with the young Aribah woman. Granddaughter of Pearl. And, while we're on the topic of LBB you seem to know him better than I would have thought. Pardon my asking, but are you—"

"My goodness, No! In point of fact, I have never met him in person! All of our communications, and they have been extensive I must admit, have been by phone. Several by Zoom. As I said, none in person."

"You know a lot about him for only having a phone connection to him."

"For one thing, he's in Texas and I'm in Florida. For another, it's to our mutual benefit to share information, to trust each other. I get a great insight into the art world and he... he gets to know what the government is doing at any given time. Most important to him, he receives a fair appraisal of value for the few pieces he parts with. Unlike the Kumars, who are constantly one step ahead of indictment, LBB always has a clean tax record."

"Tell me about granddaughter Bates Aribah. What should I know about her?"

"That woman's nothing but trouble. Trouble with a capital T. I don't like her one bit. Only in Bates' mind is there any relationship between her and Little Billy Bob. You can trust me on that," Ghana assured Leslie. "As I'm sure you know, she recently acted as an intermediary in a somewhat controversial art transaction involving one of the few remaining original da Vinci's."

"The Salvator Mundi," Leslie acknowledged. "Auctioned last year for over four hundred fifty million."

"According to our analysis of the situation, the Mundi is now in the possession of your friend Bishop, via Miss Aribah. She was working with Andino, who, by the way, is ex-cop and a friend of

Jakowski, to deliver the Mundi to the real buyer, who we believe to be Prince Badr bin Abdullah Al Saud."

"From your tone, I assume you have your doubts."

"You, of all people, should know that in the high stakes art world nothing is as it seems. The official story is, as you said, the Mundi was sold at auction to the prince through intermediary Queen Baribah, who now goes by Pearl Aribah, grandmother to Bates."

"If what you said before about LBB owning the Mundi is true, it follows that the prince owns a fake."

"The prince, by refusing comment as to whether he has the original or not, hasn't helped the situation. He won't confirm that he even has the Mundi!"

"And you can't get to the bottom of it? Why?"

"As I said, the prince won't give a statement and he's out of our jurisdiction, so we have no pressure. LBB has let it be known to his Seminal Society cohorts that he has secured the Mundi, so we're taking him at his word."

"What about Andino?" Leslie asked. "You said he was the one who transported the Mundi from Christies to, I assume, the real buyer. If a substitution was made, he was the logical person to have made it."

"He, or Bates. She was right in the middle. In fact, she's the one who certified to the prince that she picked the Mundi up at the auction house and it never left her possession until she delivered it to him in person."

"If the prince ever learns she lied, then what happens?"

"Bates' days would be numbered. Nowhere in the world would be safe for her. Not even Thunder could protect her then."

"I dare say, you're here to see what you can squeeze out of Andino. I'm right, aren't I? But Andino's gone missing!"

"That's true enough. But that's only a byproduct of my mission. The cover as you will. Let me be blunt, Leslie. The IRS wants you to come work for us. Frankly, my instructions are to 'seal the deal'."

Leslie sat back in her chair and took a long moment to process what she had just heard. Her first instinct was: *Hell no! I'm not working for the IRS!* Instead, she asked, "And just why would I consider making a change? I've only worked for Lee County going on four years. As investigators go, I'm still cutting my teeth."

Ghana studied the detective, then said, "You're serious, aren't you? At first, I thought you were pulling my leg about being inexperienced. You may have been a detective for only four years, but you've been a cop for fifteen. More important, you have one of the highest homicide arrest records in the country."

"Right place. Right time," Leslie answered, playing down Ghana's praise, while realizing Ghana's offer had come from much higher up.

"One arrest, two, maybe. But you're credited with six! And not only that, the billionaire art collectors, the ones such as Morris Dexter Stratis with the penchant for substitution and deception, have let it be known that they will no longer consider any acquisition that has its roots in Southwestern Florida. You got their attention big time. The IRS powers that be like that. They believe with you working as an agent, the IRS can significantly increase tax revenue."

"I'm flattered, don't get me wrong. But it just doesn't feel right. It just doesn't."

"Maybe it'll feel better when I tell you that your starting salary will be in excess of one hundred twenty-five a year. Plus benefits. That's not counting overtime and a travel allowance. And... and here's the best part—for you. You won't have me for a supervisor. We'd be colleagues."

"What's that mean?"

"You'll have your own team. Develop your own network. Work your own investigations. You'll train in Georgia for fourteen weeks, then be assigned a location. Maybe Florida. Maybe somewhere else? Where would you like to work?"

Overwhelmed, Leslie managed, "I haven't thought much of it, frankly."

"What're you thinking? Yes? No? Maybe?"

"Have to think on it all's I can say," Leslie managed.

"I'll put that down as a maybe. Next class starts in exactly one month."

"Don't I have to qualify? Pass some sort of a test? Have a background check? Tox screen?"

"That's all been done. Just say yes and you're in. Easy as that. I told you they want you."

Coming back to earth, Leslie said, "I'm not the first detective to solve crimes—even homicides. That's what we're paid to do. So, what's the real reason?"

"Way above my pay grade, Leslie. You did graduate with the highest, or one of the highest, scores ever. You have almost total recall. Photo memory I'm told. And, most important of all, you must have picked up a rabbi along the way. A rabbi with powerful connections—and an unlimited IRS checkbook."

Names—and faces—passed across Leslie's internal vision. Leading the parade was Little Billy Bob Bishop, the Texas rancher who Leslie had enjoyed having two private dinners with. She could still taste the barbecue, along with the fantastic key lime pie, she had consumed as he had talked about his rare collection of Seminal Society Firsts and the ends to which the billionaire collectors—he had referred to the other collectors as rivals—would go to secure a First. "The most devious and cunning one of them all," he had confided, "is Dex Stratis out of Pittsburgh. His collection, I am led to believe, is even more extensive than mine. But then again, Dex is not above smoke and mirrors, bait and switch, so no one really knows what he has and doesn't have."

Leslie's mind then went to Sanjay Kumar, the silk-suited billionaire electronics wizard. The vision of Kumar's gorgeous wife Riya, lingered in Leslie's mind a few extra beats, the Indian woman's eyes smiling with her passion for art originals. "The masters are alive, Leslie!" Riya had said when they had last met. "Alive in my private space! Can you imagine being in complete harmony with da Vinci, Botticelli, Picasso, Vermeer for hours with nothing standing between you and them?"

Forcing herself back to reality, Leslie addressed a practical question to Ghana. "What exactly would be my function with the IRS? I'm not an attorney, nor am I particularly good with numbers. I'd be useless with audits and things like that."

"Investigations. Tracking down suspicious high-value artifact movement. Making certain the proper people paid their fair share, as they say, of taxes. Skimming even one percent from a ten-million-dollar profit on the sale of an item is big money. These folks either forget to pay altogether, or when they do declare, they establish a low value for the art piece. Since the sales are often private, it'll be your job to track them down and document the true transaction. Separating genuine from fake becomes the real challenge. When these high rollers buy, it's always a genuine First. When they sell, suddenly their precious artifact becomes a fake."

"What about criminal activity? Is that—"

"FBI. Or local police. Like you and I are doing right now. I'll tell you what you won't be doing. You won't be running through the streets with guns firing around you as you risk your life to arrest a petty thief. More important, you won't end up as your partner did."

Focusing on her deceased partner again got Leslie's attention. She carefully reviewed what had been said. Then added, "I didn't know we were going on the clock right now. Are you telling me something?"

"Just that a FGCU student found what she called 'scarf fabric' tangled in a tree behind her dorm on the south bank of the lake where Tac Jacobi drowned. The Internet had shown an artist's rendition of a parachute landing in the lake causing her to think about the guy who "fell from the sky." The student equated the fabric to parachutes and called the Lee County Sheriff tip line. CIA Hillard called her back almost immediately and asked her to secure the material. An hour later the remnant the co-ed found was on its way to the FBI for analysis."

"I didn't know anything about all that! Why didn't they—"

"You've been otherwise occupied. What with Cox's death and all you've had on your hands. Anyway, the material's a perfect match to a sketch from a da Vinci notebook describing parachute material he was working on. Without hesitation, I'd say it's full bore, game on!"

SIXTEEN

"RODRIGUEZ," LESLIE SAID INTO her phone when the young detective answered. "You've drawn the short straw! You're now working with me on the Jacobi case. That's the man who drowned in the lake last week. Pull the file, read everything. Meet me in the Pit in two hours ready to discuss the case. Ask Hilliard to join us."

"You got it, Skipper! See you in two."

On the way to the office, Leslie bit the bullet and called Jakowski.

"Leslie!" he exclaimed, "you're the last person in the world I expected to hear from. What a pleasant surprise!"

"Don't read anything more into this than just me gathering information."

"If, by *information* you're referring to the status of the divorce, then—"

"That information, as you well know, I could get from the public record. No, I just had a visit from Ghana, and—"

"She must have gone to the Cox service. Sorry about the loss of your partner. I know he rubbed you the wrong way. I also know you respected him—and will miss the guy. I thought about coming down but deep-sixed the idea."

"I agree. Pittsburgh is where you belong until... until your divorce is resolved. Then perhaps we'll see." Leslie struggled to keep her voice neutral.

"Sounds to me like you've had a change of heart. Am I no longer—"

"I said we'll talk when your Pittsburgh business is finished. It's pointless before that." In point of fact, she wanted his divorce to be independent from her feelings for him, which were, if she was being honest about it, more negative than she was yet willing to admit. Maybe it was Cox's death, maybe something else. But in any event, she now didn't feel as though she had a solid footing. And that bothered her.

"If it's not about our future what then?"

"Two topics. First, tell me about Andino. Heard you and he were buddies."

"Not exactly buddies. When he worked on the Pittsburgh force, we had occasion to match notes. As you know, Verona, where I work, is just up the Allegheny River from Pittsburgh. We shared information. Once in a while we'd have a dual operation."

Recognizing this was Jakowski's way to say a lot and impart little of value. She knew the big cop only did this when he was shielding important info, so she countered, "Jak. You're in deflection mode! Give it to me unfiltered."

"Busted! You know me way to good. When Andy quit, he moved out to Greensburg, that's an hour East, and opened a one-man Private Eye operation. Did okay for himself."

"I'm not visualizing him taking candids for wronged spouses. What aren't you telling me?"

"Deliveries. He specialized in securely picking up and delivering valuable objects."

"Such as?"

"Jewelry mostly."

"And? Keep going! You're still holding back."

"The occasional art piece."

"Art piece? As in some old old guy giving his prized Warhol, the one that hung over his fireplace for a quarter-century, to his son across town? Or art piece, as in a Seminal Society First being loaned from one museum to another?"

"The latter—mostly."

"Then, can I assume that in your capacity as facilitator for Morris Dexter Stratis, you and Andino did business?"

"Occasionally we did."

"Jak, you're exhausting me! Please stop the cat and mouse and fill me in on Andino!"

"Look, I don't have much more. The man was good at what he did. Move items from one location to another. Yes, high value items at times. I hired him from time to time, but I never instructed him to do anything other than point-to-point delivery."

"I take that to mean that people other than you gave him instructions. Those other people might have been working for Stratis."

"Might have been. I'm not confirming one way or the other 'cause I don't know."

"I'm sure you've heard rumors that substitutions have been made during an Andino delivery? You're confirming the truth of those rumors."

"I wouldn't doubt the rumors, that much I'll say."

"Did he ever work with a woman named Bates Aribah?"

"Granddaughter of Queen B. Piece of work, that one. I've heard the rumor. Personally, I think they worked on at least two, possibly three, deliveries. But I don't know for certain. I'm done on this topic. You said you had two."

In her line of work, knowing when to tromp the brake is just as critical as knowing when to mash the gas pedal. This was brake time. "I've been offered an investigative agent job—I don't know exactly what they call it—with the IRS. My own team and all. What does that mean?"

"Means you're on a waiting list. Along with a thousand other detectives, who, in the end, will be rejected. Coveted job. Great pay. Great pension. Great work. Clean. You never even arrest anyone. You file a report. If the Justice Department agrees with your investigation, they send Federal Marshals to do the dirty work. Never get your hands dirty. The only downside, you might work one case for years until you get what you need to close it—or recommend indictment. Or worse, come up dry!"

"Sounds boring."

"Maybe to young ears. But trust me, chasing felons through the streets, dodging bullets, gets old real fast. As we both know. You've been on the job, what? Four years now? Took two bullets that I know about. A fraction of an inch one way or the other for either of them and you'd be spending the rest of your life needing assistance getting on and off the toilet—or worse! Six feet under like Cox!"

Leslie had to accept that Ghana's offer came because of Cox's death. It wasn't just a timing accident that the proposal had come at her most vulnerable moment. It had been by design, A cold calculation on the part of whomever controlled such things that it was only a matter of time until she took a bullet. That told her one very important characteristic of her new boss. He or she was prone to manipulation. Out of one frypan directly into another is how Leslie saw this opportunity.

"You're awfully quiet, Leslie. Talk to me. What about us?"

Ignoring Jak's question, she ducked the elephant hanging over their relationship. "I think you answered my questions, at least for now. Thank you."

"Not so fast. The divorce is finally back on track and frankly I miss being with you. I know you've banished me from your part of Florida, but—"

"Pete, I think it best we continue with the plan. I'm knee deep in what appears to be a homicide investigation and breaking in Cox's replacement isn't going to be easy. A rookie of all things. I don't need anything more on my plate."

"Sorry if I'm a burden to you. I certainly don't think—"

"That came out wrong. It's just that... that I'm overloaded and... and frankly in mourning. I shouldn't have called. I'm sorry."

"Have it your way, Leslie. Just be sure you know what you're doing. Most important, just know I love you."

The line went dead without Leslie having time to respond.

Replaying the conversation, Leslie concluded it had been for the best that Pete had not given her time to reply, conflicted as she was.

Leslie was not even to her desk when Rodriguez appeared, seemingly from behind a row of filing cases. "Your first interview on the Tac death," the rookie began, was with a young woman who first found him in the water. Her name, nickname really, is Star. Full name is—"

"Orion Skyler," Leslie filled in. "Granddaughter of William Paxter Skyler. Made a fortune when he sold his shoe store chain to Amazon. According to Star, he's got a home in Sag Harbor, one down here, and one in the 'Hills of Italy' where he's visiting friends. What of it?"

"So, it's real! I've heard rumors that you have total recall, but I didn't believe it! Until now! What a gift!"

"You give me too much credit. I just reread the file. Continue, please."

"Star also said that her grandfather is off chasing after Michelangelo—or da Vinci. She couldn't recall which one."

"And that means what to you?"

"Well, for one, I read your older files on The Seminal Society, so I know about billionaires chasing after Firsts. But truthfully, I couldn't find anything about anyone going after parachutes. In fact, I don't even believe da Vinci invented the parachute."

"Don't forget the Euphon from Chladni. If it's a First, they're all in. With respect to the parachute, there are certainly mixed thoughts as to whether or not that is a true da Vinci First. But he did make sketches that are contained in a codex gathered by the 16th century sculptor Pompeo Leoni."

"I saw on Wikipedia that Bill Gates paid thirty million for a da Vinci codex. Is that where the sketches are located?"

"Wrong codex. Gates owns the *Leicester* Codex. The Codex with the parachute is the *Atlanticus* and all twelve volumes are in Milan at the *Veneranda* Biblioteca Ambrosiana. In July 2000,

Adrian Nicholas, a British skydiver, jumped from a hot air balloon with the intent to prove da Vinci's design worked."

"So, did it work?"

"So far as it went, the experiment worked. But... but what I find interesting is that da Vinci had drawn a pyramid constructed from pine struts covered with wax impregnated linen cloth. Nicholas, however, listened to critics and naysayers who predicted the structure would land so heavily on him that he would be crushed. When Nicholas got near the ground, he cut the contraption off and used a conventional parachute to complete his descent. The da Vinci parachute landed so slowly that nothing was damaged.

"That's exciting! Love to talk to Nicholas. Want me to call and see if he could shed any light on what Tac was up to? Why design a parachute if airplanes didn't exist?"

"Unfortunately, Nicholas died in 2005. But that was a good thought. But I know at least part of the answer to your question about parachutes and planes."

"Why then?"

"Buildings were getting taller and taller. In case of fire, use a parachute."

"Not very practical but makes sense for da Vinci. I know he was interested in flight, so it makes sense for him to dwell on parachutes. It's too bad Nicholas died. I would have liked to... Hey, I just had a thought! Could our guy Tac have been trying to recreate the original parachute?"

"For what purpose?"

"To be the first person to prove da Vinci was right by going *all the way* to the ground instead of ending the descent early. Maybe Tac was going for the whole enchilada?"

"But the material found in the tree was silk, not linen."

"Waxed linen, you said."

"That was what da Vinci said to make the chute from. But look what I just found online," Leslie held her phone up for Rodriguez to see. "Mariano di Jacopo, a man who died the year da Vinci was born was, like da Vinci, an engineer and an artist. Jacopo drew the first parachute, and he lived in a community that housed silk traders and weavers. What's more, he was known by the name Taccola."

"Could our Tac be a relative? Want me to check it out?"

"Go for it. Nothing else is making sense!"

SEVENTEEN

"LESLIE, I'M SO THRILLED YOU AGREED to have lunch with me," William Bishop, said, doffing his oversized white hat as he took an exaggerated bow. "I'm looking forward to the pleasure of your company.

"Red Robin is not exactly your penthouse suite at the Ritz-Carlton, and it certainly doesn't hold a candle to your Texas Barbeque, but they do have good hamburgers. I know it doesn't matter to you, but I'm buying."

"If that's what it takes to enjoy your company, dear lady, I will gladly accept your kind offer. Lead the way."

"Leslie," her lunch partner began when they were seated in the far corner with Leslie having a clear view of the front and side doors as was her habit, "I understand you've had more than your fair share of trauma in your life. This highlights just how dangerous your job is. Please accept my condolences on the loss of your partner. I'm truly sorry."

"Thank you, Mr. Bax—"

"Please! I thought we were beyond that. Billy Bob works. Close friends, which I consider you, call me LBB. May I call you Leslie? Or do you prefer Detective?"

"For now," Leslie said, mentally kicking herself even as she spoke, "I think Detective would be the proper way to go." Adding, "At least until this investigation is over."

"What investigation is that? Or am I not allowed to ask you that? I thought you were on leave."

"I ended the leave early. I'm investigating a drowning that occurred last week. A guy jumped from a plane over Miromar Lakes. It was—"

"I'm very much familiar with Tac's death. Thought it was an accident."

Leslie studied her companion a moment trying to ascertain his level of interest in Tac and the circumstances of how he died. "We're not ready to announce one way or the other. You have input, I'm all ears."

"I suppose you think I have input because of my connection—alleged connection I should say—to the Seminal Society. Am I close?"

"Close enough. According to the Society, da Vinci's soul was passed along to Galileo. Am I close?"

"So the Seminal Society collectors believe. Does that mean you've linked Tac's death to da Vinci?"

"We're not there yet. However, in Tac's library we did find two books written about someone named Mariano di Jacopo. This Jacopo guy, who was called Taccola, died in 1453. That's just after da Vinci was born. Apparently, Taccola, who was an artist and inventor like da Vinci, sketched parachutes. I don't think it's a coincidence that the deceased called himself Tac. After all, he was an avid skydiver." Leslie again paused, this time to choose her words carefully. "I should also add that Tac's neighbor is believed to have been involved with transporting the Salvator Mundi—and the substitution thereof. That, of course is what brings to mind da Vinci and his parachute sketches. And, from our prior discussions, I gather you're an expert in collecting da Vinci."

"If you're looking for a da Vinci expert, you should speak with Bill Gates, he owns—"

"Da Vinci's Codex Leicester. It's the only copy of a da Vinci manuscript that resides outside of Europe. No, it's not an expert I'm looking for. It's knowledge of recent da Vinci transactions."

"Can you just imagine owning such a treasure?" Bishop said, refusing to take the bait. He leaned back and closed his eyes, a satisfied smile on his face. "Among other things, those papers cover diverse topics, such as the diffusion of light in the heavens, musings on why the moon is luminous, and a study of hydrodynamics. And that's only a small sampling."

"I take it you've seen the Gates Codex."

"Oh, several times, in fact. I happen to be an early investor in Microsoft. Gates and I go back a ways. As you must know, in the mid 90s he paid thirty million dollars or so for the Codex. A while back, I offered him a blank check. But the offer fell on deaf ears."

"There's a rumor the Codex will be going on tour. Do I have that right?"

"You do. I think it's a bad idea, but security's over the top."

"When has that ever stopped the Seminal Society collectors?" Leslie quipped, laughing to cover the bluntness of her comment.

"I take exception to that. The only collector I know who gets tangled up with security in any negative way is Stratis, usually with your Pittsburgh cop friend somewhere in the mix."

"Talk about taking exception," she quickly responded, her face setting hard. "May I remind you that you owned the security company that transported Newton's manuscript when it managed to go missing in a substitution. A substitution that resulted in one of your employees being shot and killed."

"Touchè! Thanks to your stellar investigation, the perp's awaiting trial. A sad story all around."

"I notice you haven't commented on the whereabouts of the original Newton. Or who financed the transaction."

"It certainly wasn't me, if that is what you're insinuating."

"If the shoe fits, then—"

"That shoe is much too large for me, Leslie. Much too large. Can we—"

The waiter interrupted, ready to take their order. When he left, Leslie, said, "I think you changed the subject on me. I was discussing da Vinci and his parachute sketches, and you moved onto the Gates Codex. What's troubling you about da Vinci?"

"What makes you think I'm troubled?"

"Wouldn't be much of a detective if I couldn't read you."

"Not many can, Leslie. Not many can. Here's the thing about the parachute drawings. They're contained in another codex called Atlanticus. You're right, I would love to possess *that* codex. It's very securely held by the *Biblioteca Ambrosiana* in Milan. Tis a shame."

"From my perspective, LBB, the only shame would be if those drawings were to be removed from public access and held in a private collection. That would be the real crime."

"That's what I love about you, Leslie," Bishop said, gently placing his hands over hers. "You say what you believe. Not many do. I admire that. I really do."

The warmth of his fingers was comforting. At least for the moment she didn't want time to pass.

The waiter chose just that instant to appear at the table. "Okay, who gets the one with no fries?"

"That would be her," Bishop said, sitting back in his chair. "I'm a fries man all the way."

They ate in silence until Bishop downed his last potato. "What's this I hear about you moving over to the IRS? I suppose that's a real tribute to your abilities, but... but I can't say as I'm happy about the prospect."

"I have two questions," Leslie commented, surprised at LBB's bluntness. "One, how the hell do you know about that? And two, how does that affect you?"

"Answer to your first question: A little birdie told me. Answer to your second: I take the fifth. But I can tell you this much. You better keep a sharp eye on Ghana. She's not all she wants you to believe she is."

"LBB! You can't leave me hanging like that! What are you talking about?"

"I suppose I can tell you. Despite all the rumors, I now own the Salvator Mundi."

"And what may I ask is the connection between the Mundi and Ghana?"

"Not only do I own the Mundi, but I have possession of it as well."

"You're avoiding the Ghana connection."

"It was Agent Maxine Ghana who personally delivered the painting to me."

"I've been looking for you," an excited Rodriguez called from halfway across the Pit, motioning Leslie over to the chair next to his desk that he hastily cleared of files. When she sat down, he admonished her. "You had your phone off. You never have your phone off. Where were you?"

"That's not your business! What's so important that it couldn't wait until after my lunch break?"

Rodriguez leaned in close. "I had a call just an hour ago with the director of the Martin Luther King Jr. Memorial Library in D.C. And—"

"Why that library? And what has this to do with—"

"I think you know that the Codex Atlanticus, that's where da Vinci's aeronautical sketches were drawn, are maintained at the *Biblioteca Ambrosiana* in Milan. Well, as it turns out, the codex was on display last year in D.C."

"Continue. You have my attention."

"As I said, I spoke to the director and it turns out that the IRS had an art expert inspect the codex to make certain it was genuine."

"And?"

"And, according to the director, he was assured all was in order with the Codex."

"Did the director tell you why there's any question about authenticity in the first place?" Leslie asked, leaning back from her partner.

"I asked him that very question. He said he was puzzled at first as to why the IRS was interested in the Codex. Said he checked into it and it seems rumors are floating that a substitution had been made or was about to be made. They increased security, but nothing happened."

"That they know about," Leslie added. "Or will talk about."

"There is that possibility, yes," Rodriuez conceded.

"I'd like to talk to whoever the IRS used to examine the Codex. Happen to get a name?"

Rodiquez studied Leslie's face a long moment, moving even closer than before. When he finally answered, his voice was barely a whisper. "The person's name was—and don't shoot the messenger—Agent Maxine Ghana, at the request of... Detective Leslie Hodges."

EIGHTEEN

LESLIE WAS STRUGGLING TO UNDERSTAND the implications of what Rodriguez had just told her when, upon returning to her desk, she found a note.

SEE ME! ASAP!

There was no mistaking whose handwriting it was. Her boss, Captain Karen Stetson. Leslie could only guess how much time had elapsed since its placement. There was no guessing as to the tenor of the note. Angry. She could also only guess as to whether Boots was cooling down—or even hotter since writing the missive.

Since Rodriguez hadn't said anything about Boots, Leslie was certain the invitation had not included him. Typically, an ASAP command from her boss triggered a quick response. Jogging to the boss's office would not be out of character for Leslie, except this time she required time to process what she had just learned from her partner—and what she had learned from LBB. *Why the hell would the IRS use her name? And why in hell would Ghana deliver the Mundi to LBB? Maybe it wasn't the IRS! If not, who?* The possibilities seemed endless.

Leslie was barely through Boot's doorway when Stetson barked, "There you are!" Duplicating exactly the greeting Leslie had received from her partner upon her return from lunch with Little Billy Bob. "I've been waiting for your return. Have a good lunch with your Texas friend?"

How—and most important, why—Boots knew of her lunch plans was troubling. Leslie forced her smile to remain in place. "I wouldn't exactly call Bishop a friend. To answer your question, yes, the hamburger was excellent."

"That really wasn't my question," Boots barked. "Now, was it?"

"You want to know if I got anything useful from LBB. Truthfully, I'm not certain one way or the other. There's one theory we're working—and this is Rodriguez's idea—is that Tac Jacobi's death is in some way related to parachute drawings made by da Vinci."

"Sounds like a lot of wheels are about to be spun chasing after drawings made in the fifteenth century. Who the hell cares? I don't believe da Vinci ever made a parachute. If I'm right about that, then this Tac character didn't jump from a plane with a parachute stolen from some da Vinci collection. People die all the time from misadventures—and this feels like a misadventure to me. Sorry to interrupt. You were telling me what you got from LBB."

"Bishop seemed to know a lot about the parachute and particularly that the original drawings were on display not long ago at the Martin Luther King Jr. Memorial Library in D.C. Tac appeared to have had a high interest in those drawings. Apparently, Agent Ghana also inspected the Codex." Leslie purposefully didn't reveal that her name had come up as having validated Ghana.

"You're grasping at straws," Stetson responded. "Wrap it up sooner than later."

"FYI. There is a little smoke. Tac's friend and neighbor, man named Andy Andino, was rumored to have been involved with a substitution of a Seminal Society collector art piece seems to have gone walkabout. Nothing definite yet. Rodriguez is on it."

"How's the kid doing?"

"So far, so good," Leslie answered, happy the spotlight moved away from her. "He's got good instincts."

"Glad to hear it. Don't waste a lot of time on Tac's death. I'm willing to sign off on accidental. Goodness knows, we have enough on our hands, we don't need to be chasing our butts."

"I hear you, Captain. Do what I can. But I just learned that the Mundi painting was delivered to LBB by Ghana as well. Where there's smoke..."

"Okay. Do what you deem best. Only don't waste resources. Oh, I almost forgot. I understand you got a job offer. What's that about?"

"How the... the dickens did you—"

"Ghana herself called. For once she's playing nice. That in and of itself is worrisome. She assured me the poaching's coming from far above her. Wanted me to know it wasn't her who initiated it. Seems her management's hot to trot."

"Hotter than I am, that's for certain," Leslie assured Boots. "Money's good, I'll say that much. But candidly, I love what I do. Need to think long and hard on it."

"Sheriff'll be happy to hear that. Tell you this much, with your high-profile homicide closing rate, that man'll do anything to keep you. As would I."

"I hesitate to ask you this, but I don't know who else to ask. Why's IRS so anxious to hire me? I'm barely past rooky stage and hit a bit of good luck is all."

"First off, Leslie, in your case luck may have helped, but you have an intangible. Don't know how to explain it, but you lock on and don't let go. You read people as well as anyone I've ever known in the business. You hear them, really hear them. When they're lying, you know it. And that never-forget-anything mind is... well, priceless."

"I can name a room full of cops that fit that bill. You for one."

"Thanks. But my day's come and gone. Retirement's in my headlights. You have your professional life ahead of you. Between me and you, I say go for it! Hey, don't get me wrong. You have a great future here in Lee County and I'd do anything to have you stay."

"But why me? They have their pick."

"Truth is, and this is only an educated guess on my part, the big money buyers—the LBB's, the Stratis's of the world; the Kumars, those folks—are frightened of you. And the Feds know it."

"Truth is, I haven't arrested any of them. Sure, I've managed to nail the people who've facilitated their acquiring Seminal Society Firsts. But I've not even come close to nailing any of the real money collectors."

"The way those guys work with layers of intermediaries—facilitators as you call them—it's no wonder. I'd say that's why the Feds want you. If anyone can bring them down, you can."

"More credit than I deserve."

"Cash in when the getting's good. The ones I mentioned, Bishop, Statis, Kumar, as well as that specialty insurance guy, what's his name, Great Southern—"

"Jack Silver."

"Yea, Jack Silver. They all take your calls. There's a reason for that. I can't name another cop who even has their private numbers, let alone who scores an answer when their phone rings."

"Jakowski has access to Stratis."

"Only because Jak facilitates for him. And speaking of Pete, he's someone you can talk to about working for the IRS. Oh," Boots said, reading Leslie's face, "hit a sore point, did I? I thought you two were... tight."

"That's over... at least until he gets his divorce. Then we'll see."

"I thought the timetable for that divorce passed. I must have—"

"It passed alright. Divorce was postponed for some reason. Don't understand it, but—"

"But you're having second thoughts?"

If Leslie had been talking to anyone else she would have immediately shut down this topic. But to her Captain, she replied, "We enjoy each other's company when we're together. But there's something... something I just can't—"

"Deception. Hate to say it, but Jak wrote the book on it. Facilitates for Stratis by setting up complicated deals around the world that allow precious artifacts to be put in play. Stratis pays him handsomely for that work. Then, to keep it all legal, he informs for the IRS so they can get an insight into Stratis' financial dealings. Doing the IRS bit allows him to keep his detective shield. In the last five years, Stratis has accumulated for his own private collection close to three billion dollars' worth of art. IRS is no closer today to finding that Stratis has done anything illegal than they were before Jakowski became involved. I'll leave it at that. Should I assume you haven't told Jak of your offer."

"Correct. But I think he knows."

"Best to keep it that way. Your little IRS secret will stay with me as well. Just promise you'll think long and hard on it. And I'll be the first to know when you decide. Correct?"

Leslie nodded her consent. Anxious to get out of Dodge, she started for the door.

"Before you go, one more thing."

"Captain?" Leslie said, turning back to face her commander. "What?"

"When you decide what your relationship is with Jak, please let me know."

"Ay, ay, captain."

"Leslie, again thank you for agreeing to meet me for lunch today," the voicemail message from Bishop began. "I always enjoy our time together immensely and today was no exception. I welcome an opportunity to continue over dinner. How about this evening at seven? Or whatever day or time works best for you. I'm thinking of the Veranda. Never been there, but I understand it's comfortable—and dare I say, romantic. I can pick you up."

Her first impulse was to decline. To that end, she dialed his number. Her call went directly to voicemail. "Hodges, here. I'm afraid..." A voice from deep within her brain interrupted her words. *Go for it! the voice sternly instructed. Go for it! You enjoy his company. You're excited by him, the voice pressed. Say yes and see what comes of it.* "... I can't make it," Leslie continued, then surprised herself by adding, "at seven. But seven-thirty will work just fine. I'll meet you there."

"Are we meeting someone?" Rodriguez asked, adding, "Sorry, but I couldn't help overhearing your conversation."

Leslie had no idea how long her partner had been standing over her. "No, this is private," she answered defiantly as she had come to do with her former partner.

Unlike Cox, Rodriguez simply said, "Sorry, didn't mean to intrude. I was just coming over to update you on what I've been doing in your absence. I want to be certain I'm on the same page as you."

"Appreciate that. So, what have I missed?"

"Possibly nothing. I went over the inventory of the home of the deceased. Found a bunch of books and articles on da Vinci's notebooks. Some are organized in what they call a Codex, folded pages bound together. On his phone were text messages between him and two other people pertaining to a particular Codex. I'm assuming that's where the parachute drawings are located. Both are Tac's neighbors."

"I'm guessing one of these guy's named Donatello Andino."

"Correct. Goes by Andy."

"The second?"

"William Paxter Skyler. He's supposedly in Italy doing—"

"His granddaughter, Orion, is the one who found Tac in the lake. I interviewed her. Goes by Star. Wife's deceased."

"Skyler was last seen at a museum in Milan examining parachute drawings from someone named Mariano di Jacopo. Hillard and I are heading over to Skyler's to see what might have been over looked. You want to join us?"

"Think I will. How many homes does this Skyler have? You know?"

"Hillard believes it's four. Perhaps one or two more."

"From what I recall," Leslie added, "he sold a shoe store chain about four years ago. One of his homes is in the hills of Italy. Star says he's visiting friends and that he buys Firsts for resale to the Seminal Society. According to his granddaughter, he's off chasing after Michelangelo—or da Vinci. She didn't know which of them. Has Hillard reinterviewed Star?"

"By telephone. Seems that kid, and her friends, are always going somewhere. Never seem content anywhere. Only thing I know Hillard got was some confusing comments on sheets of material of all things."

"What kind of material?"

"Not sure. I think two sheets. One silk. The other, some kind of oiled cotton. Star wasn't sure."

"Context?"

"The Old Man—that's what she calls her grandfather, The Old Man—was angry about some missing material. He had brought it back from somewhere and it disappeared from his house over in Miromar Lakes. She said she had never seen him so angry. Kept repeating, 'That nutcase stole it!"

"Skyler file a police report?"

"Not that I could find."

"This 'nutcase', do we know who she was referring to?"

"Star guessed Tac. But didn't know for certain."

"Her guess was based on?"

"Hillard pressed Star on that. Star would only say that the silk material she had previously seen at her grandfather's house looked like what she saw in the lake when she found Tac. But she wasn't certain."

Both Leslie's and Rodriguez's phones sounded in unison. Their screens came alive. GOING TO THE SKYLER PREMISES.

"Okay. Let's go." Leslie's communicator sounded. Holding it near her ear, she announced, "Hodges, here," then went silent, waiting for dispatch to relay a message.

A moment later she said to her partner, "Case just went sideways! Palm Beach Sheriff's Office pulled Donatello Andino from Lake Okeechobee about an hour ago. Tentative cause of death, crushed skull. A bag of rocks was tied around his ankles. Been in the water long enough for the canvas bag to split open. Preliminary estimate, five days, give or take a day either way."

"Suppose we should head over to Andino's place. See what we can see."

"Can't do that! For now, Palm Beach has declared it their scene."

"How's that even possible?"

"Above my pay grade. That's political BS that the sheriffs will have to work out."

"Hope they do it fast. Oh, one more thing Hillard learned from Star. They, she and her friends, were in Paris for the Olympics with front row tickets to beach volleyball."

NINETEEN

LESLIE WAS UNCHARACTERISTICALLY nervous thinking about her upcoming dinner with the Texas billionaire. She had gone home, taken a long shower and then carefully selected the dress she would wear, changed her earrings three times, finally settling on pear-cut green sapphires, her favorite given to her by Junior, her deceased husband, on their fifth wedding anniversary.

The need for the long shower, she told herself, wasn't so much her excitement about dinner as it was with her frustration over the Tac death investigation. It was going nowhere and now she was under pressure to label it an accident and move on. Loose ends, such as material obtained by neighbor Skyler in Italy, the material having a pattern similar, or so Skyler's granddaughter thought, to the material of Tac's parachute, nagged at her. Skyler himself having seemingly disappeared, rendered it impossible for her to speak directly with someone she considered a Person With Relevant Knowledge.

Now another neighbor, and friend of the deceased, Donatello Andino, having been found dead in Lake Okeechobee, threw Leslie over the edge. Small threads she knew, but more than she was willing to ignore. Her agitation was compounded because the Palm Beach Sheriff's Office had taken exclusive investigative control of Andino's house. Leslie was certain the Andino death was related to Tac's, but she could point to no real connection.

Captain Stetson had called Leslie personally to be certain she understood the orders. That call had come in just as she was dialing Bishop to cancel their dinner. "Hell with it!" Leslie had exclaimed to her empty car when Boot's line went dead, "At least dinner with LBB will take my mind off this mess!"

"What a delight you came!" Bishop said, standing to greet Leslie when she approached his table. "I half expected you to cancel. I mean with the news and all."

Leslie stood awkwardly facing the billionaire. Hugging was inappropriate, yet a handshake seemed too cold.

Bishop broke the tension by coming around the table and pulling the chair out for her.

Sitting down, she confessed. "I was going to, but..."

"But what? Go on. Finish your thought," he said, his hand on her shoulder pressing ever so slightly. "I'm just happy you're here."

"I was hoping to get away from it for a few hours. And this seemed... seemed the right way to do it."

Taking his seat, Bishop smiled the comfortable smile Leslie remembered from their prior dinners and said, "I'd promise to do just that. Only with all the news coverage it'll be hard."

Losing the internal battle to stay away from the topic, Leslie relented. "So, what are they saying? I don't even know what's public and what's not."

"A bass fisherman—known only as CH—cast into the shallows over on the east side of the lake and instead of the prized fifteen pounder he was hoping for, he snagged one Donatello 'Andy' Andino, who happened to be on the Palm Beach Sheriff's Office Person of Interest list."

Leslie remained silent.

Bishop continued, "An astute reporter questioned whether the death of Andino had anything to do with the parachuting accident in Lee County last week. The one in which Marino Jacobi lost his life."

"And just why would they be linked?" Leslie asked, fishing to see what was known.

"Primarily, because the two men were neighbors, perhaps even friends. There's also an unconfirmed report that Andino was last seen in the company of, the dead parachutist. Just why am I telling you something you already know?"

"That's enough business talk. Okay. I'll have what you're having," Leslie said, nodding to the mostly empty wine glass sitting in front of Bishop.

LBB caught the eye of the waitress and held up two fingers. When she nodded, Bishop turned back to Leslie. "In the interest of full disclosure, and I promise after this no more shop talk, I need to confess that the collector community is—"

"The collector community? You mean the Seminal Society?"

"Among others. But yes, particularly the Seminal Society collectors are extremely interested in Leonardo da Vinci's work. In fact, even as we speak, you know the Olympic games have just concluded. All of Paris has been turned upside down so to speak. Did you happen to catch the opening ceremony?"

"Part of it. I must confess, I'm not really into sports."

"It isn't the sports the collectors are in Paris for. The grand prize of them all, of course, lives along the Siene."

"The Mona Lisa! You gotta be kidding! I've heard nothing."

"I'd be surprised if you had, Leslie. Public will never hear anything negative about the most famous painting in the world. Under cover of the fireworks and other special events, you can assume attempts were made to compromise the great lady. How successful they were is open to speculation."

"Are you telling me something?" Leslie demanded, shifting backward in her chair, suddenly uncomfortable.

"I am. But not what you're thinking. Frankly, Leslie, I value your friendship far too much to put it in jeopardy over a possession. Even that possession! I'm remaining out of the Mona Lisa fray. I've made my intentions clear on that point."

"Clear to whom, exactly?"

"The other collectors with the desire—and wherewithal—to secure the Mona Lisa, should she have been set free to wonder the earth."

"Wouldn't it be obvious if she's missing?"

"Yes and no. Back in 1974 she was on display in Tokyo and a visitor sprayed her with red paint. In 2009 her protective glass was smashed. In each instance, the public statement was that the great lady was unharmed. Maybe. Maybe not. Public will never know."

"Do you know?"

"Now we're getting into trade secrets, and I'll plead the fifth. I said I was remaining out of the current scramble, and I mean it. To be completely upfront and full disclosure, I am interested in da Vinci's parachute material. But I'll remain out of that as well. You must know he didn't invent the parachute. That came from a guy named Mariano di Jacopo. Died in 1453. About seventy years before da Vinci was born. In point of fact, the parachute may have been first conceived by a Muslim inventor, Abbas Ibn Firnas, who leapt from the minaret of the Cordoba Mosque in the year 852 with a parachute strapped to his back. He landed with only minor injuries—or so the story goes."

"You're quite the expert on parachutes, I see. And the people who conceived them."

"Firsts. As you know, I'm afflicted with the need to have Firsts."

"But if da Vinci wasn't the first to invent the parachute, then I don't see—"

The waitress set the drinks in front of them. "Do you want to hear the specials," she asked, "or do you need more—"

"Please give us a little time," Bishop said. Looking across the table at Leslie, he asked, "Perhaps I misspoke. Would you like to order now?"

"I'll wait. Go on with your story."

When the waitress moved off, Bishop continued. "Well, da Vinci may not have conceived of the idea of a parachute. However, the material to allow it to function properly is another thing. The great man described a linen cloth sealed around a wooden frame. There is rumor—and rumor only—that he constructed such a cloth. A roll of it to be exact."

"And you want that roll! Is that what I'm to believe?"

"Exactly! Rumor also has it that he actually jumped off a mountain using some part of that roll for a parachute. Maybe yes. Maybe no."

The passion in Bishop's eyes was undeniable—and contagious. Leslie leaned forward, as far as she could, as a child might at a father's knee, waiting for the climax of a story. "I thought da Vinci never actually jumped. Did he?" she asked, caught up in his excitement and anxious to hear the answer.

"Rumor—so far as I know. But one never really knows. So much is lost to history. But I do want what remains of that original cloth. That much I can tell you." He paused, then added, "But, as I said, I'm stepping back."

Regaining control of herself, she settled back in her chair. "When you say, 'original cloth', what do you mean?"

"Good question? My guess is that a parachute uses about two hundred square feet of material. That's based on an assumption that the bottom opening is about four feet on a side. The material is stretched over a wooden triangular frame—a twenty-three-foot-high pyramid if you will. From what I can determine, da Vinci specified linen. I believe the artist in him would have required a cloth with a pattern."

"Any particular pattern?"

Bishop's eyes regained the intensity Leslie had seen a few minutes earlier. "I speculate here, so I might be mistaken. But he was enthralled with what he called, the Vitruvian Man. According to him, a perfect man would fit exactly inside a square that is bound by a circle."

"A man inside what?"

"Visualize a man with outstretched arms. No matter where he moves his arms—or legs for that matter—they would touch the boundaries of a square. The square, in turn, is bounded by a circle. Here, let me show you."

Bishop produced a pen and drew a circle on a napkin. Inside the circle he formed a square. And inside the square he drew a man with outstretched arms and legs. He then proceeded to draw more arms and more legs, each in a different position, but with the common factor that they all touched the boundaries of the square. "I give you," he announced with a flourish, Vitruvian Man." Bishop paused a moment, then added, "This, according to historians, depicts the blend of art and science, forming the basis of Renaissance proportions theories in art and architecture."

"I have to admit," Leslie said with interest, "that you've captured my attention. I can see why you're interested in historical items. How much would this material be worth?"

"To most people, very little. It's enough to see it in a museum for a minute then move on to something else. For true collectors, however, a hundred million for the original material is a good base number."

A thought jumped into her head. She studied Bishop a long moment before asking. "Is it something—I mean the da Vinci material—that you'd consult with that lawyer Showers about?"

"Thunder? I've no need for his services! I could buy and sell the Cook Islands, that's where he does most of his business, if I had half a mind. My collection is far too large for the likes of him."

"I'll confess, Bill. You've captured my imagination," Leslie again confessed, drawn in further by the depth of his passion.

"Then by all means, Leslie, you must come with me to Texas. You'll appreciate my entire collection. Everything's based on science and art. And they're all originals. Touched by the great ones themselves."

"I'd love to," Leslie responded, surprising even herself. "But—"

"We can have dinner and drive over to Page Field. I wasn't planning on going home any time soon, but anything's possible. Plans are always flexible. Whatever suits your fancy."

Not certain what Bishop had in mind, she equivocated. "As you know, I'm in the midst of a murder investigation at the moment. Any travel on my part will have to wait."

"People tell me all the time, work comes first. It's a concept I've never had to bother myself with. And thank goodness for that, I must say. You too can cut yourself free any time you wish. Come with me and you'd never have to work again."

Still not certain she knew what was being proposed and not ready to find out, she simply said, "Work does come first, I'm afraid."

"If and when you become available, the offer will still be open. I'm a patient man. Just call and I'll make it happen. No strings attached."

Gathering her courage, Leslie blurted, "I had occasion to speak with Bates Ara..."

"She's delusional—at best! Pay no attention to that woman! She's blowing through her grandmother's Persian fortune faster than I'd believe possible! Another year—two at most—and they'll be out on the street."

"She thinks you'll marry her."

"Goodness no! I've given her no reason. And believe me when I say that won't ever happen."

"Have you invited her to Texas?"

"Not on your life! As I said, she's delusional! And on that note, no more shop talk. Tell me about your childhood. Unless I have it wrong, you grew up in Gulfport, Mississippi."

"You've done your homework I see."

"As have you, I'm certain. Would you expect less of me? I'm hoping this is the beginning of a long, beautiful friendship."

"Said Captain Renault to Rick as fog settled over the runway in *Casablanca*."

Bishop raised his glass. "Here's looking at you."

It had taken all of Leslie's resolve not to spend the night with Little Billy Bob. This had been her third dinner with him, the other two had been pleasant enough, but essentially work-related. This one had a totally different feel—personal and, dare she think it, intimate. The more than just friends hug when they parted said it all. The feeling was certainly mutual—and they both knew it.

Her decision to not start anything new before she finally settled her relationship with Pete Jakowski was real. She also knew deep down that she had already crossed that line. There'd be no retreating, regardless of her ultimate Billy Bob decision.

Thinking of Pete, brought to mind her recent conversation with her boss concerning the Pittsburgh cop. *Why was Boots so interested in her private romantic life?* It wasn't like the captain to be involved with her underlings' personal lives. Leslie recalled her conversation with Boots where Boots had confessed to a brief relationship with Jak back in the day. *Has that romance been rekindled? Was Jakowski behind the IRS job offer to get her out of the way? If not, who was? Certainly not Little Billy Bob? Who then?*

The questions continued, switching from Boots, to Jakowski, to the dead jumper, Tac. Then onto the dead neighbor, Andy

Andino. Finally, after what seemed like hours of twisting and turning, the real issue surfaced. The loss of her partner, Simeon Cox. The tall, lanky good-ole-boy, with the Tennessee twang and unruly ash-blond hair, somehow had managed to penetrate her defenses. He had become the best partner she could imagine. Tireless energy—and smart. She even missed his constant harmless sexual innuendoes. She now realized it had been his awkward way of reminding her that she needed to keep her human side if she were to survive the "street".

At some point, sleep took hold of her and she found herself on a jet heading west over Texas. She knew it was Texas because the letters T-E-X-A-S were visible, one after the other, on the ground below. Then, after seemingly flying forever, an arrow appeared: A large arrow stretching to the horizon.

The window next to her suddenly flew open and her head was sucked out. She screamed, but no sound came. In the far distance she could make out a new letter.

An *I*.

No, not an *I*. An *L*.

Then a *B*.

Then another *B*.

An alarm buzzer sounded. At first it was faint. Then it grew louder and louder. The plane's nose suddenly bent downward, and the plane headed toward the ground below! The letters *LBB* were now more clearly visible and growing larger by the minute. The sound of the buzzer increased.

Then a giant image of Bishop appeared. The letters becoming large arms snaking upward toward the falling plane. She fought to bring her head back inside, but the harder she worked the larger her head became and the closer the arms got. Fingers appeared at the end of the arms; fingers that searched for her face.

The buzzer grew louder and the fingers grew longer. Gathering as much strength as she could, Leslie worked her head back inside the plane, only to have it jam solid halfway through the porthole. She pulled harder and harder to no avail. Then, without warning, her head broke free and popped back inside the plane.

Her eyes flew open and in the early morning light her bedroom slowly came into focus. Her cell phone on the bedside table gave one last buzz, then fell silent, the name RODRIGUEZ slowly fading.

TWENTY

"YOU, OKAY?" LESLIE'S partner asked when she returned his call a few minutes later. "You sound... well, out of it would be polite."

"Just coming awake, Lewis. Give me a moment to orient myself."

Unlike Cox, who often called her even earlier in the morning, this was a first for Rodriguez. The fact that he hadn't greeted her with, 'Am I disturbing something special?' was a definite plus. That didn't mean that she wasn't missing her former partner and grieving over his death. His constant dwelling on her personal life had become a real point of contention, but she missed him more than she was willing to admit. "It's six in the morning," Leslie managed. "Can't wait to hear what couldn't hold an hour or two."

"A friend called. A guy I grew up with up in Kissimmee. Went to the Academy together. He's over with Palm Beach. Says they're finished with Andino's house and the brass are trying to make a case for searching Skyler's place."

"Skyler's? They find something linking Skyler to Andino?"

"Friend's not privy to all they have. Piecing it together he believes Andino was Skyler's delivery guy. There's also talk about some kind of material found in Andino's home that's somehow linked to Skyler."

"Friend have a name?"

"Mind if I keep that to myself for now? You know what'll happen to him if anyone over there finds out he's talking to us."

"As you wish. What do you have in mind?"

"Meet me at Skyler's at seven. I have a locksmith friend who'll do me a favor."

"Won't need that! There's a key under a stone outside the lanai. Got that much from Star. Skyler's granddaughter. See you there in thirty. Be sure and notify CIA Hillard and her team."

"Hillard can take it from here," Leslie instructed Rodriguez several hours later. "Looks to me that Skyler covered his tracks carefully. Makes me suspicious when there's not a single financial transaction to be found. Not even a receipt from a restaurant. Nothing."

"Yeah. But we did find notations—confirmations—of Olympic tickets. They were in the granddaughter's room. Most important, I think, are the timelines of the events she—or someone—had tickets for."

"And Lewis, that's relevant because? I'm not following your line of thought."

"Because several of the venues are not sporting events as you might think. The Louvre being one of them."

"Are you telling me Star and her friends went to the Louvre?"

"Those tickets were for the opening day—actually night—of the games. July twenty-fifth to be exact. The Louvre was closed to the public then."

"Any evidence Skyler was in Paris at that point?"

"Interpol is working it now."

"Him being at the Louvre squares with a rumor that—and I stress rumor—that the Mona Lisa was, for a lack of a better word, substituted for that night by one or more of the guests. Compromised may be a better term."

"I haven't heard—"

"You won't! Louvre will say nothing. Maybe Interpol will shed some light."

"I'd think the Louvre would make a racket!"

"You'd be wrong. They deeply care about privacy. Security is one of their biggest expenses, with specialized measures taken for their priceless items. It's not only a major embarrassment if the Mona Lisa were to be compromised, but it's a certainty their revenue would suffer as well. My sources assure me they'll not make a public fuss."

"Are you thinking the Seminal Society collectors are involved?"

"Right down their alley, isn't it? I see you've studied my files. That's good. Can you think of a better target for them? The most famous painting ever. A true First."

"I once read that the Louvre had about fifteen hundred security folks on staff. I can't even imagine how—"

"That doesn't stop dreamers from dreaming—and billionaires from scheming. Nothing appears to stop those... those men!"

Rodriguez fell quiet, processing what Leslie had just told him. Uncomfortable with the silence that had fallen over the room, he finally said, "I can't believe tickets to the Louvre are in any way related to a guy whose parachute ripped apart over a small lake in Southwestern Florida. That's a stretch on a good day."

"If da Vinci hadn't dabbled in parachute design, I'd agree with you. I may be swinging at shadows, but truthfully we're not exactly swimming in leads. Hey, and speaking of parachutes, we didn't find the material we thought we would." Now it was Leslie's turn to go silent, processing the information she had received from insurance man Silver, as well as from Bishop.

"Find out from Beth when Riya Kumar will be arriving and where she'll be staying. If that name doesn't ring a bell, check my earlier files. Also, a new name, not yet in the file, Hugh Showers. AKA Thunder. Have Beth track him down. I believe Kumar and Showers are meeting and I want to be there when they do."

"The best Beth can do," Rodriguez told Leslie ten minutes later, "is to place both Riya Kumar and Thunder at Page field at nineteen hundred-thirty hours."

"When?"

"Today."

"That's an hour from now," Leslie noted, checking her watch. "Mind driving?"

"Not a problem. Thunder's jet is scheduled to fly out at twenty-three hundred."

"Dinner meeting?"

"Anyone's guess, but likely."

On the way to Page Field, Leslie, who was prepared to leave a stern call back message, called Maxine Ghana. The IRS agent answered on the first ring, negating the need for the message. "To what do I owe the honor of you taking my call?" Leslie inquired, trying to mask her surprise. "You don't usually answer."

"Truth is, I was just fix'n to call you. Give you a heads up. Lady Kumar is in your neck of the woods and according to our sources is meeting with an offshore guru lawyer named Showers. Meeting's set for eight. Won't be a long one. Showers has dinner with your Texas friend Bishop at nine."

"What's that about? I thought Bishop didn't need Thun... I mean Showers'... services."

"Best guess. It has something to do with parachute material. But truthfully, I would have thought you could spread some light on that, seeing as though you and he are—"

"Are what?" Leslie demanded, her temper rising and her face getting hot. "Just what—"

"—friends. That's a good thing Les. A really good thing. Up to now LBB has kept to himself. We believe he has the largest collection of Firsts in the world. He keeps such a low profile that not many would even know about it. Far as we know, he's clean. He appears to declare everything he sells—which, I might add, are few and far between. Of course, we have no good way to know how much he sold a particular artifact for, but we do have reason to believe he's been straight with us. For that matter, we really don't know what he paid for a particular artifact. But he's better than the others. With them it's cat and mouse."

"Kumars?"

"Meeting with Thunder should tell you something. The wife's as cunning as she is charming. They are under constant scrutiny."

"Can you work your magic like you did a few months back and ground Shower's plane until I release it? He lands in fifteen minutes. That gives me a half hour before Kumar. Should be enough—for now."

"You got it. Let me know what you get."

"You heard," Leslie said to Rodriguez when she hung up from Agent Ghana. "We'll interview Thunder on his plane. Should prove interesting."

"While you were on the phone, I contacted Page Field. Showers plane is seven minutes early. Landing on runway FMY05 and assigned to ramp D. We'll be escorted to the plane. Our firearms have been cleared."

"Good work."

"Mind my asking? What do you have on Ghana that she helps you as she does? I've asked around about her and I have to tell you, she's not known for that kind of behavior. At least not what people tell me."

"Truthfully, I don't know. Didn't start out that way. But we've... we've evolved you might say. Helps that I stay off her turf and confine our investigation to underlying crimes, if any. And I feed her information on our investigations."

"What exactly do you expect to get from Thunder? We don't know about any underlying crimes in Jacobi's death, so we can't press him along those lines."

"This is the exception that proves the rule, I suppose. You might say I'm working on the theory that where there's smoke there's fire."

"When you say smoke, just what are you visualizing?"

"Too much da Vinci in the air. Marino Jacobi—Tac—an experienced parachuter, falls to his death. He was apparently an ardent student of da Vinci and his parachutes. Coincidence? Maybe. But... but then we have Orion Skyler, the co-ed who found Jacobi. She's the granddaughter of a da Vinci buff, who just happens to have tickets to the Louvre where da Vinci's most famous painting is housed on a day when the building is closed to all but the very privileged. Add to that the rumors of a Mona Lisa heist—substitution to be exact. Then we have Riya Kumar—a Seminal Society collector and a person known to be interested in da Vinci—flying into town to meet with a lawyer known for his ability to protect wealth in foreign countries."

"Does Kumar live here in Florida?"

"Good question. I'd guess California—or Texas—but truth be told, never thought to ask."

"Where's the Thunder law firm based?"

"Don't know that either," Leslie confessed, feeling less prepared for this meeting by the minute. "I just assumed Texas."

"Why Texas?"

"Isn't everything larger than life from Texas?"

"Hadn't thought of it that way, but I suppose you're right about that." Rodriguez stopped the car in front of a small building with a D flag flying from the pointed roof. Two uniformed Lee County Port Authority Police officers hurried toward them. The woman wore a supervisory white shirt and black slacks and the man's shirt was navy blue. Leslie and Lewis stepped from the car, both holding their Lee Country credentials in front of them.

"Timing's perfect," the supervisor said by way of greeting. She turned back toward the building.

The other officer said, "Follow us." He turned and hurried after his retreating boss.

Leslie and Rodriguez fell in behind, the four of them arriving at the plane just as the boarding stairs touched the ground.

"Go on up," the supervisor instructed. "Max here will wait to escort you back to your car when you're finished. Is there anything else you need from us?"

"Thank you," Leslie said. "I don't suppose we'll need anything further."

The door slid upward when the two officers reached the top platform, allowing them to enter the plane. The contrast from bright sunlight to the dim interior was stark and disorienting.

A man's disemboweled voice, emanating from a few feet in front of them, announced, "Welcome aboard!"

"Oh!" Leslie exclaimed as her eyes began to adjust, "I didn't see you there! Sorry. I'm Detective Leslie Hodges and this is my partner, Detective Lewis Rodriguez."

"Yes, I know who you two are. Can't say as though I'm happy to have you barge in this way. I'm Hugh Showers and this," he waved his arm around proudly, "is the law office of Showers and Moore. You have exactly thirty minutes to ask whatever the hell you want to ask. After that, you're out of here! I don't give a shit if I'm grounded all night. Believe me, in the end you'll pay a higher price than I will. And while I'm setting the ground rules, let me be very clear, like I said, you can ask anything you want. I reserve my rights to only answer what I deem appropriate. Attorney-client privilege and all that. Understood?"

Not willing to show intimidation, Leslie replied, "Mind moving back so my partner can get fully into the pla... your office? Your law office I believe you said."

Showers took several steps back. "That better?"

"Much better. Ground rules are good, Mr. Attorney Showers. I'll take you at your word that we're now standing in your law office. Are we to assume then you're licensed to practice law in Florida? And that all your State fees are in order? Should I check with Tallahassee?"

When Showers didn't answer, Leslie said, "I'll take your silence as an acknowledgement that you're not licensed to practice law—or anything else—in Florida. That being the case, let's just have a civil conversation and we'll be gone before you know it. Fair enough?"

"What is it you want to know?" Showers replied, the belligerent tone now gone.

"For the record," Leslie asked, "where are you licensed?"

"Texas, for one. New York for another."

"Texas. By any chance do you know William Bishop the Second?" Hearing herself pronounce LBB's formal name sounded funny.

"Little Billy Bob! Everyone in Texas knows LBB!"

"He a client of yours?"

"I never divulge who I represent—or don't represent. That's confidential."

The way Showers glanced away led Leslie to conclude that he, in fact, did represent her friend. She moved on. "We understand that your legal specialty is providing offshore protection for property. Just what does that mean? Give it to us in lay terms if you will."

"In its simplest form, we help establish ownership of property in countries other than the country where the owner of that property resides."

"What other countries are we speaking of?"

"Nevis, for example."

"That's in the Caribbean, isn't it?" Rodriguez commented.

"Yes. Eastern Caribbean."

"What about the Pacific? Anything there?"

"The Cook Islands."

"So how does it all work?" Rodriguez pressed.

"The real short version. We set up a trust in one of the offshore places and transfer title of whatever property you want to protect to the trust."

"Does the property need to go... offshore?"

"Depends. That's best. But not always possible, or desirable."

Leslie pressed. "If the property's cash, that's relatively easy I suppose. But if we're talking stuff, like artwork, then I assume it's harder."

"You have something in mind, Detective. Spit it out."

"Paintings come to mind. If I owned a famous painting, could I keep the painting here in Florida and set it up in a trust in the Caribbean?"

"You could."

"Would that protect the painting?"

"Depends upon from what?"

"Tax liability?"

"Depends."

"On what?"

"I'm not a tax advisor. I do the trust documents. Others do the tax and other planning. Sorry, I can't elaborate further."

Leslie studied Thunder for several long seconds before asking, "By any chance have you heard about a theft of the Mona Lisa?"

"I have not. To my knowledge, that painting is still in the Louvre where it belongs."

"So, nothing you are currently handling involves the Mona Lisa?"

"That's correct. But if I were, it would be stupid of me to tell you."

"Are you handling any other famous artwork?"

"No comment."

"What about da Vinci?"

"What about da Vinci?"

"You doing any work involving anything created by da Vinci?"

"No comment."

"Let me ask the question another way. Have you any knowledge of da Vinci's parachute material?"

"For that, I refer you to a man named Andy Andino. Best I can do."

"Do you represent this Andy Andino?" Leslie asked, not letting on that Andino was now lying in the Palm Beach County Morgue.

"As I told you, I won't divulge client's names. One way or the other."

"Dead or alive?"

Concern flickered momentarily in Thunder's eyes. "Are you telling me something?"

"Sorry. Can't divulge police business."

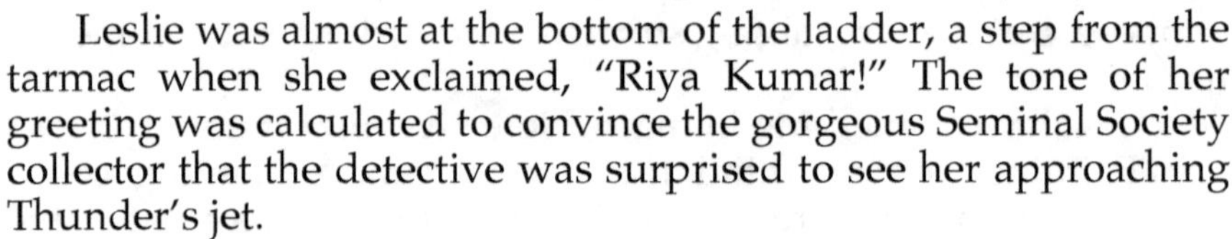

Leslie was almost at the bottom of the ladder, a step from the tarmac when she exclaimed, "Riya Kumar!" The tone of her greeting was calculated to convince the gorgeous Seminal Society collector that the detective was surprised to see her approaching Thunder's jet.

"Oh, hello, Detective. I was just—"

"Riya Kumar, this is my new partner, Lewis Rodriguez. Lewis, this is the woman I was telling you about, Riya Kumar. She and her husband, Sanjay, are art collectors, dealing mostly in Firsts."

"This is not the same young man I met up in Tampa," Riya commented, "now is it?"

"No. You're right. That was Simeon Cox. Unfortunately, Detective Cox—"

"Oh, sorry! I hadn't remembered his name. Now that you said it, I read where he was... shot. I'm so sorry. That must be just horrible for you."

"It is, to tell the truth. So, what brings you to Florida if I may ask?"

"I really should say it's not your business! But since you have just been on this plane you know who it belongs to. You know I'm meeting with Thunder."

"Mind telling me why?"

"Of course I mind. It's legal business. And confidential."

"But this is Florida. Mr. Showers just got finished claiming he doesn't practice law in Florida. And, again unless I'm mistaken, you don't have a residence, or a business, in Florida."

Anger flashed across her eyes and was gone within an instant. "I wasn't aware one had to live in Florida to meet with a friend."

"I thought you just said it was legal business. Which is it? Legal? Or a friend?"

"Friends do all manner of business with each other," Riya said, clearly struggling to regain her balance. "And they do it when and where it is convenient. We both just happen to be passing through your lovely state, so here we are."

"So, this... this conversation with your friend doesn't have anything to do with the rumors I've been hearing about the Mona Lisa?"

"The Mona Lisa? I don't know what you're talking about."

"Rumor has it that a substitution has been made and that the original is available."

"There are always rumors pertaining to the Mona Lisa. None of them pan out. And besides, that great lady would be far out of our range, even if the rumors were true."

"What would be in your range?"

"That, my dear, is not something I care to discuss. But rest assured, there are many Firsts floating around. There is no limit to available art."

"But Firsts are what *you* collect. There are only a limited—"

"da Vinci himself had any number of Firsts! There are several of his out there."

"For example?" Leslie pushed, taking advantage of Riya's clear agitation.

"For example, his parachute material is known to be down here in Florida. Last seen in the possession of my friend, Pax. I was hoping—"

"Are those detectives giving you trouble?" a booming voice from above them asked. "If so, I'll have them removed for trespassing!"

Leslie knew it was Thunder even without looking up. She also knew she wouldn't get any useful information from Riya with him hovering nearby. "We were just leaving. For the record, I'm standing on Lee County property. Trespass is a distant stretch—even for a *licensed* Florida lawyer, which you claim you're not." Turning to Riya, Leslie added, "I did want to speak to you about da Vinci and the parachute material. I believe you have my number. Call anytime. We just might be able to help each other. One never knows. Have a good visit with your *friend*."

"What do you make of Riya?" Leslie asked when she and Rodriguez were back in the car.

"Lying all the way. She was clearly distressed that we knew who she was meeting with—and why."

"I know her as calm, cool, aloof even. I agree, tonight she was agitated. I can't make up my mind if it's the Mona Lisa, or the missing parachute material that has her upset. My money's on the parachute material."

"If Skyler and Tac don't have it, then who do you think does?"

"Andino. Being Skyler's logistics person, I'd bet on him."

"Not found there either," Rodriguez reminded his partner. "Maybe we have this backward. Could it be Kumar who has the parachute material? Maybe that's why she's meeting with that lawyer jerk."

"Assume you're right, what would she do with the material? Hard to display it. Tac wanted it for jumping. To proclaim to the world that he jumped using da Vinci's original parachute. That's not Riya."

"Arguing for taking it offshore. Selling it to, say, a museum for display."

"That would be right in Mr. Thunder Shower's wheelhouse! The trick for Riya is not getting blowback from Italy if and when the material goes on display. Showers provides just that kind of immunity. I think you nailed it Lewis. I think you nailed it."

TWENTY-ONE

BE IN MY OFFICE PROMPTLY at zero nine hundred hours, the message from Captain Stetson that Leslie received just before midnight had read.

"Let me guess what this is—" Leslie called from the doorway as she was being ushered into her boss's office the next morning. Realizing Sheriff Radcliff was standing in the far corner, she stopped mid-sentence and came to attention. She had arrived prepared for a reprimand for continuing to pursue the Tac drowning death. *Good heavens, the big boss himself! That suggests the visit to Thunder the previous evening! If so, Showers indeed carries major clout. His Thunder moniker is well earned!*

"At ease," Boots said. "You look as though you just got caught with your hand in the cookie jar—or worse. Anything you want to confess? The sheriff and I would love to hear it."

"No," Leslie managed. "Only I didn't expect... Oh, nothing."

Radcliff walked over to the desk and picked up an envelope. Ripping it open, he turned to Leslie, "I hope this is not premature. Before we proceed, please finish your sentence."

Leslie looked to Boots for a hint but saw nothing helpful. Sucking in her breath, she said, "I was going to apologize for not converting the Tac death to accident status and for interviewing Attorney Showers over at Page Field. Truthfully, I believe there's more going on than—"

"Say no more," Radcliff said, "Good on you! We've been pussy footing around Showers long enough. Hope you can tag him with something."

"Afraid not yet, Sir. It's early on that account. But he's on my screen."

"Nail him if you can! And make it stick!" Extracting sergeant strips from the envelope, he handed them to Leslie. "You've earned these—in record time I should add."

"Congratulations!" Boots said, standing behind her desk and reaching across to shake Leslie's hand. "Well deserved. Well deserved."

"You're a credit to our department," The sheriff added. "Keep up the good work."

"Thank you, Sheriff. Thank you Boo—Captain—for believing in me."

"Just keep up the good work, Sergeant. As I said, we've been trying to interview that Thunder character for some time now. How you managed it I don't think I even want to know. I'll be interested in your report. His name pops up in every major Florida bank robbery investigation. Nothing illegal mind you, just there. He's an annoyance at best. Money movement type of annoyance."

"You can add valuable art artifacts to your list. I don't yet know how—or even if—he plays a role in the actual movement. Where there's smoke.... That I know."

"Keep on it. Oh, sorry about the loss of your partner. I know he wasn't everyone's cup of tea. But the kid was ours, and it hurts. Governor's been on my case over it. Just you take care out there."

"Will do, Sheriff. And thank you again."

"No need to thank me. You earned the stripes. There's more to follow." With that, the sheriff saluted and left the room, closing the door behind him.

"Congratulations," Boots again said. "Fastest ever. You're on your way, Kid. Keep up the great work."

"Okay by you if I continue on the Tac case? I'm not yet comfortable calling it an accident."

"And just why's that?"

"Too much da Vinci. His parachute material. Neighbor Skyler is interested in da Vinci. The Mona Lisa is in play. Another neighbor and friend, business partner actually—Andino—homicide. The Mundi passing through his hands. Riya Kumar in town to meet with Thunder. I keep asking myself what's an offshore wealth specialist doing here in Florida? Something big's going down—or about to go down—and I'm not ready to call Tac a coincidence."

"Follow your hunch. Just don't go crazy. How's Lewis working out?"

"Can't complain. He's not as intuitive as Cox, nor does he put in the hours Cox did. That guy never seemed to sleep. Don't know how he kept it up. He was always working something. On the other hand, it's refreshing to not be constantly fending off his innuendoes. I'll say this, Lewis is certainly clever. In the long run, he could prove to be even better than Cox."

"I agree. Cox was an administrative shit-show. The saving factor for him is that you two made a great team. I'm glad you stuck it out with him. In the end he was worth the paperwork. Frankly, I'm sick over his loss."

Holding her sergeant insignia, Leslie acknowledged, "These stripes are half his. I can never forget that." Wiping a tear from the corner of her eye, she added, "May he rest in peace."

Leslie was almost back to her desk when Rodrigues caught up to her. "I heard about your promotion… Congratulations! Fastest ever, I'm told. Sorry to—"

"I just found out, not two minutes ago! And you already know!"

"Boots' assistant wasted no time. The second the door closed behind you she was on the horn. The world knows by now. You can bet on that."

"I don't know what to say, other than thank you."

"You don't have time to say anything. We have a real brouhaha going on over at Sampsons. Come, I'll drive. Get in my car!"

"The funeral home! What the hell's the trouble?" Leslie's mind immediately reverted to a major incident she had been involved with in Tampa. A crime boss had been shot. His family was midway through the second day of what was scheduled to be a three-day wake when tempers began to flare because the line to park was so long that traffic was backed up for miles. Not a good formula when dealing with Tampa's crime captains.

Leslie had been assigned coverage of the parking lot. It seemed to her that every living soul in Tampa was coming to pay homage. She had called for backup that had not yet arrived when the door to the chapel flew open and people, mostly men, poured out of the building and raced to their cars. Yet unknown to Leslie was that two brothers of the deceased had been fatally shot while they prayed over their brother. A colossal jam resulted in the parking lot and despite her best efforts, it was midnight before she could untangle the mess, made worse when the homicide team arrived, along with the Medical Examiner, and halted all movement while they investigated the fatal shootings.

As expected, not a single person; not the mother, not the wives, not the children, not the hundred or so visitors, had seen who pulled the trigger. Every one of them had had their backs to the shooting or were looking in the opposite direction.

A block from Sampson's Funeral Home Rodriguez turned to his partner. "You're in your own world over there. Haven't said a word since we left the office. Thinking about the promotion?"

"Far from it. Thinking about a funeral brouhaha many years ago. Don't go telling me people were killed over at Sampsons."

"Not killed. No, not yet. But a hell of a lot of yelling and screaming. From what I can piece together, the funeral service for a male suicide was about to begin or had just begun—don't know which—when a middle-aged woman appeared in the doorway and ran to the closed coffin. She threw it open. Here I'll play you a tape from the funeral director. The woman you first hear is the woman who burst into the funeral home. Don't know much about her. Preliminary check says her name's Clare Ricks. Has three kids. Here goes."

"Oh, Ed!" the tape begins, "I was told it was you! You're not getting away again! No, you're not! Stop this funeral right now! You think this man's name is Ed Monsune. You're wrong about that! Big time wrong! That's not who's in this casket here! This guy's my husband, Ed Ricks! I demand you stop this funeral!"

Rodriguez stopped the tape. "This next woman you hear is someone named Kay Monsune, the deceased's wife. They have two children. Ready."

"Go," Leslie said, wondering where this was heading. "Make it fast. Sampsons is just around this corner."

"Here goes."

"Whoever you are! Get out of here! That is certainly my husband, Ed Monsune! Been married ten years! Now get out before I... before I do something I'll regret!"

The police car came to a stop under the funeral home portico behind two empty sheriff cars, their lights flashing. "There's more," Rodriguez told Leslie. "It got really heated. Threats back and forth. That's when Sampson called 9-1-1."

"I'll listen later," Leslie said. "That's Sampson over there. The guy in the black suit. Starched white shirt. Thin tie. Recognize him from the TV commercials. 'Customer's always right,' is his motto. Except, I don't know who the customer is. The deceased—or the person paying the bill."

"Can't really be doubt about that," Rodriguez replied to Leslie's retreating back. "Can there really?"

"Your officers are inside," Sampson said in his practiced calm voice. "You the sergeant they said was on the way? The one in charge of the situation we have here?"

"I am. Name's Detective Les... Detective Sergeant Leslie Hodges. This is my partner, Detective Lewis Rodriguez. What seems to be the problem?"

"It's more than a seems to be, Detective. It is a problem! A big problem, let me tell you. We have two women, my client, Mrs. Kay Monsune, the wife of the deceased, a man by the name of Ed Monsune. Then we have a woman who claims her name's Clare

Ricks and says, at the top of her voice, that the man we are about to inter is Ed Ricks—her husband!"

"When you say, 'inter,' I think of cremation. Is that what the plan is? To cremate the man deceased?"

"It certainly is. The service was supposed to be concluded by this point and Mr. Ed Monsune would be on his way to the crematorium now. Let me assure you, Detective, I have cross-checked the documentation provided by the wife and—"

"Which wife?" Rodriguez asked. "Apparently there are two."

"A man can have only one wife! Period! I don't know anything about a second wife. Kay Monsune is his wife! She hired me to inter her late husband. Poor man committed suicide. As I was saying, all the documentation is in order. Can't cremate without all that. I'm meticulous in what I do. You won't find anything amiss, I can assure you of that."

"I'm sure you did everything right, Mr. Sampson. Yet there is a person saying there is an error. She must be taken seriously. Did you check to see if this Kay is, in fact married to the deceased?"

"Usually, we don't ask for marriage papers if the name is the same, which I assure you it is. In this case, Kay—Mrs. Monsune—had all her legal papers in her car." The funeral director handed Leslie a document. "Here's the marriage certificate, Detective."

Leslie momentarily examined the document, then handed it to her partner. "Looks to be in order. We'll keep it for now. Is everything quiet inside? Calmed down?"

"Mostly, I believe. Every time I go back inside, that woman, Clare, starts screaming. She's calm so long as I'm out here."

"She knows the ceremony can't go forward without you."

"I suppose that's how she thinks. But I can't have her disrupting the orderly process. My reputation is at stake here. She's trespassing! Please take her away. I'll press charges if you need me to. Just get her out so we can proceed with as much dignity as we can possibly muster."

"We'll do our best, Mr. Samson," Leslie promised. "Please remain out here while we go inside. That will be best."

"But this is my—"

"Please remain outside, Mr. Sampson. You said yourself that the second woman is calm if you're absent."

"Make it fast. We have another... Just make it fast."

The two detectives went inside and had to wait a moment for their eyes to adjust to the dimness. While in the corridor they heard voices coming from a room off to their left. A moment later they walked slowly to that room and opened the door. Every one of the twenty or so heads in the room turned in their direction.

The two children who had been running between the chairs stopped for a moment, then resumed their game—or whatever it was they were doing.

Clare Ricks was easy to spot. She was also the only adult, other than the two uniformed officers who had positioned themselves at either end of the casket. She was also the only adult dressed in what appeared to be beach clothes. She started toward the newly arrived officers, causing the uniforms to move to intercept. Leslie held her hand up, simultaneously announcing, "I'm Detective Sergeant Leslie Hodges and this is my partner, Detective Lewis Rodriguez. Everyone please remain where you are." Focusing on the woman continuing in their direction, Leslie calmly said, "Am I correct in thinking you are Clare Ricks?"

The woman stopped in her tracks. "How the hell...! Yes, I'm Mrs. Ricks. That man in that coffin over there—that dead man—is my husband, Ed Ricks! He's the father of my three children—the ones over there. I want this cremation stopped!"

"Mind sitting down over here," Leslie asked, moving back toward the door and away from the anxious looking group sitting in a circle around a woman dressed all in black, "so we can discuss this calmly—and in private?"

"There's nothing to discuss! That dead man is Ed Ricks, not Ed Monsune!"

Ignoring the outburst, Leslie motioned Lewis to take a seat in the back row near the door. She turned a chair around from the row in front of Lewis and gestured for Ricks to sit. Leslie sat next to her partner.

Clare turned back toward the group of people, took a step in their direction, saw the two deputies tense, thought better of it and walked over to where the detectives were positioned.

"Sit, please," Leslie instructed.

The woman looked around, studied the room a moment, then slowly settled in the chair.

Before she could say anything, Leslie said, "Clearly, you're aware that the man in that casket is deceased. You've said so many times. May I assume you have not lived with that man, the man you call Ed Ricks, for many years?"

"I call him that because that's his friggin' name!"

Ignoring the outburst, Leslie continued. "How long have you lived apart?"

"Little over twelve years. Right after he was arrested it was."

"Twelve years ago he was arrested?"

"Yes. Robbed a liquor store he did."

"What state?"

"Right here. In Fort Myers it was."

Leslie nodded to her partner who immediately started punching information into his communicator. To Clare she said, "And you never got a divorce?"

"He might have, I don't friggin' know. And don't really care!"

"So why are you here? Disrupting his funeral service?"

"For my kids!"

"What's for your kids? So they can see him?"

"Hell no! I don't want them having any part of that no-good bum!"

"So, what do you want then? I'm confused."

"Social Security death payments due my kids! He was their father and I want what they are entitled to. If he's buried as Ed Monsune they get nothing! If I can prove Ed Ricks gone and killed hisself, then they get paid 'till they eighteen. I'm not givin' that up no how!"

"Let me understand, you—"

"Pardon me a moment," Rodriguez interrupted. "I have it here that an Ed Ricks was arrested and convicted twelve years back. Only his conviction was for disorderly conduct, not—"

"Must have pleaded down! But that was him. Indeed it was."

"As I was saying," Leslie injected, "you don't care if the man over there, the man you call Ricks, but others call Monsune, is cremated. You only care that your children get their Social Security allowance. Do I have that right?"

"Right as rain!"

"So, if you get proof of who's in that coffin you'll be satisfied? Do I have that right?"

"Proof that holds up! Yes. That's what we're entitled to."

"What about if we take his fingerprints and his DNA? Will that be good enough for you?"

Clare Ricks sat quiet, apparently going over everything in her mind. When she next spoke it was quiet, deliberate. "Yeah. That be enough," she finally said. The tone of her voice was that of a person who was more accustomed to being ignored than to getting what she believed she was entitled to. "I don't suppose Social Security can argue with that, now can they?"

"I wouldn't think so," Leslie replied. To Rodriguez she instructed, "Get the ME out here for prints and DNA. Tell them they have an hour, two at most. I'll speak with the wife. Tell her what we are doing." Turning back to Ricks, she said, "I'm going to send that uniformed deputy over here. I want you to leave with him. You can wait outside until the Medical Examiner comes to take the prints, or you can leave. Your choice. But you're not remaining inside here. I give you my word there'll be no cremation until prints and DNA are secured. You okay with that?"

"I don't need the cop. I recorded your promise in my phone." Ricks held her phone up for Leslie to see. She stood, called her children over and slowly made her way to the door.

"That was clever how you defused the situation," Rodriguez said, smiling for the first time since being assigned to handle this matter. "I thought we'd have a hostage situation on our hands. The negotiating team is seven minutes out. I'll have them stand down."

"First, make certain Ricks is gone. Then change of plans. I need you to brief the Monsune woman. A call came in I have to take. I'll be out in the car if you need me."

"Rodger that, boss. Oh, this just came in from Beth Hillard. Apparently, the guy over there in the casket was given the name of Edward Monsune at birth. Sheet on him says he was abandoned at a fire house when he was about a week old. Adopted by a family by the name of Ricks. He did marry Clare. They did have three children. He was divorced about two years after his conviction. No record of him being married again, but he did resume using his birth name of Monsune. Beth didn't find any court order for that."

"All that stuff's for the lawyers to work out. All we need do for now is be certain we know who's being cremated. Prints and DNA will be enough for that. I'm certain the ME will sign off, so Sampson can get on with the cremation. Explain it all to both Sampson and the grieving widow. Let me know if there're problems."

"Roger that."

"Congratulations on your promotion," Agent Ghana said, when Leslie returned her call. "I'm happy for you, and I trust it won't impact your decision to come with us."

"Thank you. I won't ask how you knew so fast. I don't want to know. I must say your offer is a good one, but... but I haven't decided one way or the other. And, as I said, I won't until Tac's death is resolved one way or the other.

"Understood all too well. It's been a long time since I've been buried in the bowels of a murder investigation. One thing drummed into me by my then boss was that when nothing added up, I was most likely missing a key element. 'Go back to the beginning' was his mantra. 'It's always lost at the beginning!' So go back to the beginning, girlfriend. You missed something."

"That's always sound advice. I think I'll—"

"Tell me about that weasel, Showers. What did you find out?"

"For starters, he appears to have been protecting money and property for people of substance for a long while now. The fact he's not been arrested by any jurisdiction, coupled with the fact that the IRS needs to ask me, makes me believe he's good at what he does."

"Nailed it. We've come close on tax evasion several times now. But can't ring the bell. We'll try to seize property from someone of significant wealth, only to find the property is owned by an offshore entity that we can't touch. Guess who the lawyer is in almost all cases? Guy's a wizard!" Agent Ghana sighed.

"I sense you're more interested in Kumar than in Showers. What do you suppose she's moving offshore?"

"That's why we're talking! The Kumars have skirted tax payments for years. They negotiated a settlement a while back and paid most, but not all of it. We tried—and failed—to seize some of the art pieces they own. Showers built an impenetrable wall. Frustrating. We're hearing rumors about some da Vinci artifacts, like the Mona Lisa and some cloth, parachute material, that is being moved around. Sniffing around Thunder I was hoping you'd pick something up."

"Sorry to disappoint, but I don't even know what she—they—have going on. I've heard the same rumors. The Mona Lisa appears to be safely held at the Louvre. So, who knows? It's frustrating."

"Don't underestimate a theft at the Louvre. On the record, Interpol is a blank on the rumored theft. Off the record, well that's another matter altogether. If I were a betting woman, I'd put my money on your friend Riya having—or more likely, brokering—the great lady. Can't imagine why else she'd be meeting with Thunder in person when encrypted text would work just fine."

"Abundance of caution you're thinking."

"Something along those lines. Yes. It may be more than property she's worried about."

Leslie thought about what she had just heard from a federal agent, a woman who had far more access to sensitive intel than a sheriff's deputy. If Ghana wasn't comfortable saying the real part out loud, then neither should she. "Thank you for the information," she responded. "I'll act accordingly. Talk soon."

Rodriguez appeared at the car window just as Leslie hung up with Ghana. "Interrupting anything?" he inquired.

"Just finishing up with Ghana. I don't know if she was sending a message, but she stressed going back to the beginning with the Tac investigation. I'm thinking of doing just that. Start by reexamining his house, this time with a fine-tooth comb. You with me on this?"

"It's your call. If it's a go, I'll brief Assistant ME Goodrich. His ETA is now—" Rodriguez glanced at his watch. "—five minutes out. He'll be alone. He said he knows you from the Tac drowning. Goes by Brat. You thinking of tonight?"

"Already too late. First in the morning works for me. Say eight?"

"How about I ask Brat. See if he's willing to retrace his steps."

"Be sure he doesn't get the notion we're second guessing him."

"When he's here, we'll take his temperature. Doesn't impress me as someone who gets over worried about things. I'll put it on us."

"Speaking of temperature," Leslie said, "how'd you kept that Ricks woman under control out in the parking lot? She's a handful."

"Told her one more outburst and we're putting Monsune in the oven immediately. Shut her right up. Money talks loud and clear."

"Ain't that the truth. At all levels."

TWENTY-TWO

LESLIE DROVE THROUGH THE Miromar Lakes front gate at exactly eight A.M. Two cars were parked in the driveway of Marino Jacobi's house. She recognized one as belonging to Rodriguez. The other, she assumed was the Assistant ME's.

"Thanks for doing this for us, Brat," Leslie said, her hand outstretched in greeting when the young Australian doctor stepped from his car. "We're at a dead end and thought we'd—"

"Your partner explained it all last night. I'm happy to stretch my legs in the field. Nice break from staring through a microscope all day. I hope I can be of help. Mind you Mate, I haven't any idea what we're looking for."

"Join the crowd, Doctor. We're running blind on this one. Anything out of the ordinary. Anything at all. We need a thread to pull on. A sliver will do. Right now, we have essentially nothing."

"Where shall we begin?" the lanky doctor asked. "Our typical procedure would be office, owner's bedroom followed by any work area. In that order. After that we'd do the kitchen, then the remainder of the rooms."

"Works for me," Leslie answered. "I'm not that organized."

"Don't let her fool you, Doc," Rodriguez commented, joining them, "she's the most organized person I've ever worked with."

Twenty minutes later Leslie called out, "This is interesting!"

Both men stopped what they were doing and joined her at a built-in white veneer desk straddling a corner in Tac's office with a clear view of the lake in which he had drowned. The right-hand middle drawer was pulled open and Leslie held what appeared to be a business checkbook having three checks to a page.

"It appears as if this is a rather new account. Only four and a third pages, thirteen checks, have been issued. Look who the twelfth check was written to!"

"Consultation with Thunder," Brat announced, reading over Leslie's shoulder. "Ten thousand dollars. Should I know this... this Thunder?"

"No reason you should. Not yet any way," Leslie was quick to point out. "Law firm out of Texas. Specializes in protection of property, using offshore trusts. I've asked Beth Hillard to round up everything law enforcement knows about the firm. I expect later today we'll have a report of what the law firm does. We now know that Tac was consulting the same lawyer as Kumar."

"What do you make of that?" Rodriguez asked.

"Not much yet. The linkage to the Kumars is worth noting."

Brat, his curiosity peaked, asked, "You think Tac was trying to move something offshore? Or perhaps he was seeking something already offshore?"

"From what I gather about the lawyer, he doesn't actually move the items. Just set's up ownership in another country."

"Truth is, he could be the one moving merchandise. A sideline to his legal business so to speak. Anyone challenging him, he claims legal privilege. Ties them up in court type of thing. Just saying."

"Possible, I suppose," Leslie acknowledged. "Looks like we've exhausted the office. Now for his bedroom."

"Ready to do the garage?" Rodriguez asked less than fifteen minutes later when it became clear there was nothing in the bedroom of importance to their investigation.

"Let's do it," Leslie agreed.

"If I recall," Brat injected, "The garage was immaculate. So was his car, a Mercedez AWD. Pristine interior." Consulting an electronic pad, he continued. "Vacuum of the back boot showed traces of plastic film. We surmise that came from a pre-delivery protective covering. The rest of the garage was almost sterile."

"I see what you mean," Leslie acknowledged as she opened the door from the laundry and visually observed the interior of the garage. "His car's here. One work bench along the far wall. A tool chest is positioned next to the work bench. When we originally went through this space, I was curious as to where the normal garage clutter was."

"That's the question you put in the case file," Rodriguez confirmed. "Couldn't answer then. Don't suppose this time'll be any better. Hey," the young deputy called, "what's this?" He was standing in front of the work bench pointing to a barely visible dark spot, the size of a small fingernail.

Brat consulted his pad. "That spot was there when we first went through this garage. Let me see if we sampled it." The assistant ME interacted with his pad for several minutes, before saying, "Look at this! Originally, we determined it was a fingerprint smudge. The copy we took proved to be inconclusive. Could have been because it was badly smudged. Or the person lifting the print didn't get it all. We can fix that."

"How will you do that?" Leslie pressed.

"Out in the car I have one of our newer microscopes. It's not designed for field use, but if one of you helps, we can bring that bad boy in here and get at that smudge.

"I'll help," Rodriguez immediately announced.

A few minutes later, as the two men came back into the garage carrying a heavy looking piece of equipment between them, Brat said, "I don't usually bring this to a crime scene. It's not designed for travel. From our discussion last night, and our poor result with the print the last time, I thought this would be better than the portable one we normally bring to the field. This baby is internet connected and fast as hell. I dubbed it 'Big Ben'." He set the device on the work bench and focused the lens on the spot. "Here goes," he announced, flicking the ON switch. "This should not take but a... ah, here it is already! Told you Big Ben's fast. Oh, bugger!"

"What now?" Leslie inquired.

"The problem before wasn't the technique used by the technician in lifting the print. The problem is that the print is inherently defective. Kinda like someone sliced it in half. Never hold up in court. But... but there's something else as well. Here, take a look." The Aussie motioned for the detectives to look at the screen. "That small crater near the center, that's a cut mark in the surface. I'm winging it now, but I'd say the cut mark was made by an X-acto knife with a number eleven blade. There are fibers buried in the slot."

"Fiber? As in fabric fibers? Or some other kind of fiber?"

"Appears to be fabric fibers. With some kind of coating. Unfortunately, the system is blank on what type of fabric or coating. I'll keep working it. Let you know when we get something."

"Okay, let's do the—"

"Got something!" Brat announced, reminding Leslie of a kid in a candy store. "Got a match for the fiber!"

"So, what fabric is it?"

"Can't tell you that. Sorry. The match is with a sample we originally took from the parachute—the one from the lake."

"You don't know what the fiber came from? Cotton? Nylon? Wool?"

"I do know there's an eighty-three percent probability that fiber came from a linen sheet," Brat said, his attention diverted to a file that came up on his pad. "Oh, lookie here!" he exclaimed. "You're not going to believe this! The best match to that partial is IRS Agent Maxine Ghana!

TWENTY-THREE

A NOTE WAS LYING OPEN on Leslie's desk when she returned later in the day, the embossed name Debi clearly visible across the top.

To whom it might concern:

I was speaking with Kurt, a neighbor of mine who plays bocce with the guys on Fridays and learned that the Sheriff is looking for information pertaining to that poor man who was found murdered over in Palm Beach.

This might mean nothing, but for what it is worth, two days before his death was reported on the TV news, I saw a woman banging on his front door. I wouldn't remember the incident, except a while ago her picture was also on the TV. She is the granddaughter of Queen B. I forgot her exact name. Kats Arib or something like that. I hope this helps.

Yours,

Debi

"Rodriguez," Leslie called, "Follow up with this, will you? My interview with Bates Aribah is in the file. I want anything you can find on Aribah's interactions with Andino. Here's what bothers me. The file from the Palm Beach search of Andino's place is devoid of anything linking Bates and Andino. But—"

"I know you asked Bates if she knew Andino. She adamantly denied knowing him. That's all consistent. So, what's troubling you?"

"I didn't believe her at the time! I'm convinced she and Andino had a relationship with respect to the Mundi painting—and possibly more! That guy Skyler, Star's grandfather, seems to be a major source of First artifacts. Andino was a delivery messenger for Skyler. Aribah, by her own admission, has the Mundi. She's either working directly for Skyler or... or they're using Andino for a cut out. I need to piece together a time frame for both of them, say, going a month back."

"I appreciate that instinct is critical to what we do, Leslie," Rodriquez commented. "I get that. I really do. But we have nothing."

"That's what's troubling me," Leslie acknowledged. "That's exactly what I want you to create! While you're out interviewing this Debi woman, I'll go through the Ring door video footage, see what I can find."

"Good luck with that," Rodriguez skeptically replied, crossing the room on the way to his car. "Palm Beach found nothing of interest."

"Let's hope you do better. Oh, Beth! I was just going to call you. Great timing. Walk me through the Andino Ring file."

"At least they put the entire digital footprint in the file," Beth said. "The rest of their Andino file is a hot mess."

"How do you know the full Ring file's there?"

"The new software is amazing," Beth answered. "I asked it to tell me if any part of the file between last Tuesday midnight and Friday at noon is missing. Here is exactly what it responded." Beth handed Leslie a sheet of paper on which was printed: RING DIGITAL FILE 23601, FROM TUESDAY 00:00 TO FRIDAY 12:00 HAS BEEN REVIEWED. EVERY SECOND IS ACCOUNTED FOR.

"His death was reported on Friday. He was seen alive on Wednesday," Beth said. "I've confirmed that. It's all loaded on your computer."

Leslie turned to her keyboard and typed in: FILE 23601. IS THERE ANY PERSON ON WEDNESDAY?

Almost instantly the computer screen came alive: RING DIGITAL FILE 23601, WEDNESDAY A WOMAN WAS PRESENT FOR SEVEN MINUTES AND TWENTY-THREE SECONDS BEGINNING AT 10:12. SHOULD I PLAY THE VIDEO? AND THE AUDIO?

YES, YES, Leslie typed.

The front walkway to the Andino house immediately came alive showing Bates Aribah walking toward the camera, a wrapped package under her left arm. The Ring chimes sounded and Bates, her face now in profile, stood, waiting. Almost a minute passed before the door opened. Bates took a small step backward, her face filling in on the screen while an off-camera male voice said, "I didn't expect you. You shouldn't be here. Not now. Not ever. I suggest you—"

"You're working for me, Mr. Andino. Not the other way around. Need I remind you? Here, take this." Bates then thrust the package forward. It passed mostly out of view of the camera.

"Is this the—?"

"No need to go into that now! Take it and deliver it to the normal destination!"

"I thought—"

"I said, no need to get into all that! Do as I say!"

The door closed several seconds after that. Bates turned and walked back down the front walkway. The video turned off when she was out of sight.

"What do you make of that?" Beth asked. "I'm confused. I—"

"Hey, wait!" Leslie exclaimed. "Something's in that last shot! Looks like another person was standing just behind Andino."

"I didn't see Andino. He wasn't captured by the camera."

"No. But a third person's hand was. I'll play it back."

A moment later, Leslie said, "There! See that! A hand, I'd say a man's hand! Here, I'll play the last minute back in slow motion."

"You're right," Beth confirmed, as the video slowly replayed. "Appears to be an arm behind Andino. Very faded. Don't know how you saw it! The owner of that arm had to be standing directly behind Andino."

"If there were any faces, I didn't see them. Maybe the lab can work their magic. Could that have been the deceased guy, Tac?"

"Anybody's guess."

"Palm Beach didn't note that exchange in the file summary," Beth commented. "I wonder—"

"Probably didn't see it. That's my guess."

Other than several visits from Tac, the last one the day before Andino was found dead in Lake Okeechobee, Andino's door camera yielded nothing more of interest. Leslie was just about to bring up the written forensics file when her phone rang. She was surprised to see the name PETE pop up on her cell. "Jak," she exclaimed, "I thought we weren't—"

"Strictly business," Jakowski responded. "Just business."

Thinking about his pending, but highly prolonged divorce proceedings, Leslie was cautious. "Cop business or marriage business?"

"The former. No change in the later."

"I'm all ears," Leslie said. The statement came out sharper than she had intended, her harbored doubts that he was serious about leaving his wife rising to the surface. In an odd way his divorce procrastination was comforting. It validated her tentative decision to move on with her life, a decision she had come to several months back, but was unwilling to admit, even to herself. Her romantic mind was now focused on William Bishop. "What's up?"

"What do you know about the Mundi—Salvator Mundi—other than da Vinci painted it?"

"Sounds like an exam question. I'll parrot what I read on the Internet. Salvator Mundi is Latin for Savior of the World and is a subject in iconography depicting Christ with his right hand raised in blessing and his left hand holding an orb, often surmounted by a cross, known as a globus cruciger. How'd I do? Want more?"

"I'd give you an A-plus for background knowledge, but—"

"If it's transactional information you're seeking then I would answer that the Mundi was likely purchased by Mohammed bin Salman, the crown prince of Saudi Arabia, through a proxy. The painting has not been seen publicly since the sale. However, rumors have it that it was acquired by Abu Dhabi's Department of Culture and Tourism for eventual display in the Louvre."

"So, you *are* aware that U.S. law enforcement believes that it is in the possession of Queen B? More accurately, in the possession of her granddaughter, Bates Aribah?"

"Jak, I know you're law enforcement and all that. But you also know I can't talk about an ongoing case. Let's just leave it at that. Okay?"

"I take it then that the Mundi's an ongoing case. Okay. That's good to know. Then I'm not wasting my time. Now hear me out. You can say nothing if you wish. I'm assuming you're working the death of that Tac guy who was found in the lake. Mundi only comes into the picture because some versions were painted by da Vinci."

"How does Mundi tie into Tac? I lost you there."

"Only that Tac was, from my understanding, desperate to get his hands on da Vinci's parachute material. That's why he and that other dead guy, Andy Andino, were friends. Tac was working with Andino to obtain da Vinci parachute material. From what I've learned, the granddaughter Aribah was the messenger for that."

"The actual supplier, in your version of the story, is who?"

"Guy named Skyler. William Paxter Skyler to be exact. He usually works directly with Andino. Not this time for some reason."

"This time?"

"As I said, Bates Aribah. Here's the kicker—Aribah sold the material to Tac. Price: Twenty-five million! How Tac came up with that amount remains a mystery. Along came another buyer. Your friend LBB to be perfectly honest. Price: Don't know exactly, but sources claim over a hundred million. See the problem?"

"The problem Bates had—maybe still has—is selling the same material twice. So, how did she solve that?"

"Have no idea. Sorry."

"Changing the subject. What do you know about Andino?"

"He ran errands for Pax Skyler, who, as I assume you know, is a Seminal Society player. Pax made a billion when he sold his shoe company. He's spent his life since then traveling around the world pursuing all things da Vinci. Story is he managed to get his hands on the da Vinci material. Hand-painted da Vinci impregnated linen to be exact."

"Where is the material now?"

"Unless I miss my guess, it's offshore."

"How'd he pull that off? The man's been out of the country since—"

"FYI. Skyler landed last night. He's at his Miromar home as we speak."

"You didn't answer my question," Leslie said, masking her excitement about finally getting to meet the man at the center of so much turmoil. "How'd he get the da Vinci material offshore if he himself hasn't been in the country?"

"That's what messengers are for. Andino and Aribah."

"Neither of them has been out of the country, far as I can tell."

"Let's just say a little birdie flew it offshore for him."

"Birdie have a name?"

"Need to know only"

"Birdie fly out of Texas?"

"That's a fair assessment."

"Birdie go to law school?"

"You're a detective. Told you more than I should have."

"So, why'd you call?"

"Be careful, all's I can say. You need to be careful."

"What the hell's that mean?" Her thoughts flashed to her partner, Cox. whose life was lost to a felon's bullet. He was always careful, but sometimes being careful just isn't enough. "How the hell's a cop supposed to be careful?" She threw back at him. "I need more than that!"

"Oh, I hit a tender spot, did I? Sorry. Didn't mean to. One friend to another; shit's going down all around you. All's not what it seems. Be careful."

The line went dead before Leslie could probe further.

Leslie resumed her fast-forward review of the Ring file and was rewarded when fifteen fast-forward minutes later the front door opened and Andino walked out carrying the package that Bates had brought three and a half real-time hours earlier. At the edge of the camera's range, he handed the package to a mostly unidentifiable person. Andino immediately turned and retreated into his house, quickly pulling the door closed behind him.

Leslie replayed that segment of the file several times but was unable to identify the recipient other than to note a brief flash of blue. Isolating the blue in the file proved elusive, but the color lingered in Leslie's memory. Suddenly, she exclaimed, "Bingo! Got it!"

"Got what?" Rodriguez asked, startling her.

"Oh! Didn't know you were back. Quick interview. Get anything?"

"Nothing important."

"Write it up anyway."

"So, Leslie, what did you get?"

"Oh, I now know who Andino gave the package to."

"What package? What are you—"

Leslie filled her partner in on the Ring file, then said, "Blue flash I saw was the exact color of a shoe someone was wearing. I just can't bring up who was wearing that shoe. It will come to me in time. Right now, I want to focus on Skyler. Just learned he's supposedly in town. Call him and set up a visit. Better yet, tell him we're on our way."

TWENTY-FOUR

"THANK YOU FOR SEEING US," Leslie said to Skyler after introducing herself as well as Detective Rodriguez. "I know you're on a busy schedule and I appreciate you taking the time."

"Don't kid yourself for one blessed moment that I made time for anything! This young man told me in no uncertain terms that you and he were coming. I can't very well stop you, not if I ever require your services. I suppose I could have gone about my business and left you to an empty house, but hiding has never been my way and I won't start now. State your business as succinctly as you can!"

William Paxter Skler stood at six foot three and was in remarkably good shape for a fifty-eight-year-old. That much Leslie knew from the profile CIA Hillard had prepared. What surprised her was his vitality. Deciding to take him at his word, she asked, "What do you know of the Salvator Mundi painting?"

"Savior of the world! In most circles it's attributed to Leonardo da Vinci. I'm not convinced it was all him. More likely he sketched it and his pupils filled it in. Rumored to be in bad condition. Sold for a high dollar value. Hasn't been seen for years. Should I continue?"

"Let me be blunt," Leslie said, pushing back against Skyler's tactics. "Do you have possession of the Mundi?"

"I do not."

"Is the Mundi in this house?"

"No!"

"Has the Mundi been in this house in the last month?"

"Next question!"

"I'll take that as a yes," Leslie responded. "And I thank you for your honesty."

"Take it anyway you wish, Detective. I don't have it."

"Do you know a man, now deceased, by the name of Andy Andino?"

"I did. He's—was—a neighbor. From time to time I hired him to run errands for me. Best in the. business. I'll miss him."

"Did you purchase the Mundi from a woman named Queen B? Or her granddaughter, Bates Aribah?"

"Next question please."

"During the recent Olympics did you visit the Louvre at any time?"

Skyler paused before answering, "By invite. Yes."

"At any time during that visit to Paris did the Mona Lisa come into your physical possession, even for a moment?"

Again, the pause. "I see no need to answer that question, other than to say I did visit the grand lady and I did spend quality time with her."

"Alone?"

"As alone as one can be at the Louvre. Best security anywhere."

Leslie took a moment to phrase her next question in a manner to elicit as much information as possible, realizing now that Skyler wasn't prone to lying, nor was he about to incriminate himself. "If I were to intercept a Mona Lisa here in Florida, would I be correct in assuming it is the original?"

"Great question, Detective! Great question. I've been pondering that very question for several days now. Based on your questions, I assume you've heard—through Interpol I imagine—that a substitution has been made at the Louvre for the most valuable portrait ever created. As you must know, I'm a da Vinci disciple. If it were possible, I'd own anything and everything he ever created. But, alas, I don't. To answer your question more directly, there most definitely is a rumor floating that the Mona Lisa has been set free. It is also true that forensics is not able to provide a definitive answer to your question. Knowing the players involved, I'd put my money on the *floater*, if you were to be so lucky as to intercept such, being the genuine article."

"Thank you again for your honesty. In your opinion what are the odds of me locating the *floater*, as you called it?"

"My, you're blunt. Refreshingly so, I might add. Let me be just as blunt. Zero! You have absolute zero chance of intercepting the Grand Lady."

"What makes you so certain?"

"Andino was the best I've ever known in the business. He was hired to transport that treasure. Not by me, I should add. If anyone could pull it off, Andy could. That fact alone got my juices moving. When he didn't show up in Paris I walked away. End of story."

"Who hired him if you didn't?"

"Next question."

"'Best in the business,' is what you called Andino. My question: In what business?"

"Moving extremely valuable artifacts. Particularly when their owners would rather not have the artifact moved. From jewelry to portraits to valuable documents. He handled it all. Alas, the poor man met his match over in Okeechobee. A great loss to the underground art world I must say."

"The underground art world? I suppose that label applies to those who desire to separate art owners from their possessions?"

"My dear, in the art world, it is often difficult to identify one from the other. Let's just agree Andino was a gifted courier. Period. Said enough. More than I should have. Now I have a question of my own."

"I'll answer if I can."

"I had in my possession a quantity of da Vinci parachute material. Let me clarify that. Leonardo gave very specific instructions as to the treatment of linen so that if the treated material were to be wrapped around a wooden frame one could safely jump from great heights and land comfortably on the ground without serious injury. I found—and secured for myself—what I'm certain is the original da Vinci parachute material made by his own hand. When I was last here in Miromar Lakes I had that material in my possession. I engaged Andino to handle a final provenance certification. My question to you is: Did you find the da Vinci material in Andino's possession?"

"Could you please describe the material? For example, did it have a pattern? That type of thing." Leslie was stalling, hoping to be able to form an acceptable answer.

"Linen. With chemicals soaked in."

"Any pattern on the material?"

"Vitruvian Man. I don't suppose you know—"

"da Vinci's study of the human form," Leslie immediately answered. "The Vitruvian man is meant to demonstrate the perfect ratios and proportions found in human anatomy."

"How in the world! Could I convince you to come work for me young lady! You're most definitely wasting your talents working for the Sheriff. With a mind like that, you could—"

"I'm perfectly content doing what I do, Mr. Skyler. Thank you just the same."

"Can I take it from the fact that you know about the Vitruvian Man that you've seen the material?"

"I wouldn't go that far," Leslie truthfully replied. "Let's leave it at me discussing the material with an interested party."

"Let me impress on you, then, that should you come across the material I want it back. It's priceless! And I own it."

"I can't promise anything. But I do suggest you file a theft report."

"Just do this for me then. If the material comes into your possession, please keep it local. Don't allow the Feds to take it."

"Why is that?"

"They have sticky fingers. Property goes into a black hole and it never surfaces. Look, please just keep it local."

"I'll try. It would help if I knew why."

"I've said enough. You're a cool lady—that's what Star calls you—a cool lady. Being a cool lady only gets you so much. Look, the job offer's open. Money's good. Nothing illegal I promise."

"That's kind of you to offer. But I don't—."

"Think about it. One further thing you should know."

"And what's that?"

"I had a second parachute. Sold to me as an original. But I have my doubts on that. In fact, I'm positive it was a clone. A fake."

"How would I know? Does it also have the Vitruvian Man pattern?"

"Goodness no! It's orange and yellow. Broad stripes of orange and yellow."

"For what it's worth, Mr. Skyler, that describes the very parachute Tac was using when he landed in the lake."

"Please let me know when I can claim that chute. It might be a fake. But it's certainly an expensive fake. Anything further you need, please call my lawyer. Good day, detectives."

Skyer walked across the room, turned a corner and was gone. The detectives were left alone. Leslie noted the confused expression on Rodriguez's face and decided they had been the beneficiary of more information than she normally received on a visit such as this. She wasn't certain her own face didn't appear as bewildered. Nodding toward the door, she followed her partner out to their car.

"Hi, Beth, you have something for me?" Leslie said in answer to her Criminal Investigation Assistant's call. "Rodriguez and I are just leaving Skyler's house. Guy's a piece of work. Before I forget, I want you to take the Tac parachute into your personal custody and secure it well. Apparently, it's more valuable than we thought."

"Will do. Two things for you. First, two guys just walked into the Outreach Center at Gulf Coast Town Center and asked for you. Something to do with the casino over in Immokalee."

"Tell them to wait. We're just across Ben Hill Griffin. Be there in five. And second?"

"Second. Item LCS24307-156, labeled TAC WORKBENCH, is puzzling to say the least. Blood DNA is a seventy percent match for IRS Agent Maxine Ghana!"

"Ghana! What the hell's going on? Brat just read the smudged print using a device he called Big Ben. The print was a partial and his best guess was that it also comes from Agent Ghana!"

"That doesn't sound possible. I'll keep working it. Can't wait to get to the bottom of this mess."

"Names? Of the two men waiting for us."

"Richard and Dave."

"Good afternoon, gentleman. My name's Detective Sergeant Hodges and this is my partner, Detective Rodriguez," Leslie said to the only two men in the lobby. "I understand you have information for us. Which one of you is Richard?"

"That'll be him," the guy wearing the Ace in the Hole T-shirt said. "I'm Dave."

"I understand you gentlemen asked for me. Pertaining to?"

"On TV," Richard answered, "they asked anyone with information pertaining to Andy—Andy Andino, he's a neighbor over at Miromar Lakes—to contact you. I saw Andy over at the casino in—"

"Before you go on, let's go back to a room where we can talk in private," Leslie interrupted. "Follow me, please."

When the four of them were seated around a small table in a claustrophobic room, Leslie asked," Mind if I record this conversation?"

"Okay by me," Richard nodded.

"Likewise," Dave added. "I don't have much to say anyway."

"Let's begin then. Who wants to go first?"

"As I started to say," Richard began, "we saw Andy over at the Seminole Casino in Immokalee."

"I suppose you see many of your neighbors over there. Casino's a popular place. Why tell me about Andino?"

Dave leaned forward only to have Richard wave him back. "It's not that he was there. You're right, I see a lot of my neighbors over there. It's how he was acting. As if he didn't want to be seen. No, I said that wrong. Let me be clear about this. It's not so much that he was trying not to be seen. It's that he appeared not to want to be seen with the person he was meeting."

"Please clarify."

"Dave and I were playing Twenty-One in the private room. There were five tables active at the time. He came in, studied the room for a moment, then selected a table with a single player off to the left of ours. He played several hands, all the time studying the room as if looking for someone. I'd say he stayed at that table maybe five-six minutes before he got up and went to a closed table at the back of the far end of the room. Over by the restrooms. The next time I looked his way, a woman had joined him. I hadn't seen her come in. I assumed she was staff. They spoke for a while. Don't really know for how long because when I looked over she was gone. He sat for several minutes by himself before walking slowly across the room, passing our table on his way out the door."

"Dave," Leslie asked, "what can you add to what you just heard?"

"Nothing. Only that when I went to the bathroom, I looked to see how the woman could have come and gone without us seeing her. Didn't notice anything obvious. There are mirrored walls in that area. I assume it's possible there's a hidden door or two."

"Can you describe the woman?"

"Tall. Taller than you even. Stocky. Solid built. Short curly hair. Round looking face."

"White woman? Hispanic? What?"

"Not white. Dark skinned. If pressed, I'd say Hispanic."

Leslie glanced over at her partner. He nodded but said nothing. "Anything further either of you can add?"

"Nothing I can think of," Richard replied.

After going over the date and time of the sighting, Leslie handed each of them her card. "Appreciate you coming in. Please don't hesitate to call or drop a note if you think of anything else. Remember, details, however trivial they might seem, are important."

"Did you catch that description?" Leslie asked Rodriguez when they were back in the car. "I'm thinking we have a major problem on our hands."

"That's a perfect description of Agent Ghana! Her name's popping up everywhere. I agree, can't be a good thing."

"Where there's smoke. I'll have Beth call the casino, see what they'll tell us. If anyone has video, they'll have it in spades. Hopefully they'll share without too much of a fuss."

"Hi Beth," Leslie said to their CIA when she answered her phone. "I have Lewis on speakerphone with us."

"I'm okay with that," the always upbeat CIA responded. "Hi, Lewis."

"What's going on, Beth?" Rodriguez said by way of greeting.

"Same old."

Leslie went on to explain what she was after, and why. Beth then said, "I know Luca Maikoh. He's the manager over there. Do you want to take a drive or shall I set something up on the phone?"

"It's less than forty-five minutes. I'm for going over."

"See what I can arrange. When?"

"How about now?" Leslie said, looking toward her partner to gage his reaction.

"I agree. No time like the present," Rodriguez replied, nodding his concurrence.

"Hear that?" Leslie said into the phone. "Set it up. We'll start in that direction. Call me to confirm. Oh, and Beth, keep Ghana's name out of the file—for now."

"Too late for that. Her DNA set off all kinda bells. Sheriff himself called me. This is getting hot."

"Crap! Well, it is what it is! Let me know what you work out."

"Have you shared your findings with Palm Beach?"

"Fix'n to now. Frankly, I was slow rolling until I spoke with you. They haven't shared a thing with us." Leslie thought of the file they had been working from. The Ring video they had reviewed. "That's not exactly accurate. We've seen that interesting video."

"If you're talking about the Ring file you should know that it came from Agent Ghana's team. Palm Beach's files remain closed I'm afraid."

"What the hell's that about?"

"That's exactly what Boots said when I briefed her 'bout an hour ago."

"Okay, set up our casino visit. We're on our way."

Leslie's call to Boots went immediately to voice mail. They drove in silence. Traffic was light until they hit Lehigh Acres, less than a mile from her house, where a fender-bender brought traffic to a virtual stop. Leslie reached to turn on the lights and siren just as the name BOOTS popped up on her phone. "Thanks for calling me back," she began and was immediately cut off.

"What the hell you get us into now?" Leslie's highly agitated Captain barked. "Sheriff's all over me!"

"About what?"

"You going to the casino to see surveillance videos is what got his drawers in a knot. Haven't seen him this worked up in a long while. What gives here?"

"I'm following a lead in the Tac investigation. Since when—"

"Seminole Police are all over him! Got themselves in a real tizzy, they have! Claims they should have been notified if you were investigating in their territory."

"That's pure BS! Their agitation's premature at best. It's video at a casino that has nothing at all to do with them. I'm just confirming a lead that two people of interest met at the casino. I misspoke when I said it was a Tac lead. It's really a direct lead in the Andino case. It's peripheral in Tac."

"Telling me is unimportant. Sheriff's up my ass. I'm up yours. I think this all has to do with Ghana's blood, and perhaps a partial print, being in Tac's garage. Now that I think of it, if what that video shows is a direct lead in Andino, then I bet Palm Beach got wind of it! Palm Beach got onto the Seminole Police, gave them a hard time. If that's the case, I understand why the Sheriff's so wound up. He and Palm Beach have been in a feud for a while now. Has to do with resource allocation. Above my pay grade."

"We'll turn around. But we need to confirm the lead at some point."

"Never mind. Until you hear from me directly, continue to the casino. I'll call a friend over in Palm Beach. He's the captain in charge of the Andino investigation. Over the years we've handled several matters together. Name's Wine. Jerry Wine. Straight shooter. He'll be interested in what you've heard."

"Aye, aye, Captain." Hanging up, Leslie turned to her partner, "Turn off the lights and siren. We're in no hurry now."

TWENTY-FIVE

CAPTAIN STETSON SOLVED THE problem by inviting her counterpart to join Leslie and Rodriguez at the casino to view the video. Leslie's instructions were to wait just inside the front door for the Palm Beach captain.

"I'm Jerry Wine," the short, pudgy guy with a slight limp said to Leslie. "You must be Leslie Hodges. Tall, lanky, wearing aqua slacks. Boots nailed you perfectly. What I don't understand, is how she knows your pants color?"

"It's Friday," Rodriquez volunteered. "Everyone knows she wears aqua on Fridays. Tomorrow it'll be blue, followed by—"

"One less thing I need to decide in the morning," Leslie said, defending her behavior.

"Sounds OCD to me," Wine commented. Quickly adding, "But hey, each to his—or her—own. Oh, by the way, you and I met once before." Responding to Leslie's puzzled expression, Wine continued. "At your husband's funeral up in Tampa. From the stories I heard, he was certainly a good man and well-liked. Your husband died a hero and the least we could do was come up and honor him. Oh, I'm sorry for bringing up painful memories."

"It was all so over whelming." Cops had come from every corner of Florida to pay their respects to Junior who was killed in a bank robbery gone bad. Leslie had met so many law enforcement officers, women as well as men, that it was a blur in her otherwise near faultless memory. "Pardon me for not remembering you."

"I would have been shocked if you had. There were close to five hundred. Some, I imagine, didn't sober up for a week! Not me, I should add. I was in the middle of an investigation. Now that I think of it, it was a robbery of an art artifact from the Norton. And a near homicide."

"May I ask? What art piece was involved?"

"Maybe none. Maybe Botticelli's *Adoration of the Magi*. It was on loan from the *Uffizi Gallery* in Florence. You into art?"

"How'd it go down?" Leslie asked, ignoring Wine's question.

"Perp hid away. Two hours after the museum closed, he opened the main door and was most of the way out of the building when a guard arrived. A shot was fired and the guard went down, hit in the chest just below the heart. Took a lot of fancy medicine, but he survived. Curator reported nothing taken, but rumors in the art world dispute that, claiming the Botticelli was substituted."

"I take it you never found the perp."

"No trace. Nada."

"No fingerprints? No DNA? No images?"

"As to the prints and DNA, nothing. We do have an image, images actually. All useless."

"Mind if I see them?"

"My pleasure." Wine logged into his iPad, clicked several times and handed the screen to Leslie. "There are three pics. One worse than the next. Scroll through them as you wish. FBI took their best shot at reconstruction. Gave us nothing."

A moment later Leslie, confirmed, "I can't even tell if it's a man or woman. I agree the image looks male, but—"

"Can't be certain. We've enhanced them and still a blank. Can't even get an accurate height—or a reliable weight for that matter. Talk about useless security. That's a prime example, sorry to say."

Leslie flipped the iPad closed and was about to hand it back to Wine when she realized she had just seen a familiar color. "Mind bringing that up again? I think I saw... yes, there it is! That blue! See, at the very bottom of the screen!"

Wine enlarged the image to the maximum, then said," Blue blob. I wouldn't even know it was blue, except that's what you called it. I'm thinking it's a shoe."

"Very much a shoe!" Leslie confirmed. "Seen that color before! Outside Andino's house on his Ring camera. I'm thinking the shoe is being worn by a... a courier. I'm assuming that the person wearing those shoes is a woman. But even that is open to question."

"I'll go with woman. Now, how about telling me what's going down. Why am I here?"

"We have reason to believe Donatello Andino met with IRS Agent Ghana here at the Casino, I believe, shortly before he was killed." Leslie went on to provide Wine with the date and time, repeating almost word for word what Dave and Richard had said.

"In other words," Wine commented when she finished, "you have a witness, witnesses, who saw them together and you're not comfortable giving us their full names."

"Correct. When identity is important to your investigation, I'll be happy to give you what you need."

"Reliable?"

"No reason to think otherwise. Totally disinterested. The thing I don't understand; why meet here? I mean with all the security cameras you'd think both of them would stay clear. Neither of them is naïve."

"Let's go look at the video from that day. That shouldn't be a problem. Wait here—or at one of the tables if you like."

"Too rich for my blood. I'll use the restroom and we'll wait for you in the gift shop over there."

"Speaking of places too rich for your blood. That place certainly is, at least for mine. I'll make this as fast as I can."

It took Wine exactly seventeen minutes to find the manager, select and copy the video, actually several videos, showing either Andino or Ghana. He texted Leslie to meet him in a currently unused private baccarat room.

"That was faster than I anticipated," Leslie exclaimed when she joined him.

"Pays to have friends in high places."

"More like they want to remain open, cooperate with the authorities, if I were to judge."

"A little of that as well." Wine placed his iPad where all three of them could see the screen. "Here goes. We'll see just how accurate that source of yours really is."

A moment later, Rodriguez said, "Pretty accurate I would say. That's certainly Andino, as well as Ghana."

"I repeat," Leslie added, "Why would two savvy people be so public about a meeting?"

Wine nodded his agreement and added, "For now our job is to take what we see and run with it. Somewhere down the line, we'll make sense of it."

"You sound like Junior," Leslie remarked, pain permeating her voice. "But that's the life we selected for ourselves. Is it not?"

Wine again nodded. "I suppose I should answer the question you haven't asked. What is the status of our investigation? In a word, zip! We're convinced Marino Jacobi was the last person to see Andino alive. We found no abandoned car anywhere close, so he may have even driven his friend Andino to the lake. We just don't know. Jacobi's dead, so unless we get something further, case suspended."

Walking out of the casino, Leslie turned to Wine. "We do have some new forensic evidence from Tac's garage. I'll see that you get it. Mind lifting the restrictions on Andino's house? We're still investigating Tac's death, and I'd like to have a complete file."

"I thought that was a suicide. Or an accident. What gives?"

"In truth, we don't really know. Chalk it up to instinct I suppose, but I think we're missing something."

"I live on instinct as well. I'll get you everything I can. Break your neck. And, hey, thanks for including me on this."

"Hey partner," Rodriguez called hours later when they were both getting ready to knock off for the day. "I was looking at Andino's Ring video and had an idea. We've been thinking granddaughter Bates was an owner of the Salvator Mundi and sold it. What if she was only part of the transportation? Does that change anything?"

"Certainly possible, Lewis. Even so, that doesn't really change much, I'm afraid."

"I suppose not," Rodriguez acknowledged just as his phone rang. "Hey," he immediately called to Leslie, "It's Beth with information for us. She tried calling you but your phone's off."

"Oh, hell! I had it off for our visit with Wine and forgot to turn it back on. Put her on speaker." Rodriguez did as instructed.

Leslie said, "What's up, Beth? Sorry about my phone being off."

"No problem. Got something for your Tac investigation. I got to thinking. If Agent Ghana was meeting with Andino, it would be in her official log. But it isn't!"

"How do you have access to that information? It's restric—"

"Better you don't know. Anyway, that caused me to dig further. I found nothing of any consequence in her official log, other than her meeting with you."

"So?"

"So, I didn't find official plane travel to Paris either. I did find evidence, again from another source, that she had gone over and back around the start of the Olympics. I'm waiting for airport video from her departure and arrival. See if anything pops up."

"Good work! You're keeping all this from her, I assume. Nothing's going in the official file."

"Affirmative. But someone must have said something to the wrong person because there's a block on what *she* can access directly. They haven't taken her off her investigations, but everything that she does or accesses is carefully screened. I understand the FBI's investigating. They're very much aware of your investigation."

"Okay. That's all we can—or should—do for now. Good work!"

"Glad to help. I have to say, this whole thing with an IRS Agent being part of the illegal activity puzzles me. And quite frankly, is depressing."

"You're not alone, Beth, that's for sure. Nothing makes any sense. Not yet anyway. Here's Lewis. He has something for you."

Ten minutes later, Beth was back on the line. "Bingo!" she said into Leslie's phone with as much excitement in her voice as she ever allowed. "We have Granddaughter Bates driving through the Miromar main gate. As luck would have it, camera caught a glimpse of a package on the seat beside her. Size consistent with the Salvator Mundi."

"Sounds promising," Leslie replied. Adding, "As you well know, that's not conclusive of anything other than the fact Bates lied to me. It's time for a second conversation. I think we'll do that here. How are you coming with the airport videos?"

"They're stonewalling, as usual! Boots got directly involved, said she has a friend who'll come through. Call you when... hold it! That's her now! Hold for a moment." The line went silent but didn't drop. Leslie took the opportunity to bridge her partner on. He was in his car, just pulling into his favorite pub to unwind.

"Beth," Leslie said when their CIA came back on the line, "I took the liberty of adding Rodriguez."

"That's fine. There is footage of Ghana! Both going to and coming from Paris! It's conclusive. She boarded a plane at RSW that connected in Atlanta to Paris. She arrived back at RSW via the reverse route. What's more, the package she was carrying on her way off the plane is identical to the one beside granddaughter Bates in the car entering Miromar Lakes, which, of course, matches the one visible in the Andino Ring file. It now appears that Agent Ghana is working directly with Bates—and with the deceased Andino. That's the good news."

"And the bad news?"

"FBI has declared William Paxter Skyler's premises off-limits, and—"

"There's more?"

"Any cooperation we may have had from Palm Beach with respect to the Andino murder is gone. We fly alone from here on out."

TWENTY-SIX

ON THE WAY TO WORK THE NEXT morning Leslie received a message that she and Rodriguez were to report directly to Stetson's office. The Captain was uncharacteristically pacing from one corner to the other when Leslie came through the door, her partner a few steps behind. "Close the door," their Captain barked, not breaking stride. "And sit! The both of you!"

Not until they were both in their seats did Boots' pace change ever so perceptively. "What the hell's going on?" she demanded. "With the Jacobi case? As if homicide isn't enough. It's apparently linked to the Andino homicide over in Palm Beach! To make that worse, you triggered the FBI! Last thing we need around here is the Feds sticking their noses where they don't belong."

"For the record," Leslie began, pushing back on her commander, "I never spoke to the FBI. Nor did I authorize anyone else to do so. If you recall, we got a tip that Ghana met Andino at the casino. I wanted video to confirm that meeting. The casino refused. You set it up with your friend over in Palm Beach, Detective Wine. If the FBI got a tip, it came from over there. Not here."

"That meeting in the casino took place only hours before Andino managed to get a bullet in his brain."

Leslie remained silent knowing she was at the limit of her control.

"In any event," Stetson continued, "you'll have nothing further to do with the Andino homicide. Leave it alone! You understand me? And as for Tac Jacobi, I have no choice but to insist you—"

Leslie, in anticipation of being told to drop the Jacobi homicide as well, leaned forward in preparation of leaving the Captain's office, but not before she resigned.

"—have twenty-four hours to wrap it up. Bring charges — or drop it. Am I perfectly clear on that as well?"

"Perfectly," Leslie said, standing and walking to the door. Before leaving, she turned to face her captain. "What I don't understand, is why."

"Why what?"

"Why would we ever *not* pass on information pertaining to a homicide to an investigating officer?"

"You'll have to take that up with the sheriff! Feds are all over him. That's all I'm going to say on the matter. You got twenty-four hours."

"How the hell did you keep your cool in there?" Rodriguez questioned on their way back to the Pit. "We did nothing wrong. In fact, we're one hundred percent by the book."

"Cap's never acted this way before. Something else's going down. Most likely with the sheriff. We just don't know what it is. I think we... I... stepped into something I'm not yet seeing."

"Gotta be something to do with Agent Ghana. Nothing else makes sense."

"We gotta concentrate on putting Jacobi to bed." Leslie noted, focusing on their main problem. "We have a cut in a parachute, a back-up parachute at that, and very little else.'

"Don't forget the partial print and the partial DNA, whatever that means."

"Means we're nowhere and have a day to get answers quickly. That makes me uncomfortable."

"You know, boss, it's always possible Boots is right. Jacobi just might have been an accident, despite the *theoretical* parachute cut. Afterall, we don't have hard evidence that the chute was cut. At this point its ninety percent speculation. Could be time to hang it up. Appears the real action is between Agent Ghana and Andino."

"If it's not homicide, I agree it's accidental. Certainly not suicide. Tac committing suicide doesn't feel right. But to tell the truth, Lewis, I'm not comfortable with accident. That razor cut in the work surface with the imbedded shreds of parachute material, while not conclusive, is more than pure speculation! If we assume the cut was made by Ghana, which appears to be accurate, it's not such a tall leap to conclude Ghana committed homicide with respect to Tac's death."

"If you prove right, then what do we do about it? After all, she's a federal agent."

"Treat her the same as any other perp. As you point out, we don't have enough to go after her. Call Beth, see if she has anything more."

Rodriguez retrieved his phone. "Shit! I turned this off when we went into Boots' office. Missed several calls from Beth. Damn!" He hit the callback for the last call.

"Been waiting for you," their CIA said instantly. "Got some updates for you."

"On?"

"The Tac case. You know that piece of material where we recovered the partial print?"

"Go on."

"It's now clear that it was cut by an X-ACTO knife just as the ME said. That makes it deliberate. All the experts I've spoken with are in agreement. The chute that was cut was not the da Vinci chute."

"If not the da Vinci," Rodriquez responded, "what was cut?"

"It was a second chute—an emergency chute—Tac was wearing."

"Why would he wear two chutes?"

"Been kicking that around with the team. Our consensus is that we assume he didn't trust the da Vinci."

"Or," Leslie injected, "he didn't believe the da Vinci was really a da Vinci! It seems the artifact world is riddled with what I'll call, *close seconds*. Fakes to be blunt about it. Tell me, Beth, is the cut enough to affect stability of the chute?"

"Sixty-four-thousand-dollar question at trial," Beth answered. "We've run a series of tests. Bottom line is that the cut is long enough to affect both stability and speed. Our take is that the chute would be useless to stop a fatal rate of descent."

"We would be justified in calling Marino Jacobi's death a homicide. Is that what you are saying?"

"Most definitely. The final ME report will classify cause of death as Homicide."

"And we have a partial print of Agent Ghana."

"We do; however there's a major problem. Ghana's prints have been—"

"Let me guess! Restricted!"

"How the hell did you know? Not restricted. Removed! By the FBI no less!"

Lewis gave Beth a quick version of their earlier meeting with Boots, then added, "Never saw Leslie so upset. I thought she..." Seeing his partner draw a finger across her throat, he said, "...handled herself well, all things considered. Call me if anything turns up."

TWENTY-SEVEN

BOOTS WAS NOT AVAILABLE when Leslie stopped by her office twenty minutes later. "Tell the boss I need to see her," she said to a blank-faced substitute sitting at the assistant's desk. "Case you're wondering, I'm Detective Sergeant Hodges."

"Do you spell that with one 'd' or two?"

"Spell it anyway you wish. Just give her the message."

Leslie was immediately angry with herself for being snippy with the helpless clerk who found herself thrust into a job she was unqualified for. She turned around to apologize. Just then her phone sounded and the letters LBB appeared. "Mr. Bishop," she said into the phone, "you're the last person in the world I expected to be calling. I'm busy—"

"Please be outside your office in five. We have to talk." The line went dead.

Exactly five minutes later, a silver Bentley Continental GT hardtop rolled to a stop directly in front of where Leslie was standing. Bishop leaned across the front seat. "Get in. Time's not on our side."

"Wha—"

"No time. Trust me."

Leslie opened the door, thought about alerting her partner, changed her mind and climbed in. The car was moving before her door was fully closed. "What the—"

"It'll all make sense in a few minutes."

"Where are we going?"

"Page Field. Your lawyer friend's plane's about to take off. I think—"

"Lawyer friend? You referring to Thunder Showers? Or to—"

"Yes. Showers."

"Hey! Slow down! Speed limit's—"

"Won't get there in time if we do that. Trust me."

"Then we should be in my car!"

"Won't work. Showers is keyed in. Don't really know how, although I have my suspicions. The moment you go into the system as responding to Page he'll be alerted and abort."

"Abort what? What the hell we doing anyway?"

"If we get there in time, and if all goes right, you're going to be in possession of a genuine Salvator Mundi. Those are two big *ifs* I know. But *if* they hold, this'll be a big day for you."

"Just don't get in an accident, that's all I can say. Tell me again why I can't notify my partner?"

Bishop swerved around several cars stopped at a traffic light, then wove his way across the intersection against the light, dodging several cars as he went. Safe on the other side, he said, "Your partner's okay. I'm not certain your communication hasn't been compromised. Someone far up in your food chain's in on this."

"Federal level you think?"

"Certainly at the federal level. I also believe at the county, or state level as well."

"What value are you putting on Mundi?"

"Round numbers. A billion when all is said and done."

"And you know about this just how?"

"You can't stop being a cop, can you?"

"Isn't that why I'm here?"

"Good point."

"Again, I ask, how do you know about the Mundi and the timing?"

"Because I'm the buyer. Or so the seller believes. Payment will occur when the Mundi is secured in Nevis."

"And who's the seller?"

"Bates Aribah. Among others."

"Bates? The granddaughter?"

"That's her."

"Alone?"

"I was afraid you'd ask that. She's the front person. There's a long chain of people. Call them intermediaries if you like. In the espionage world they're known as cutouts. An IRS agent by the name of Ghana seems to be the lead in all of it."

Leslie sat quietly, processing what she had just been told. "What I don't understand," she finally admitted, "is if you arranged for the transportation of the Mundi as you claim, then why in the world am I here with you now? I mean what's in this for you? With me involved, you certainly won't get the Mundi. What can be so—"

"You! I want you. It's that simple, Leslie."

That stopped Leslie cold. Words disappeared.

They turned a corner and Page Field was on their right. "There" LBB said, "is Shower's plane. I think you know it. The one with the thunder bolt across the tail."

While Leslie was struggling to respond, Bishop asked, "Thoughts on getting onto the tarmac? I'm hoping you know someone who works here. Someone from the Lee County—"

"As a matter of fact, I do! Junk! My former partner up in Tampa! I forgot about her! She transferred down here about a year after me."

"Junk, you say. What's the origin of that?"

"Waymetta Junksotta. She got a nice promotion to join the Lee County Port Authority Police Department. Works both Page and RSW. We had lunch a few times, then drifted apart. Haven't spoken to her for a while."

"Get her on the line! You—and her—need to get onto that plane in the next few minutes."

Leslie dialed her former partner's number. Waiting for the connection to go through, she said to Bishop, "I have no idea of her work schedule, or even if she's still assigned to Page. I saw that she was promoted to Lieutenant last week and I've been meaning to call to congratulate her. Oh, shit! It's ringing busy!" Turning to LBB she said, "See that gate entrance over there near Thunder's plane? Park near there. Hopefully, Junk'll call me right back and she can get the gate open fast enough. If I go inside the terminal, the red tape'll kill us—not to mention tipping Thunder off."

Leslie's phone rang almost as soon as she hung it up. "Junk! Glad you called back. I need a giant favor. No time for questions."

"What can I do for you, *Sergeant*? Your wish is my command."

"I'm over here at Page and... and I hope that's where you are right now."

"I am. Just walking out the door. What—"

"I need you to let me onto the tarmac. There's a plane about to take off. Thunder bolt painted on its tail. I can't come through the terminal. I'm outside the gate next to the plane. You and I will board the plane for a stolen property search."

"What is the nature of that property?" a suddenly very interested voice asked.

"Please keep this confidential. I have been reliably informed that a stolen Mundi is on board."

"I don't have—" Junksotta replied.

"Time is of the essence!"

"I can't open the gate because I don't have the key. It'll take about ten minutes for me to get someone there."

"We don't have ten minutes!" Leslie pleaded.

"Yes, you do, my friend. Yes, you do! I just put a silent hold on the plane. It won't go ten feet."

Leslie debated asking the next question but decided to err on the side of protection for her colleague—friend—should she want to back out now. "Will lack of a search warrant present a problem?" Leslie tentatively asked, hoping her former partner will turn a blind eye to the legal problem.

"Here's the thing with that plane. We have reason separate from you to believe it's being used to move, or to facilitate the movement of, stolen goods under a false bill of lading. We already have a search warrant that can only be used with the stipulation that we pre-identify, and file with the court the exact object we are looking for. Until you gave us the Salvator Mundi, we couldn't execute the warrant. That guy Thunder—or whatever his friggin' name is—has everyone bought and paid for. No loose ends. Nothing pops up. The Salvator Mundi fits the criteria for the search warrant perfectly. If we find it on board, that guy's a goner. And so's his plane. See you in a few at the gate."

Turning to LBB, Leslie said, "I suggest you drop me and get away from here. Otherwise, you'll be part of the trial workup. Truth is, you might be either way."

"I'll take off if you don't mind. I have every reason to believe the Mundi is genuine and I'd like to remain out of any criminal probe if possible."

Leslie stepped from the car, but not before LBB took her hand in his. "Don't forget, your invitation to visit is always open. Take care. I'll be at the Ritz Carlton in Naples. Please come soon." He blew her a kiss. "I'll be waiting."

It was never good to be across the desk from Captain Stetson in her office, particularly with the door closed. This was no exception. Leslie felt her forehead getting warm as her boss's eyes narrowed. "What do you mean," Boots demanded, her voice leaving no doubt about her seriousness, "there's nothing about Little Billy Bishop in the file! Yet, on the one hand you say he planned to pay for the Mundi when it landed in Nevis, and on the other I'm supposed to believe he tipped you off to the painting being on that plane. That would be contrary to his own interests—and frankly contrary to logic. Pardon me for thinking your story's not making sense!"

"I didn't think it important to include his name," Leslie repeated for perhaps the third time. "He simply told me about the stolen painting being on Thunder's plane at Page Field. Based on that tip, I called my former Tampa partner who now works for the Port Authority over there and met her at the airport." Boots knew about the warrant they were holding and that Junksotta thought the information Leslie had given her was credible enough to trigger the search, so there was no reason for Leslie to repeat that part of the story. "They've now recovered a billion-dollar artifact, not to mention a fifty-million-dollar jet plane. Sheriff's front and center on the news. I don't understand, what can be bad?"

"The IRS being in the middle for one! Agent Ghana for another! The saving factor for you is that the boss is in his glory. That's fine and dandy for him. For you, I'm not so sure. He might privately credit you for the bust, but the fact of life is that the cameras are lining up outside Junksotta's office. That's all on the positive side." Boots studied her newly minted sergeant for a long moment, then in a calmer voice continued, "I'm troubled by the why of it. Why did Bishop even tell you? He had everything to lose and nothing I can see to gain. Also, there's the small matter of how you got over there. Your partner's report states clearly that he learned of the incident while at his desk. He then drove over and brought you back to the office. That is accurate, is it not?

"It is. LBB took me over." Remembering how warm and comforting Bishop's hand had felt, her face flushed and she turned away.

"What the hell's that about? What aren't you telling me?"

"Its personal. That's all I want to say."

"It's not your call, Leslie. If it has anything to do with the file—no matter how remote—then you err on the side of over inclusion. You know that as well as I. Let's have it with no more omissions."

Leslie turned back to face her boss. "Look Captain, I put everything in the file that I believe belongs in there. Anything more is speculation. Except... except perhaps for one fact. And that is that, as I told you, LBB said he was the potential buyer."

"You didn't tell me at least two other *facts*. One, why LBB told you he was the buyer. And two, *how* did the Bill of Lading for a *billion-dollar package* get signed by an IRS agent! There are simply too many moving parts missing from the story."

"As to the *why* LBB told me about the Mundi: I have to admit that *is* perplexing." Leslie sucked in her breath and let it out slowly before saying, "He has asked me to go to Texas with him. Frankly, I don't know what he means by that. We had no time for discussion." Leslie again sucked in her breath and clenched her fists. "Before you ask. No, we haven't had sex." She surprised herself by adding, "Not that I haven't thought of it. I have."

"I didn't know it had become that serious between you and him."

"That's the thing. We've had dinner a few times. This last time, he invited me down to Texas to see his art collection and stay as long as I wanted. He's made it clear we can travel the world together. And... and he'd stay away from activities that would compromise my sensibilities."

"You thinking of taking him up on his offer?"

"Haven't really gotten that far," Leslie lied. Her mind again focusing on his warm hand—and that blown kiss. She could see herself living on a Texas ranch, traveling the world with Bishop, buying whatever art hit her fancy, never ever again worrying about how to pay for anything. Forcing herself back to the present, she said, "Especially not while I'm investigating Tac's death."

"What's the death have to do with LBB? You telling me something?"

"Quite frankly, Boss, I don't know what I'm telling you. One minute I'm thinking Tac's death was an accident. He packed his chute wrong type of accident. He was an expert at packing, so it's hard to believe he screwed that up. Then the next minute I'm thinking it's a homicide. The cut on his work bench, coupled with parachute fibers mixed into the bench wood fibers. Add to that what appears to be a fingerprint from Ghana and the homicide theory takes on a life of its own."

Boots came around her desk to put her hand on Leslie's shoulder. "I can see why you're going in circles. The only thing I can add, for what it's worth, is that I've known Agent Ghana for a lot of years. She may be many things, but expediting a Bill of Lading for a stolen property is not one of them. That's simply not her! And her taking a life! That's out of the question! I can't even imagine it! That's what has me so exercised, how can I be so wrong! If you're serious about working the case, then go back to the beginning, something's been overlooked."

TWENTY-EIGHT

GO BACK TO THE BEGINNING. Even as she slept, the words played repeatedly in Leslie's head, sometimes being yelled from a megaphone at an unfamiliar airport and sometimes on a banner being dragged across the sky. The pilot of the plane being none other than Sylvan Pecking, smiling broadly.

First thing the next morning she said to Rodriguez, "If you haven't already done so, I need you to come up to speed on that pilot, the one who flew Tac when he jumped to his death. Guy's name's Pecking."

"Yea. Sylvan Pecking. Goes by Roo. What do you want to know?"

"Good you've read the file. Good start! What's your take?"

"Boss, I hate to say it but maybe we're missing something here. We need to go interview that boy again."

"I agree. Call and set up an appointment. We can talk to him here or at his home."

"As luck would have it, I was on assignment several weeks ago over on the school campus lending a hand to the campus police. Every noon without fail a guy matching Roo's description has lunch over by the ball field. I'm thinking how many mohawk cut, red-headed FGCU students can there possibly be? I say let's pay a visit to the campus at noon. Gotta be him."

"Fine by me. Just let your police pals over there know. Don't need to be stirring up a turf war."

"Roo, remember me? Detective Hodges." Leslie began when they walked up beside him. "We met—"

"Oh, hell..." Pecking exclaimed, quickly jumping to his feet, his sandwich falling to the ground, "I didn't exp—"

"Sorry to startle you. If you'd like, we can buy you lunch."

"No need," Roo said, bending to pick up his half-eaten lunch. "A little dirt never hurt anyone. What do you want from me? I already told you what I know."

"Let's just go over it again. I have a new partner here. His name's Detective Lewis Rodriguez. I want him to hear everything directly from you."

"I have class at one, so I have to eat now."

"Go ahead and eat and tell us about that morning when you took Tac—Marino Jacobi—up for a ride."

"It wasn't for just any ride! It was so he could do a parachute jump over a small man-made Lake Como. That's over there in the Miromar Lakes community."

"Right. Just tell us in chronological order what happened, what was said, etcetera."

"Do my best," Roo replied, finishing off his sandwich and washing it down with a Pepsi. "As I think about it, tell me you're investigating Tac and not me. If it's me you're after I plead the fifth!"

"It's Tac. Not you. You have my word on that."

"Okay then. So, here goes."

Roo then repeated, almost word for word what he had told Leslie and Cox the first time.

"You finished?" Leslie asked when he stopped talking.

"All I have to say," the red-head replied. "That's everything."

"Tell us about Tac's last words. Did he say anything when he jumped?"

"It wasn't like him to yell anything, if that's what you're getting at. No, Tac was business-like. Opened the door and out he went."

"Before he opened the door," Leslie asked, "did he say or ask anything?

"He didn't ask anything."

Rodriguez moved closer to Roo. "Okay, he didn't ask anything. By chance did he say *anything*? Tell you anything?"

"Like what?"

"That's what I'm asking."

"Nothing."

"Anything about the parachute?" Leslie added. "What it was made from? Who made it? Any concerns he might have had? Anything?"

"Now that you mention parachute, yes, he did talk about the parachute. It was an odd shape, as I said. Wood slats. When I questioned him, he said he had tied on a backup just in case."

"In case of what?"

"I couldn't hear him all that well. Lot of noise and the tower was in my ear as I said."

"Do your best," Leslie encouraged.

"You know he was a Leonardo da Vinci fan. He always wanted a da Vinci-constructed parachute. I thought this was it. He had told me a week or so earlier that he had finally managed to get his hands on an original da Vinci. He was so excited! On jump day I asked him if this was the original da Vinci he had told me about."

"What did he say?"

"That's what I didn't fully hear. Sorry. I think he said this one was counterfeit. But... but he could have said that he hoped this one wasn't counterfeit. That's how hard it was to hear him."

"What makes you think he had doubts?"

"Why else would he have mentioned a backup if he had the original da Vinci? He would have trusted an original da Vinci to work properly. But not a fake da Vinci."

"And why would that be true?"

"Despite the age, he trusted da Vinci to get it right and would work to keep him safe because at least one da Vinci had been tested—and worked. That would have been enough for Tac. If it was counterfeit, then all bets were off. Hey, that's only my speculation. Can I go now, class begins in five?"

"Thanks for the time. Get in. We'll drop you."

"While we're out and about," Leslie said to Rodriguez after they dropped Roo at the Water Building for class, "Let's go over to Skyler's house and see if we can catch up with Bates Aribah."

"Why her? What's troubling you about her?"

"Hunch mostly. But I'm visualizing the Bill of Lading and I believe I can make out the initials BA in the chain of custody. I'm putting my money on BA being Bates Aribah."

Rodriguez reached for his pad and pulled up the file. A moment later he said, "Here it is. The Bill of Lading. You're right about the BA. The IRS approval to leave the country was initialed MG. I assume that's your pal, Maxine Ghana."

"Can't imagine who else that would be given what else we've uncovered about her. Problem is she's hands off. Boots reiterated that to me not an hour ago."

"Hey, look! Aribah's car's in Skyler's driveway. We're in luck."

"Park behind her. That will at least slow her down. She's arrogant enough to try and bolt."

A moment later Leslie rang the bell.

No response.

She rang it again. Same result.

She knocked and called out, "Lee County Sheriff. Bates Aribah, we know you're in the house. We have a few questions for you."

Still nothing.

"Bates Aribah, if we have to get a search warrant, this won't end pleasantly for you! Open the door so we can talk!"

Leslie gave it thirty seconds, then said, her voice louder than necessary, "Rodriguez, get that warrant. Update the paperwork and add the Mundi and the initials. And the fact that her car is in the driveway. That'll throw the reasonable cause over the top. I'll wait right here."

Her partner entered the file information into his pad, brought up the paperwork from the last time, and entered the information Leslie had dictated. "Anything further you want to add?"

"Time is of the essence. Oh, and direct it to the same judge. We can only hope he's paying attention."

"Okay. Gone!" In a much lower voice, he said, "This may take hours before he gets back to us."

"Understood. We can draw straws to see who stays and who leaves."

"I'll stay," Rodriguez volunteered. "Got file maintenance to catch up on. Can do it over there under that tree."

"Just don't let Bates slip away."

"On it all the way."

Leslie's com sounded. "Maybe this'll be permission." Leslie hopefully said to her partner. A moment later she added, "Not so lucky. I've drawn the short straw to handle a theft over at the mall."

"I should go with you. The last time you did that you ended up in the hospital."

"That was Costco! This is no Costco. Seems a couple of guys walked out of a restaurant without paying. Owner has the car's license plate. Actually, the owner has pictures of three cars and he doesn't know which one of the three skipped."

"How you goin' to deal with it?"

"Go get pictures of the three car owners and let the restaurant identify the skipper. My guess some old man just forgot to pay. Can't imagine this being anything other than a mistake."

"Sounds like something I should be handling, not you. Hey, wait a minute! Beth's on the line." A moment later Rodriguez announced, "Miracle of miracles! Judge just signed the warrant. Let's go see what Bates Aribah is all about."

Leslie again rang the doorbell and knocked on the front door. This time she called, "Bates Aribah, open up! We have a search warrant! You have one minute, else we'll take the door down!"

Forty-five seconds ticked by and nothing. Then suddenly the door flew open. Bates stood defiantly framed in the doorway.

"Here's the warrant." Leslie held her pad close to Arabah's face. "Do you intend to comply? Yes or no!"

"I *will* comply," came the defiant response. "Under protest! Don't have a choice."

"That's a good decision. We'll follow you into the house."

Once inside, Leslie said, "You might have heard, yesterday a plane was seized at Page Field with a flight destination of Nevis."

"All over TV. Of course I heard."

"There was a stolen art object on that plane. A Salvator Mundi to be exact. Know anything about that?"

"Nothing at all," the young woman immediately responded. "I sold the Mundi I had. I told you that."

"Well, here's the thing. Salvator Mundi artifacts are not commodities. One doesn't go over to Costco and buy a dozen. In fact, one doesn't go anywhere to buy a Mundi because they simply aren't for sale. At this point in time, from all the research I have undertaken, there is only one Mundi for sale anywhere in the world. Yet, according to your story, you have just sold one. There was a Mundi on a private plane leaving the country illegally. That makes two Mundi's. Care to explain?"

"Perhaps your research is incomplete."

Trusting what LBB had told her, Leslie responded, "Wouldn't bet on it. I'm fairly certain there was only one. And, adding to your problems, the initials BA were on the Mundi Bill of Lading."

"I don't know what you're talking about."

"Where did you obtain the Mundi you sold?"

"I'm an intermediary."

"What's that exactly?"

"An intermediary is a person who buys an item from Person A and sells it to Person B. It's all pre-arranged. Price, timing, all."

"So you bought a Mundi from Person A and sold it to Person B?"

"Yes."

"Names please? Person A?"

"I take the fifth."

"How in the world can there be criminal liability in who you bought something from?"

"Nothing more to say on that subject. Hey! Does that warrant cover the sale of the Mundi? Or just the search of this house, which is not mine."

"Person B? Who is Person B?" Leslie continued, pretending not to have heard Aribah's question.

"If you must know, an IRS Agent by the name of Ghana. She's the one approved it to leave the country."

Working to cover her surprise, Leslie asked, "Do you often sell items to Agent Ghana?"

"Yes."

"Do you sleep in this house?"

"Yes. From time to time. Why?"

"Which room is yours when you're here?"

"The one on the right at the end of that hall over there."

"What other rooms do you use?"

"Only the kitchen. And I sometimes use the media room."

"If we search those rooms, what will we find?"

"Must I tell you?"

"We have a search warrant. We're going to search."

"The only thing you'll find is an original da Vinci parachute. Please be careful with it. It's the only one remaining, and worth... worth well, a lot of money."

"Where did you get it?"

"Mr. Skyler."

"Where's it going?"

"It was going to that guy who died. Tac I think his name is."

"What happened? What prevented it from going to Tac?"

"Something to do with Ghana and him," Bates said, her hands involuntarily opening and closing.

"What is that something?"

"He accused her of delivering what he called a forgery."

"What was Tac referring to?"

"I don't know for sure. But piecing it all together, I believe Tac bought the one still in this house from Mr. Skyler. It might have been delivered by Mr. Andino. I don't know for sure. Maybe by Ghana herself, working for—or with—Skyler. Yeah, the more I think about it, Ghana made the delivery."

"And what she gave him was, as you said, not the original."

"Correct."

"And how do you know that?"

"Well, he came over here yelling about the material being a forgery, just like she was! He demanded the original."

"What did he mean by that? Just like she was?"

"I assume it means she's a phony because she delivered phony goods. What else could he mean?"

"Did she give him the original?"

"Not that I know. If she had, how could it still be here? My understanding is that she has a buyer all lined up."

"Who is that buyer? The one Ghana believes will buy the original da Vinci parachute? The parachute you say is in the bedroom?"

"To a Texas multi-billionaire. Guy by the name of Little Billy Bob. Who else?"

TWENTY-NINE

NO MATTER HOW OFTEN Leslie reminded herself she was a Sheriff's Deputy investigating a homicide, she couldn't help but feel like a nervous schoolgirl as she crossed the wide lobby of the Ritz Carlton Hotel. Her hands were clammy, her heart felt as though it was skipping beats. Trying to stop the scenarios playing in her mind proved futile. In fact, the closer she got, the worse they were getting. *What will I do if he tries to kiss me? Will I kiss him back? Push him away? What if he touches me?*

She stepped off the elevator in his lobby and paused, not trusting herself to maintain decorum. It was in that instant that she realized she would not resist whatever he had in mind. She wanted to be with Little Billy Bob and was more than willing to move to Texas to take him up on his offer. The sudden clarity of that realization caused her body to shake. *Am I in love? We've never even kissed. Unless the blown kiss at the airport counts! It doesn't matter! I'm going with him!*

Suddenly, reality broke through. Again, reminding herself she was a professional and would act professionally, she took a deep breath, opened the door into his living room and stepped inside.

"Leslie," Bishop said, his voice as soft and comforting as it had been in her thoughts, "come on in. Hey, you look... uncomfortable. Is something the matter?"

"Nothing's the matter, Billy Bob. Nothing," Leslie responded, testing her voice and glad to hear that it sounded normal to her. "Thanks for seeing me."

"Oh, goodness, Leslie. It's always a pleasure to spend time with you. Come sit and talk to me about what troubles you. Drink?"

"No thanks to the drink. Although, I must admit that's perhaps exactly what I need. As it turns out, this visit is official. Can't drink and be on duty at the same time."

"All work and no play. Shame."

"That your way of calling me dull?"

"You dull! Never. Okay. We'll do it your way. Follow me."

When they were settled in front of a floor-to-ceiling wall of glass overlooking the blue water of the Gulf, Leslie said, "First, let me thank you for the tip on the Mundi. As you can see from the TV coverage, both local and national, it went over well for law enforcement. Sheriff's done non-stop interviews. He's flying high."

"In my world the same is true. Lit a lot of fires. All over the world I might add. Thunder has a lot of... shall we say... friends. Many are sitting on pins and needles right now wondering if they'll be next. They're wondering also if their prize possessions are safe. And those who have turned profits in the past few years and forgot to pay their fair share of taxes, are, to say the least, extremely uncomfortable."

"What I don't understand is...," Leslie forced herself to begin, not certain she had the courage to complete the question. She knew she could change the question she was about to ask. *No, Leslie, you pride yourself on being upfront, so get it out there.* "... why if you were the buyer you chose to disrupt the transaction? In effect, preventing you from taking ownership?"

"I told you. I'll say it again. I want you in my life. The only time I feel good is when we're together. There's a bond I can't explain. When you leave, there's a hole. It's as though something is missing from my life. Am I in love? I honestly believe so. I sure as hell want to find out for sure. Giving up the Mundi, something I've coveted for a very long, long time, was my way of demonstrating my commitment to you."

"You got my attention, that's for sure! As well as the attention of every law enforcement officer in South Florida. Frankly, I don't know what to say, other than I enjoy being with you as well. I even..." Leslie thought about what she was about to say and changed her mind. "Look, Bill, this is a mistake. Timing is wrong. Me even being here is wrong since I'm working an active case where for all I know you may have played a role." Leslie stiffened but remained seated. "Until the case is resolved, I simply must remain professional. Being here is anything but professional." She started to stand.

"Resign! Come with me to Texas. You can move into the main house with me. Or if you like, have your own wing of the house. If that doesn't work, then you can use the guest house. Anything you want. I would love that."

She sat back down. "Look Bill, I have obligations. A mortgage to pay. Other—"

"Leslie! Trust me, it'll all be taken care of. If you don't want to quit, take a leave of absence. In the unlikely event it doesn't work out, you can come back, resume your life."

I like this man! I should throw my arms around his neck and never let go! She again started up from the chair. *Leslie! What are you doing? Sit back down.* "Can't," she mumbled in answer to herself. "Not now." She quickly ran into the hall and didn't stop until she was in the lobby, fourteen floors below the penthouse.

Driving from the Ritz Carlton parking lot, Leslie was deeply into her own world; one moment berating herself for running from a life of luxury, and the next consoling herself for doing the right thing. Understandably, she wasn't aware of a stowaway passenger in the back seat. Agent Ghana leaned forward. "You weren't in there long enough for a sexual encounter. So just what—"

Leslie stomped on the brake pedal so hard that Ghana, who hadn't secured her seat belt, was thrown forward, her forehead making firm contact with the console between the front seats.

"Shit! What's with you, Leslie! You just gave me a concussion!"

"Seat belt must have broken! What the living hell you doin' back there anyway? Scared the shit out of me! You need a hospital?"

"Won't know for a few minutes. Shit it even hurts to talk! Jaw may be broken. Turn left and go down to the beach. We can talk as we walk." Ghana sat back, her hand on her forehead.

Nothing further was said until they were fifty feet up the beach when Leslie asked, "How's the forehead? The Jaw? Need medical care?"

"Bleeding's stopped. But it feels like a good-sized cut. Don't think there's a concussion, thank God. Going to have a nasty bruise though. Serves me right for not wearing the belt."

"Serves you right for breaking into my car—and for scaring me half to death."

"You were lost in your own world. What the hell gives with you and LBB? As I started to say, you didn't have sex. Not enough time. So, what did you do? There wasn't enough time for anything really."

"Do I ask about your private life?"

"My bad. Thought you were working a case where he could be a suspect."

Ghana being on the restricted list—and not knowing it—made this tricky. "I went to ask a question if you must know."

"Must not have been very important. Weren't there long enough. Could have handled your business on the phone."

"Need to know. Sorry, but I'll say nothing more on my cases."

"What the hell's going on? Suddenly, all my friends have gone silent on me! Started a few days ago. Files are blocked. It's as if I've been... well to be blunt, fired."

"Sorry to hear that. Boss says to share nothing. So, I'm sharing nothing."

"Look, Leslie, I didn't come over here to pick a fight with you. I'm here to follow up on our conversation of the other day. Where are you with the offer?"

Leslie didn't think Ghana was aware of Bishop's offer to join him in Texas, but she wanted to be certain. IRS agents, especially Ghana, seemed to know a lot more about stuff than one would think possible. "Of working for the IRS?" she asked.

"You have other offers I don't know about?"

"Just being certain we're on the same page." That was not true. Between LBB's offer and the IRS's invitation to join them, Leslie had thought of little else. "The answer to your question is a non-answer. The fact is, I haven't given it much thought. And I won't until Tac's death is resolved."

"That's a shame, Leslie. Right now your star is shining bright. Truth is, stars have a bad habit of fading—or falling—from the sky altogether."

"I'll just have to take my chances. When I begin something, I see it to the end. That's just how I'm built. Sorry."

"That's a good trait—usually. In this situation the offer just might melt away on you."

Leslie dropped Ghana back at her car, suggested she get the cut on her forehead looked at. She remained non-committal about when to expect an answer to the job offer. Driving from the parking lot she had her mind set on getting back to the office. A quarter mile down the road she turned the car around and headed back to the beach to treat herself to some well-deserved down time.

The sand felt cool on her bare feet. When she stepped into the warm water, the gentle wavelets felt even better. She stood, staring deep into the horizon, her thoughts of the crimes she was working as scattered as the clouds overhead. One moment she was certain Jacobi had been murdered, with the perpetrator being Ghana. The next moment her mind rearranged the evidence to make it look like a parachute accident. For a while she was certain that Jacobi had killed Andino. Then it appeared as if Bates Aribah was behind the thefts of the parachute material and the Salvator Mundi, and that Andino had also died at the hand of Ghana. Then, a moment later, everything was rearranged.

Leslie's cell interrupted her mental wanderings. The screen read LBB. The last person in the world she wanted to talk with. She allowed the call to roll over to voice mail. A moment later her partner's name appeared on her screen. That call she accepted.

"Hey partner," Rodriguez's cheery voice began, "I don't expect you back before I knock off for the day. I wanted to touch base, let you know where I was on that lunch check jumper."

"So, where are you? I forgot about that."

"A few minutes ago, I sent a picture of the car owner—along with four other pictures to create my idea of a line up—over to the waitress at the Chinese restaurant. We'll see if she can identify the check skipper. Truth is, the whole lunch was under forty bucks. We're not gonna arrest someone for making off with forty dollars, are we? I rather think not."

"If she identifies the guy, what about sending him a note—make it handwritten—asking him to drop by the restaurant and pay up. Bet it's a... a *mature* guy just forgetting. Surprised it doesn't happen more often down here."

"Aye, aye, Sarge. See you in the morning."

"Before you go, got a question. How do you see the Tac death?"

"Interesting you ask. I've spent the good part of the day going over everything we have. I've convinced myself that Tac died because both parachutes he was wearing, the so-called da Vinci as well as the backup, failed to open. The failure of the spare, appears to be because it had been sliced by someone who, I also believe, is Agent Ghana. The partial fingerprint we recovered leads us to that fact. I spoke at length with two different fingerprint experts. They're in agreement; the print we found on the workbench is a close match for Ghana's and belongs to the person who cut the chute. No doubt about that."

"You sound like you have more to report. Out with it."

"Could be something. Most likely won't pan out."

"What?"

"Turns out, on the day Tac jumped, a magazine photographer was videoing a piece on Miromar. An unattended camera was set up around noon focused on the front lake. Because of all the activity surrounding the drowning, it was decided not to publish. I'll send that video over to you. Starts at noon, but the reporter forgot about it, so it ran until the battery was gone. Around midnight."

"Anything good on it?"

"About eleven P.M. a rowboat with two men stops near the marker where Tac went in. They begin dredging for something. A few minutes later a woman who looks physically like Ghana comes by on a paddleboard."

"And?"

"And, the tape stops. Just goes blank."

THIRTY

LESLIE SAT FOR A FEW MINUTES digesting what her partner had just told her. She then started out of the hotel parking lot. Without warning, even to herself, she slammed on the brakes and pulled into the last parking spot in the lot. A moment later she had Billy Bob Bishop on the line. "Hope I'm not disturbing you," she began.

"You could never disturb me. You should know that by now. However, in the interest of full disclosure, I must admit that sometimes you do confuse me."

"Frankly, LBB, I confuse myself as well. When the case I'm working is over we can talk—about personal things."

"Problem with that, Leslie, is you'll have something new going by then."

"I can't help that. Welcome to my world." When Bishop remained quiet, Leslie said, "Speaking of my world, talk to me a moment if you will about what you know surrounding the Marino Jacobi drowning."

"I assume that's the man I know as Tac. What makes you think I know any—"

"Something you said the other night got me thinking. You said Jacobi, Tac, found out somethings he shouldn't have. What were you—"

"Oh, yes. One thing in particular. Tac was desperate to jump using a da Vinci-designed parachute. Skyler smuggled one out of France. In order to conceal the transaction, he had at least one, and possibly two, fakes made. On the surface all were identical, all except for a sealer coat or three. I think you'll find the original da Vinci parachute in Skyler's house—at least as of yesterday. Tac had possession of one of the fakes. He most likely knew it was fake."

"What makes you say that?"

"Rumors abound that he jumped with a rescue parachute. That suggests—"

"Any of a number of things actually. Tell me, who do you like for selling Tac the fake? Off the record of course."

"Off the record. I wouldn't put it past Aribah. She's the one peddling the parachute. She might have swindled Tac. If he found out, which it appears he did, then she'd be in his crosshairs. What better way to eliminate him than to put a slit in the rescue parachute to reduce its drag."

"Why not also slit the da Vinci?"

"Because without properly sizing the material, it would not have slowed him enough. Da Vinci never published the sizing formula he used, so Tac, believing the parachute that he had purchased was a fake, and also believing it wouldn't support his weight, took the precaution of wearing a backup, something I believe he didn't normally do."

"Anything more you can tell me on Tac?" Leslie urged, now anxious to get off the phone.

"That's about it. When can I see—"

"Let's wait until we make an arrest in the Tac Jacobi case. Then I'll get everything resolved." Leslie wasn't certain she could fulfill that promise in any time frame acceptable to LBB, but it was all she could think of saying.

Leslie called Rodriguez the instant she hung up with LBB. He answered on the second ring. "I need a sanity check," she said, making no apology for calling after hours. "Can you tell me if we ever released the fact that the parachute had been cut? Seems Little Billy Bob has knowledge of that fact."

"On it! Will the morning be okay?"

"Suppose it'll have to be."

"I tried to find an answer to your question last night but hit a dead end," Rodriguez explained to Leslie when she arrived at her desk shortly before eight the next morning. "Hey, you look as though you were awake all night. Hope it wasn't this that had you going."

"Matter of fact, it was. Find anything?"

"Nothing released as far as I can determine. Sorry."

"That then puts LBB squarely on the suspect list. Right alongside Ghana and possibly Bates Aribah as well."

"Latest scenario you're working with?"

"Tac Jacobi was deep into skydiving. Also deep into da Vinci. At least he was into da Vinci's work on parachutes. Goal in life was to jump from a plane using a da Vinci created parachute. He may have bought a da Vinci from Skyler. Or more likely, he thought he bought it from Skyler through Aribah, but it was a fake."

"Hold it, Les. Back up. I can understand Skyler having an authentic da Vinci parachute," Rodriguez went on, "but Aribah? She doesn't have the... the... finesse to have found an original parachute and jiggle all the systems to get it out of whatever country she found it in. Furthermore, nothing I found puts her in any position to wrangle it into the U.S. without setting off major alarm bells."

"Good point. We know she worked with Skyler. Most likely Skyler pulled off the hard stuff with Aribah running the errands. And Ghana greasing the U.S. skids. I'm thinking Tac figured out the parachute was a fake. He planned to expose Ghana as peddling fakes."

"And possibly Aribah and Sklar as well," Rodriguez chimed in.

"Could be," Leslie agreed. "I doubt if a man such as Skyler would bother with fakes. I wouldn't put that past Aribah. If anything, I bet they were scamming Tac and planning to sell the real da Vinci to a collector—not a jumper."

"Go on."

"Ghana somehow heard that Tac knew about the da Vinci being a fake and cut his backup parachute so he couldn't turn her in."

"Weak. But the best we have." Rodriguez added, "I wonder how many fakes—twins really—there are to the original da Vinci parachute?"

"When it comes to fakes, rumors abound. That's all I can say. Nothing can be taken at face value. Nothing."

"Hey!" Rodriguez exclaimed, "look at what I just received. Note from Beth. There was a breach of Ghana's files sometime yesterday. The cut backup parachute, as well as Ghana's partial fingerprint, are now both out there for all to see. That answers your question, I take it."

"It very well does. Thank you. I think that video you got from the PR person is the nail we need in Ghana's coffin. If I'm not mistaken, that woman paddleboarder, that's her! Hold it to yourself until we're ready to move forward, but I think we have enough. Unless Ghana can satisfactorily explain why she was observing, maybe even supervising, the dredging up of Tac's parachute, we have her."

At least LBB had a valid reason to know about what went on inside Tac's garage. That thought played repeatedly as Leslie tried to align her life. As she saw it, she could opt to do nothing and continue working as a sheriff's deputy, a job she loved. That, of course, was the easy thing to do. She could accept the fed offer to become an IRS investigation officer. Roughly the same life as now, only more travelling—with essentially double the pay.

The last option—moving to Texas with Billy Bob Bishop—held the greatest prospect for change, including the romantic side of being with the man whose company she very much enjoyed. On the few occasions that she had allowed herself to peek into the window of a future with him, she overwhelmingly liked what she saw. The man was kind, gentle and, above all, respectful of her. In addition to everything else, all money concerns would instantly be gone. The longer Leslie dwelled on the subject of LBB, the more solidly the argument tipped in his favor.

But love can't be bought, she continued to remind herself. *And it sure feels as if I'm being bought! Maybe when this case is over, I'll feel differently. The truth was becoming very clear. The only way to know for certain is to do it!*

Thinking about LBB recalled something she had entertained and disregarded. On impulse, she again called LBB.

"The one voice I had not planned to hear today," Bishop said, cheerily. "I hope you're calling to telling me you're coming over."

"Case is not solved yet. Perhaps soon. Since you know about Ghana's partial fingerprint found in Tac's garage, I'd like to enlist your help in completing the investigation."

"What makes you think I will—"

"Because you led me to Thunder's plane knowing Ghana had arranged that. I was just hoping to catch Ghana passing stolen goods."

"Stolen goods? To?"

"You."

"Me?"

"Well, didn't you tell me you were interested in the da Vinci parachute?"

"I am. Now assuming I go along, which is not a valid assumption—not yet anyway—what keeps me from being arrested as well?"

"My promise. She brings the parachute to you. I arrest her for possession. You never take possession for yourself. It's always for me you're acting."

"I'm assuming the reason for the arrest is so you can push her for her involvement in Tac's death."

"Right on. The fingerprint we have linking her to Tac's house is ambiguous. Close, but no cigar, close. Frustrating as hell, to tell the truth."

"Let's make the transfer at your apartment."

"I'll do what I can, Leslie. This makes me uncomfortable, to say the least. I'm not promising anything."

"Beth," Leslie explained with Rodriguez listening in, "I'm expecting the stolen da Vinci parachute to be delivered to Bishop at his place at the Ritz." She went on to outline the details, ending with, "I want audio and video of the transaction inside the building. I expect LBB to cooperate. Don't try to follow Ghana from the lot. She'll spot you, and that'll be it."

"Where will the exchange occur?" her partner asked.

"Don't know yet. Truth is, it's still preliminary. LBB has his reservations." Leslie started back across the Pit to her own desk. Changing her mind, she turned back to her partner. "Something's wrong with this picture. Can't put my finger on it, but we need to be certain we're not missing something."

"Can't imagine what that would be," Rodriguez responded. "We've gone over this a dozen times already."

"Dozen and one, then," Leslie pushed. "We're missing something. Something big."

"We know Ghana cut the parachute. Got her fingerprint, together with cut parachute material on Tac's workbench. What more—"

"Partial print. We only have a partial match. Our print expert says Ghana's lawyer will rip our side a new one if we put her on trial for cutting Tac's parachute based on the fingerprint."

"From what I've been told, Les, Ghana and you are friends. Hope you don't mind me asking, but how does that square with her being a murderer?"

"Boots asked me the same thing. Look, I go where the evidence takes me. That doesn't stop me from being uncomfortable. Big time uncomfortable. Hey, do you know if anyone, Beth or anyone, has dug into Ghana to any extent? I don't know much about her other than she was born in Trinidad, if I recall right, in 1978. I think she told me her dad came to this country when she was a young girl."

"As a matter of fact, Beth tried to do research on her when her name first came up and was blocked. I assumed the feds just blocked her because they don't want information out on their agents. But with her talking secretly with Andino before he turns up dead and all I'd think any limitation on her file would be lifted."

"You never know about the feds. They could circle the wagons to protect her for all you know."

"Okay. How about building an in-depth profile on her? Start by getting as many different instances of her fingerprints as you can. From what I understand, the partial we got is close. Now talk to me about the parachute that was cut."

"Well, all I can say is that instead of Tac strapping the backup parachute onto his back, he turned it around backward and positioned it across his chest."

"I assume that was so it wouldn't interfere with the da Vinci parachute."

"Your take is as good as mine on that. I'll run it by our National Guard folks. They do a lot of jumping. The important thing to keep in mind is that Tac most likely knew the da Vinci was a fake."

It had been over a month and the burned-out streetlight across from Leslie's driveway still hadn't been repaired. The moon was a non-factor and deep shadows prevailed in every direction. Leslie stepped from her car and, thinking she heard the rustle of clothes, instantly came to attention. When neither sight nor sound confirmed danger, she cautiously proceeded to her front door, once more stopping when she heard the unmistakable sound of a shuffled footfall. Her hand immediately rested on her weapon, stopping short of drawing it.

"Leslie," a vaguely familiar male voice called softly from the shadows behind her. "It's Detective Jerry Wine. Palm Beach. I need to speak to you. In private. Go inside and leave your light off. I'll come in behind you."

"What's this about?" Leslie asked, stalling to get her bearings and to decide how to play the situation.

"Keep your voice down! And don't turn around! I need information on Agent Ghana. I'm thinking you do as well."

"What kind of information?"

"Not out here!" he hissed. "There are two men in a car around the corner watching your house. Go in. I'll follow. Best they don't know we're talking."

Finally recognizing Wine's voice from when they had met at the Casino, and feeling more at ease, Leslie said, "House could be wired. Go around back. I'll go through the inside. Give me five."

"Got it," Wine whispered back.

Leslie heard the faint sound of movement but saw nothing. The man was good. Good enough, she realized all too well, to have put a bullet through her brain had he wanted to do so. She also realized that the men around the corner were professionals and most likely this was not their first night surveilling her house. They would already know her routines and until she did something unexpected would have no reason to inspect closer. *Being a creature of routine makes this next sequence of activities relatively easy for me.* First, I'll use the potty. Then go into the kitchen and turn the oven on. *Don't forget the living room light! And the music!*

In exactly five minutes and four seconds Leslie slid out through the back kitchen door and proceeded across the yard to a thick clump of palm fronds. A moment later, Captain Jerry Wine, the pudgy Palm Beach Sheriff's Detective, appeared. All five-foot six of him. "I don't know how much time we have out here, so I'll get right to the point. I'm positive Agent Ghana shot Andino. But two things, in addition to my Sheriff, are preventing me from taking action. One; the fingerprints on the weapon we retrieved match. Almost! And two; her cell phone places her at another location entirely. In fact, believe it or not, that location is over here in your territory, not in ours!"

"Mind giving me her cell phone data so we can match—"

"What the hell you think I'm doing here? We have your info on her—on the knife cut of the parachute, I should say. And while you won't like what I'm about to say, she *was* on the east coast at all times when that cut could have been made."

"I'll need to see—"

"When the time comes. Trust me. For now, we have shifted our investigation to them." Wine jabbed his finger in the direction of the side street.

"Are they—"

"Her management. In which case the entire IRS office is corrupt. Her handlers. In which case—"

"Where's the FBI in all this?"

"Won't talk to me. Could be because Ghana's been handling very high profile, offshore, tax avoidance cases, and they don't want to screw something up. She appears to have been officially isolated, hung out to dry. Could be a hundred reasons. I just know that you and I are also hanging out on islands all alone."

"Take away?" Leslie asked, knowing she had to get back into the kitchen within seconds or risk tipping off her meeting. She thought about telling Wine about Ghana's trafficking in stolen artwork but knew she didn't have the time.

"I'm here to tell you that if you arrest Ghana your ass'll get ground up and buried on some rotten pile of legal garbage. That, my friend, you can count on!"

THIRTY-ONE

LESLIE'S EMERGENCY ALERT went off at exactly three A.M.

"Sorry to wake you Sergeant," the dispatcher said when her sleepy voice answered. "Time's critical on this one and it's only a mile from your house!"

"Go ahead," Leslie responded, already out of bed and heading to the bathroom, studying the address that appeared on her screen as she went, "what do you have?"

"Fire in a duplex."

"Fire! Since when do I handle fires? That the boss's way of demoting me?"

"Scene reports a hostage situation! Woman, two kids, in a bedroom. Shotgun in the hall with a trip wire!"

"Fire danger?"

"They have water in the bedroom and on the roof. The building will be lost in twenty minutes unless they can get inside."

"The other half of the house?"

"Family is out. Flames under control—for now."

"My ETA is three, oh, seven. Who else?"

"We're thin to say the least. Working two major traffic accidents, and three burglaries. Your partner's on his way as well. ETA three-fifteen. Hostage team's ten to twelve out—at best."

"Before I go quiet," Leslie said into her communicator, "when a car comes available have them check a gray sedan parked around the corner from my house. Two individuals are sitting in it. Reason to believe they're monitoring my activities."

"I see here that a detective Wine from Palm Beach alerted Dispatch around midnight to those two. Car's owned by the Feds. Appears it's FBI."

"I'm almost on scene! Can't talk further."

"Fire Chief Thomas Mathews is senior. Good luck, Detective."

Leslie was no stranger to fire scenes, having worked more than her fair share in Tampa. One thing she had come to understand is that nothing happened at a fire site that didn't carry the blessing of the field commander—nothing. She parked two houses away and went immediately to her trunk to retrieve her vest and snap it around her chest.

"You the Sergeant they sent?" demanded a giant of a man with the name MATHEWS sewn across his upper left shoulder. "About time you got here! What do you know of the situation we got?"

"Tell me."

"Duplex. Both sides involved. The north side's not the problem. Family's over there," he said nodding in the direction of a group of people, including at least four children, sitting on the front lawn of a home across the street from the house on fire. "As you can see, there's only smoke now. Not true for the other unit. From what we have determined, the husband set the fire using some form of accelerant. That's not the main problem. The wife—there's a wife and two children under ten, in that bedroom up there," this time Mathews pointed to a window where a ladder was propped—claims that the bedroom is rigged with two shot guns. One in front of that window and one by the door. The guns are wired, so she says, to go off if anybody crosses their path. We're spraying the room with water to control the flames and heat, but there's not much time before we lose control. I can't allow my units in until I know it is safe. That's your job. Tell us what you need and we'll get it for you."

"Can you see into the bedroom?"

"We have some visibility, but not enough to see any trip wires. Wife says trip wires. Might be any kind of mechanism, including light, or possibly radio frequency. One false move can kill a shit pot of souls."

"Has anyone tried going into the bedroom from the hall?"

"No. Wife says there's a wire on the door. Shots were fired when we tried to go up the steps. A bullet hit one of my men in the helmet!"

"Where's the family located in the room? On the floor?"

"Floor got too hot. They're now on the bed. We're dripping water on them from the attic. This is all very unstable and frankly we're only minutes from losing complete control!"

"Can I get into the room from the attic? Or is there a better way?"

"The ceiling is the best way in because of all the trap wires. You're right about that." Chief Mathews turned to a man standing a few yards away. "Garcia!"

The man hurried forward, the name LIEUTENANT LUIS GARCIA barely visible on his shirt under all the dirt. Someone had tried to clear the grime from his face; the result being streaks across his cheeks that disappeared under his jacket. The only clean place was around his eyes, nose and mouth where he had been wearing a respirator and goggles, which were now in his hand. "Yes, Chief."

"Take this officer up to the roof and insert her through the attic into the bedroom. Respirators for the both of you. Take replacement respirators to the hostages, I don't want them running low. You're in command for structural integrity. Until the guns and whatever else he has used for traps are removed, Hodges here has command for people safety."

"Got it." Turning to Leslie he asked, "Hodges, ever work a fire?"

"Several. Up in Tampa a few years back. I got the basics. Stay low and never open a door without touching the door first."

"Good rules to follow. It's nasty up there. If kids weren't involved, the captain would've sounded the all clear and let the place burn. Take a respirator and goggles from that truck over there for yourself and follow me up that aerial. I'll get what we need for the wife and kids. Put the gear on down here. I assume you know how to control the tank. That smoke and soot'll do a job on your eyes and throat by the time you're halfway up. Frankly, I wouldn't be surprised to find asbestos in that insulation."

Leslie did as she had been trained, positioning the valve where she could easily reach it. "Good to go!" she announced a moment later, noticing her partner climbing from his car and approaching the Chief as she had done. There was no time to dwell on Lewis, as Garcia was already a quarter of the way up the aerial and moving quickly. She was assisted up onto the truck by a woman firefighter, who said, "Good luck getting the mother and kids out of there! We'll be lucky to save this house from the looks of it. That man did a real job!"

"Thanks. I'll try. Tell my partner over there I'm going in through the ceiling and to stand by in case the father's still in there."

"Hadn't thought of him being inside! Shit! This can get even worse than it is! If he's in there, all bets are off!"

"Let's hope he's not," Leslie called over her shoulder as she scrambled up the aerial trying to catch up to Garcia. Two firefighters, laden with equipment, followed her up the flexing stairs.

Garcia was on the roof standing beside a pile of respirators when Leslie appeared in the aerial bucket positioned above the roof's top ledge. Several large holes had been opened in the roof. Smoke was billowing from all of them. "Shit!" he exclaimed, "smoke's getting worse! Not a lot of time left. We'll be lucky to save any of those poor souls."

"How do I get in?"

"Follow me. Step exactly where I step. Roof's compromised." Garcia proceeded to move slowly across the roof, testing several sections with the heel of his boot before putting pressure on it. Twice the tile gave way, causing Garcia to detour carefully around the collapsed section.

Leslie, with her two escorts trailing behind, followed directly after him as she had been directed. Slowly, the entourage made its way to an already open section of roof, smoke streaming upward.

"Okay, here's the plan," Garcia said. "These two will set up a hoist for each of us. They'll lower us into the attic. From there we'll be further lowered into the bedroom where the family is. Our hope is that the attic structure remains structurally sound. We have no indication that it's been compromised, but that remains a possibility. Be ready for it to collapse. Our biggest fear right now is losing communications. Smoke's going to make it hard to see. As you know, these respirators have internal communication and have been working fine so far. We need them to remain that way. If we lose communication, then use the light pen snapped on the side. Ready?"

"Ready," Leslie answered, quickly reviewing her various rescue training sessions over the years, knowing that nothing ever prepares you for the full brunt of an emergency. She reached for the offered hoist vest, secured it around her chest and legs and walked over to the opening, positioning herself next to Garcia. He nodded and quickly stepped forward, disappearing into the smoke.

"Down," he called.

Leslie took that as her signal to also step into the smoke. The unmistakable feel of zero gravity overtook her as she plummeted downward. A second later she jerked to a stop, her feet just touching the attic floor. Garcia was nowhere to be seen in the thick smoke. "Down," she called to her unseen handlers on the roof.

"Step to your right four steps," came Garcia's voice. "There's another opening over here. I'm about to go down. See you below in the bedroom."

Leslie did as instructed, moving to her right toward where Garcia's voice had come from. On her third step she heard, and felt, the floor structure crack under her weight. Instantly, the hoist rope went limp and ran free. Meaning that her fall would be broken by the floor below, assuming of course, the floor itself was still intact.

Leslie braced for the impact that never came.

"Sorry!" a voice sounded from the respirator at the exact instant Leslie's downward motion abruptly stopped. "Floor let loose! Did I get you in time?"

"Yes! I'm still above the floor. Smoke's too thick to see. Lower me slowly." She began going down. "On the ground!" she yelled almost instantly. "Garcia, where are you?"

"Behind you. Over here by the bed. Turn to your right and shuffle move toward my voice until you get to the bed. Mother, two children, report no injury. All three are now wearing protective masks."

"Look out!" Leslie screamed, catching sight of a chunk of flaming plaster falling from the ceiling above where Garcia's voice was coming. One of the children, a little girl, suddenly came visible directly below the flaming debris. Leslie dove headfirst toward the child, arriving over her body just before the ceiling chunk landed. She rolled over smothering the flames between her and the bed. In the process the fire burned through her vest to her skin. "I'm burned!" she called to Garcia. "But we have no time. Here," she said, stripping her harness off, "the flame's out. Put my harness on one of the children. Give yours to the other."

"Not so easy!" Garcia screamed. "Don't touch them! They're—"

"Got to get—"

"Wait! Mother reports they're tied to a gun! Husband—or boyfriend—is in the hall."

"Ma'am," Leslie said, are you or your children tied to a gun?"

"Yes. My right wrist."

"What about your children?"

"No. Just me. He's in the hall."

"Are you saying the man who did this is in the hall?"

"Manuel? Yes. He did this. Bad man. Told him to leave. He did this."

"Where's the gun?"

"By the door. He said if I move, it goes off!"

"Is it a gun or a bomb?"

"Shotgun. No bomb. There he is! Do you hear him?"

"No. Where is he?"

"In hall."

Leslie listened but heard nothing. "Are you certain your children are not connected to the gun?"

"Just me. If I move my wrist, we'll die."

"Garcia. Get on the floor and crawl under or around the bed. We got to get the little ones out. She turned back to the mother.

"Ma'am, don't you move. Tell your children to go out! Through the roof. When Manuel again speaks, please tell me."

Garcia slid along the floor and stood on the window side of the bed. He pulled the little girl toward him. She pulled away, refusing to leave her mother.

Leslie, moving as close as she could to the mother, said, "I'm a Lee County Sheriff. I'm here to help you and your children. We have to move fast now. What's your name?"

"Marge."

"Okay, Marge. You need to tell your children to go with us. We're going to put harnesses on them so we can lift them out through the roof. What's your little girl's name?"

"Margie. The boy's Butch."

"Hi, Margie," Leslie said to the girl. "Let the fireman put the harness on you so we can lift you out of here."

"Go ahead, honey," Marge said to the terrified girl who clutched her mother even harder. "Do as the sheriff lady says. Let the nice man put the harness on you. They will lift you out."

"Stay with you," the child said, moving even closer to her mother.

"I will be right behind you, honey. Be brave and let the fireman put the harness on. It's all right. Everything will be all right."

The little girl moved toward Garcia and put her arms in the air. She tried to say something but choked on the smoke.

Garcia quickly slipped the harness over her head and tightened it as best he could. Worried that it still might slip off, he quickly ripped a pillowcase into long segments and tied several around the little girl. "Take the little one up," he said into the comm. "About fifty pounds."

Almost instantly, a hand appeared through the ceiling and the little girl started upward.

Garcia turned to Butch. "Now it's your turn young man. Here, slip this over your head like your sister did."

Butch complied without comment.

"That's the way. Good. We'll have you out of here in a minute."

Garcia looked up, saw the little girl's feet disappear through what was left of the plaster and said into the comm, "Boy's ready. Maybe seventy-five pounds." The rope snapped tight and Butch started upward without comment. Again, hands appeared through the ceiling opening to assist. The boy quickly disappeared into the attic.

"All's in order up here," came a voice on the comm a few moments later. "Children are outside and on their way down. Pediatric medics are standing by down there. Now let's get the bomb—or whatever else we have down there—cleared and get the mother and deputy out."

"He's talking again!" Marge called to Leslie. "I can hear him."

Leslie moved toward the woman. "Where's that tie to the gun? Don't move it. Just put my hand on it." Leslie extended her arm to allow Marge to guide her hand to the line connecting her to her husband.

Marge did as she had been told and grasped Leslie's wrist with her left hand and slowly guided it across her body to her right side where she placed it just below her elbow. She then slid Leslie's hand down her arm, stopping just above her right wrist. "Almost there! Don't move it!" the woman yelled, coughing as she spoke.

"I won't. I want to follow it."

"He said the gun's by the door. On a chair. Oh, I hear him again!"

Leslie strained to hear, but nothing registered. At the same time, she gently moved her fingers down toward Marge's wrist until she touched what she determined to be a dog collar. Tied to the collar was a nylon line stretched tight in the direction of the door. Even with goggles, Leslie couldn't see anything. Her visibility was limited to less than a foot. She dropped to the floor and slowly made her way forward, taking care not to put strain on the line.

"Remember," Garcia warned, "that we were told there were guns, or bombs, set to go off. That string could be connected to other strings."

"I *am* aware—"

"There he is again!" Marge coughed.

"By any chance," Leslie asked, "does he say the same thing each time he talks?"

"Yes, yes he does. Exactly the same!"

"What does he say?"

"He says, 'Marge, I'll teach you not to throw a good man out. You have a choice how to die. Move and you and your precious children will be shot. Don't move and you will all burn. Just like going to Hell it is for you. There's a bomb in the hall to stop fireman from saving you. So, who's boss now?' That's what he says every time!"

"Stand by to lift the mother out," Leslie said into the comm. "Five minutes, but no more. Tell my partner to come in through the front door. I'm convinced the perp's not out there, but we need to be certain. ASAP on that."

"What the hell you doing Hodges?" Garcia yelled from across the room. "You haven't cleared the hallway!"

"It's a recording! He's not out there! Nobody repeats the same thing word for word again. Don't move for a moment while I determine if we even have a gun in here."

"Hey, there's a chair here in front of the door. I can't see much, the smoke's... oh! There is a double-barreled shotgun here! It's on the chair in front of the door! Pointing at the bed. Marge, keep the string from moving!"

"For goodness sakes, be careful over there!" Garcia called. "Blow us all to hell!"

"Lewis," Leslie said into her comm, "if you hear me, don't, I repeat, don't come in the room. There's a shot gun..."

"This is Chief Mathews," a booming megaphone from somewhere outside the house sounded, cutting off the rest of Leslie's warning. "Now hear this! A shotgun's been found inside the room where the family is! All personnel take caution! Follow police sergeant Hodges' instructions!"

"This is Hodges," Leslie said, filling the silence that followed the chief's announcement. "Hold your positions! I am approaching the weapon."

Bending in close, Leslie was just able to see the string as it extended from Marge's wrist. She gingerly continued sliding her hand along it, pausing frequently to ensure she didn't accidentally bump the weapon's trigger. Without warning, and sooner than expected, the side of her hand hit something solid. A chair with a shotgun tied in place. She bent even closer and unless her eyes were playing tricks, she saw that the string was tied to the back of the chair and not to the weapon. She reported this observation over the comm at the same time she turned the chair so that the barrel of the gun now faced the side wall of the bedroom. She then fished her pocketknife from her right pocket where she always kept it. "Garcia," she said, "I just cut the string. Marge is free to be extracted. The scene is yours."

Leslie couldn't see across the room, but she heard Marge fall onto the floor as instructed. A moment later Garcia gave instructions for the woman to be lifted just as her children had been. Returning her full attention to the gun, she moved in close to make certain there was nothing she was overlooking. She checked the safety only to find that it was on. In its current condition, the weapon could not be discharged. She announced that fact to Garcia. Before she could say anything further, the door flew open and in came her partner, knocking over the shotgun. "Oh, shit!" he exclaimed. "Didn't mean to do that!"

"You knew about the shotgun! Coulda killed us all!"

"Sorry! Couldn't remain out there another second! Floor's all but gone! Gotta go out a window or something!" A loud splintering sound was heard in the doorway behind Lewis, followed by a loud crash. Flames flooded the room.

"Police are finished inside the house. Scene relinquished." Leslie said into the comm as she gathered the shotgun from the floor. "Just get my partner and I out of here ASAP! I need to know how those kids are doing!"

THIRTY-TWO

APPROACHING HOME, LESLIE'S MIND snapped back to the FBI agents who had been parked around the corner earlier in the evening. Perhaps it was the adrenalin, perhaps just her natural feistiness, but whatever, she decided to deal with it head on. To that end, she turned on the car's flashing lights and pulled up behind the still parked car. Playing dumb as to their identity, she held her shield up as she approached the driver's side window. She gave the roll down motion and paused, waiting to see what their next move would be.

Her tension level was reduced when the window went down and the two men sat calmly, not anxious to escalate the situation. "Driver's license and—"

Before she finished her request, both men held up identification badges, each containing the distinctive eagle and shield of the FBI.

"If I'm not mistaken, you've been here all night. Well, at least since I arrived home. Mind telling me what the FBI's doing out here?"

"Observant, you are. That's what makes you good at what you do."

"What's that supposed to mean?"

"Just an observation," the driver, who was the one doing all the speaking, said. "One of many. Hey, you smell like you've been burning documents all night. Anything we need to know?"

Ignoring the question, she said, "You have me under surveillance. Is that what this is about?"

"Yes and no. Believe me, Detective, if you were the target of our investigation, you'd have no clue we were out here. You can trust me on that for certain."

"If not me? Who then?"

The driver glanced at his partner before answering. "Agent Ghana, if you must know, is our focus. You've been filing some devasting accusations against her. We're following up on those."

"Out here! In the middle of the night? Next, you'll be telling me Superman really exists."

"Well, doesn't he?" These were the first words the passenger had uttered, said in a tone suggesting they were striving for even further de-escalation. "That was uncalled for on my part. Sorry. Truth is, we were waiting for you to come home so we could talk with you. In private, away from unwelcome ears."

"I live around—"

"Investigated you for the job offer you received from the IRS. We certainly know where you live. That job, we understand, remains open to you, by the way. Nothing we gave them cooled their jets—nor should it have. They really want you. Trouble is, when we got here that Detective Wine from across the state was here. His work ethic is... shall I say... suspect. We were going to wait 'till morning. Then you sped off."

"In what way is he... suspect?" Leslie's curiosity was peeked. "I don't want the case against Ghana tainted in any way."

"That's going to be hard to accomplish. Here's the thing. Your case is built, as we understand it, around a fingerprint. Problem is that fingerprint doesn't fully match."

Leslie snapped defensively. "But it doesn't not match either!"

"True enough. Wine is peddling the story that Ghana was on the East Coast at all times the print could have been left. Even though the drive time is under two hours, his argument looks solid. We've been tasked with building the case against her. Or, of course, exonerating her. As it turns out, a significant number of the art theft cases she's been assigned to over the years have ended up unresolved. That's troubling."

"She's an IRS agent. Her job isn't to catch thieves, even high value thieves, it's to catch tax evaders. What am I missing here?"

The agent in the passenger seat, the one who Leslie had determined was senior, proceeded to point out that while Leslie was right about Ghana not being tasked with catching thieves and embezzlers, she was responsible for ferreting out cheats who didn't pay tax on the ultimate sale of embezzled artifacts. The profits they reaped from such sales were now routinely in the high hundreds of millions of dollars range. He then added, "Last year alone, it's estimated that the government lost over a billion dollars in revenue."

"My evidence is strong against her," Leslie insisted. "The person who left that fingerprint rendered the backup parachute that Mario Jacobi was relying on non-operational. That directly contributed to his death. There's no one else who could have left that fingerprint. For motive, we have the fact that Jacobi, who believed he had bought a genuine da Vinci parachute, was, in fact, in possession of a fake. He was about to make that fact public knowledge, which would have, at least on a temporary basis, chilled the market. With his death, all she had to do was locate the chute in the lake and bury it. In fact, that's what we have on video. Her out there on the lake at the very spot where Jacobi was pulled out."

"We know about the video and admit it's strong, Detective—only if it proves to be accurate. Assuming she can put in evidence, as we believe she can, that it was not possible for her to have been at Miromar Lakes when that video was shot, then your case goes off the rails."

"But," Leslie persisted, "I don't believe she could produce such evidence. Do you?"

"We can't go that far. Not yet anyway. Our advice to you; proceed with caution, despite what the brass says."

"Pardon me for being suspicious, but why would two people I don't know put their careers on the line for me? What am I missing here?"

"Let's just say," the passenger side agent responded, "during our investigation we got to know you. Really know you. And truth is, we like what we've seen. Most important, we like how you've handled your partners, both here in Lee County and up in Tampa. We also like how you've handled the other men in your life since your husband's tragic death. Truth is, we've pegged you as a real asset."

Leslie was fuming long before the FBI agent finished speaking. It took all her will to remain calm on the outside. Inside, she was boiling. "What's *the other men in my life* mean?"

"Just that. You have a professional, as well as personal, relationship with Pete Jakowski. You also have both a business and personal relationship with a guy from Texas, goes by LBB, who just happens to be a billionaire and Seminal Society Collector. You've managed not to entangle yourself."

"My personal life," Leslie began, knowing full well that when working investigative law enforcement your personal and professional lives *are* inexorably intertwined. That didn't stop her from continuing, "is none of your damn business! Now get your asses out of here before we all regret what comes next!" Leslie turned her back and returned to her car, flipped off the flashing lights, took several pictures of their car and drove off. The sun was up and Leslie's day had begun. She headed home for a shower and fresh clothes, not at all certain that all of the hot water in the world would be enough to wash away the pungent smoke smell—let alone the added stench from the FBI. The clothes she was wearing were going straight into the rubbish can.

Leslie's doubts proved correct. After thirty minutes of near scalding water, and washing her hair a fourth time, and using a half bar of Dial soap, she still smelled the smoke. She told herself the smell was in her head but couldn't quite be convinced. She also debated informing Lewis about her encounter with the FBI. In the end, she decided nothing good would come from withholding information. Except that there was no need to go into the personal side of the conversation.

Her phone rang just as she stepped from the shower. The screen read LEWIS. She hit the DECLINE button and the phone immediately went silent. A moment later, perhaps thinking about what the agents had said about how she treated partners, she called him back. "Sorry, I was in the shower," she apologized. "What's up?"

"Just called to check on you. Be sure you're okay. You were in that smoke a long time. Maybe you should get checked—"

"I'm okay, Lewis. Really, I am. I'm heading to the office in a few minutes. What about you? You okay. Or do you need some time off?"

"You're the one who should take time off, if anyone should."

"I'm okay. Thanks for thinking of me."

"Okay. Then let's nail Ghana and put this all behind us. I have most of the paperwork ready. Just need—"

"Hold up a bit," Leslie said. She brought Lewis up to speed on the evidence countering the possibility of Ghana being at Miromar when the video was taken. She ended with an instruction to keep the FBI briefing out of the files. Adding, "I'll brief Boots when I get to the office."

"For the record—whatever the hell that means—I disagree," her partner responded.

"Disagree with what? Not putting it in the file or not... Hey, gotta go! Someone's at the door. Talk in the office."

Leslie was thoroughly startled and thrown off balance when she opened her front door. "Billy Bob Bishop!" she exclaimed. "What the hell you doing slumming way out here in Lehigh Acres at my front door?"

"Whatever happened to *hello*? Better yet, *won't you please come inside, LBB.*"

Leslie glanced around to see if he had anyone with him. "Looks like you're alone. What happened to your chauffeur?"

"A chauffeur is good when business is involved. I find them superfluous when it's purely personal. I saw your exploits on the news early this morning and how you saved that poor family. I checked and was told you didn't go to the hospital. You might say I was worried about you. Had to see for myself how you're doing. Now will you please invite me in?"

Stepping back from the door, Leslie made an exaggerated entry motion. "Sure. Come on in. Be warned, I was just on my way to work, so time's short."

Stepping into the house, Bishop pulled the door closed behind him. "You sure clean up well," he said after looking at her a moment. "That clip they're using of you at the fire scene doesn't do you any favors."

"Some of that is fire retardant gel on my face. Stuff does its job, but everything clings to it. As for the smoke, that's what respirators are for. Couldn't have done it without the equipment. I need to get to the hospital, see how the mother and kids are."

"From what I can gather, they're in decent shape. Thanks to you defusing the situation."

"Just doing my job. That's what I'm trained to do. That poor mother, everything she owns is gone! She's the one who lost in all this. Husband's gone. As is her house. Woman has nothing."

"She has her children," Bishop corrected. "Thanks to you I might add."

"Now what? She lost everything else! And to top it off, there's a deranged man out there who has vowed to kill all three of them."

"Two things are wrong with that statement. First, your Sheriff just announced Manuel's capture. Second, an anonymous donor has set up a million-dollar trust fund for the benefit of Marge, Butch and little Margie."

"Oh, my God LBB! I just don't know what to say. I really don't!"

"You only need say you'll let me buy you breakfast. I saw a cute little restaurant around the corner. We could go there, or anywhere else you'd like. Somewhere where we can talk."

THIRTY-THREE

WHEN THEY WERE SEATED at Joe's Cafe, the *cute little restaurant around the corner,* and Bishop having ordered a cheddar cheese omelet and Leslie two soft-boiled eggs along with dry rye, Bishop said, "You need to know, I've spoken to our mutual friend. To say she's skittish is an understatement. She told me she's under investigation for homicide and needs to move cautiously."

"If she's so cautious, then why talk to you at all?"

"Big pay day. For the da Vinci parachute—the genuine one—I offered top dollar."

"Doesn't she have enough?"

"Show me the person who ever stops collecting what they collect. Be it money in her case, or art artifacts in mine. Nothing's ever enough. You should know that."

"At least you're self-aware. That's a start."

"Just stating a fact, a fact you know all too well from your line of business. As we've discussed, I'd love to have you know firsthand what it's like to never worry about any material thing ever again."

"You know I can't—"

"I know all too well. You're still working the case, I get it. That's what I'm here for. To speed that process along if I can. As I said, I offered to buy the da Vinci parachute, but only if she brought it to my place. And did so in person. She declined, fearing getting caught. I compromised and agreed to allow her to show it to me using Face Time."

"Surprised she went that far."

"When several hundred million dollars are on the line, you'd be amazed at how those kinds of risks become easier. Here," Bishop said," handing his phone across the table, to Leslie, "tap the screen and the demonstration will commence. Tap it again to pause."

Leslie accepted the phone, turned the screen to face her and tapped as she had been instructed. "Nothing's hap... oh, there it goes. I recognize the shape of the parachute! In fact, everything, except for the colors, appears to be identical to the picture Rooster Pecking took just after Tac jumped from his plane."

"You're right. Pyramid shape is an exact copy, dimensions and all. For some reason, there is great confusion over what color linen da Vinci used. What you see in front of you, I believe, is the actual material used by the great man."

"I believe I saw Ghana's face appear right at the beginning. Is that the only time? I didn't see—"

"Ghana's careful not to get caught on camera, except the camera came on faster than she had expected. That's why she's there at all. She didn't speak at all."

"Can I play that portion again?"

"Of course."

Leslie played the clip a couple of times, trying to work out what was bothering her. She couldn't recall exactly what her concern was. She handed Bishop's phone back to him. "Why do you think he made the parachute triangular?"

"Why did da Vinci do *anything* he did? Because it appealed to some sense he had. His engineering and artistic minds blended so completely that it's often difficult to know where one leaves off and the other begins. I'm not sure he always kept them separate. You know the word parachute comes from the French word, chute, meaning to fall. Combine that with the Latin root para, meaning against. So, parachute means *against falling*! The device actually slows falling but doesn't stop it."

"Fascinating, but I don't have time for much more. Look, let me be as up-front with you as I would be with anyone else. If this parachute were to be in anyone else's possession I'd ask for it back. It is, after all, at the center of a homicide. Well, I suppose I don't know for certain Tac's death was a homicide. But it sure seems that way."

"So, you want to do what?"

"Obtain, and keep custody of, the crime scene evidence. Assuming I can get my hands on the item at all."

"I know better than to try and stop you from doing what you believe to be right and proper. You said yourself, the one in the video is a different color. And for good reasons. The one Tac jumped with is a phony! That one in the video is worth, at least to me, hundreds of millions of dollars. It's not crime scene evidence in any way shape or form."

"Where's the parachute right at this minute?"

"Sorry, not prepared to discuss that at this point. But be certain its under protective care."

"Do you know where the original was on the day Tac died?"

"Not for absolute certain. But I'll tell you what I believe to be correct. Starting at the beginning, Pax Skyler was doing the da

Vinci circuit over in Italy and France when he came upon the parachute in the basement of a house da Vinci and Machiavelli had been sharing. Skyler in the past used Queen B for transporting materials around the world. As you may know, the Queen is, shall we say aging. Her granddaughter, Bates Aribah, has taken over the transportation of high-value artifacts. Like her grandmother, Bates knows how to attract the attention of those of us who crave these items, thereby driving the price up."

"Where does Ghana come into the picture?"

"The Queen knew how to work quietly in the background. Bates is more of a bull in the proverbial china shop. Anyway, Ghana caught wind of the transaction and somehow got her hands on the genuine parachute. In the process, Marino Jacobi, Tac, got stuck with the fake."

"It's my understanding," Leslie added in a rare moment of openness, "that Tac bought the fake from Skyler's granddaughter, Orion, believing it to be the original."

"I can believe that. She's been known to deal in her grandfather's merchandise from time to time. With or without his blessing I'm unsure."

"If I told you Ghana cut a flap in the backup parachute so that Tac would fall to his death, would that change your desire to own the parachute?"

"That doesn't make sense. He had the fake, not the original. Is that what happened?"

"All I can say is stay tuned."

"What is it you need from me, Sergeant?" Captain Stetson asked even before Leslie and Rodriguez were fully into her office. "I have a busy morning and I'm hoping to hear you're about to wrap up the Tac case."

"That's exactly what we're here for. We're meeting with a County Attorney at eleven."

"You plann'n on charging? Frankly, from my perspective it's a toss-up. Those messed up prints are a problem. In my experience it goes downhill fast from there. But, hey, your record's unblemished, so why not fly a little? For what it's worth, Sheriff's on your side."

"Right this minute, I *am* planning to charge Ghana. She's in this way over her head." Leslie went on to brief her boss on what LBB had told her about Ghana showing him the original da Vinci parachute. Leslie outlined her plan to beef up security should she take custody of the parachute as she had promised Bishop she would.

"Sheriff's been on the line to me several times this morning. He's cancelled all leave and is beefing up security. Can't say as I blame him. If anyone can fake us out, Ghana can. She knows everyone. Truth is, she and the boss go back a long way. Not always pleasant, I gather from what he's told me."

"LBB won't turn it in voluntarily. I'm going to have to force the issue."

"Sure you're not too close to this? We can put another team on it if you like."

"I've worked it all out. When the arrest of Ghana is made, he'll allow me to take possession of the parachute so long as I promise heightened security.

"I'm good with it. I know the sheriff's supporting all this, but what's his real take on it? Frankly, he's confused as to why Ghana's suddenly become so front and center. Not at all like her. As a practical fallout, IRS'll have a hard time replacing her."

"Not my—"

"Okay, out now. Got work to do. Keep me in the loop."

Leslie was barely through the door when her phone buzzed. MEET ME AT THE NW CORNER OF YOUR PARKING LOT FOR A QUICK COFFEE. I'LL DRIVE—JAK

"What the hell you doing down here in Florida?" Leslie demanded even before the door closed. "I thought I told you to—"

"Aren't you the person who some time ago made it perfectly clear that you couldn't learn if your mouth was moving?"

"Good advice, my friend. Good advice. I'm all ears. What are you here to teach me?"

"You're about to make a colossal mistake."

"I am, am I?" Leslie responded, determined to give nothing away. "Tell me all about this colossal mistake I'm about to make."

"Arresting IRS Agent Maxine Ghana."

"How the hell you know what I'm about to do?" Leslie demanded.

"It's out there. Bet Boots knows."

"She wouldn't—"

"You're right about that as it pertains to Boots. I got it direct from Ghana herself."

"How the hell would she know?"

"People owe people favors. Bet there's a minimum of five people on the Lee County payroll, people who are more tuned in than you know, who, one way or another, tipped Ghana off."

Leslie was about to tell Pete how wrong he was when the list of call-backs she owed people popped up in her visual memory. Right there in the middle was Allen Smith, her former lover and now head County Prosecutor. He never called for anything other than to talk about her arrests. "Shit!" she exclaimed. "I have to admit you're right about that. Shit! And, I suppose," Leslie added, thinking through the implications of what Jakowski had just told her, "Ghana sent you over here to talk me out of filing homicide charges against her."

"It's nice working with a smart person. You're right on. How about she do one better and meet you any time, any place?"

"Do I sense your fine hand in that offer?"

"What difference does it make whose idea it was? She's willing to meet with you in person. That's what counts."

"Of course I'll meet with her. Providing there're no strings attached."

"Such as?"

"My agreeing not to arrest her at that meeting."

"Only stipulation—and I added this one—that you listen to what she has to say. Arrest her after she tells you what she wants to tell you. That's up to you."

"And my partner can attend that meeting."

"Of course."

"And not you. Or for that matter, an attorney."

"Me not being there goes without saying. I'm just an intermediary in all this. Nothing more. As for the lawyer, I'll have to get back to you on that."

"Oh, Jak, don't sell yourself short. You're a hell of a lot more than an intermediary. Only that's a topic for another day."

THIRTY-FOUR

"RUN THAT BY ME AGAIN!" Rodriguez exclaimed when Leslie told him about Jakowski's offer to set up an interview with Ghana. "Why do we need him in the middle? Why not just set it up ourselves?"

"I suppose we can do it that way, is the right answer. However, this way we know she'll show up in our jurisdiction. Going over to Palm Beach is fraught with logistics—and politics—that we'll need to work our way through."

"Trivial for our support team, you ask me. I suppose letting your friend set it up will work out just fine, just so long's our hands aren't tied about detaining her if that becomes necessary. You did say that should we decide to arrest her there'll be no problems?"

"That's certainly my understanding."

"When's this interview set to occur?"

"I'm expecting her any minute... well, speaking of the devil! Agent Maxine Ghana. Oh, my goodness! You did a job on your forehead! I know you bumped it in my car, but I didn't know—"

"I never thanked you properly for taking me to the hospital. Add a mild concussion to my stupidity."

"You okay? Shouldn't you be in bed, or something?"

"You kidding? It'll heal. Take a while, but it'll heal. Might need some plastic work down the line."

"Agent Maxine Ghana, this is my partner, Lewis Rodriguez. I don't believe the two of you have met. Lewis, as you know, Agent Ghana works for the IRS and specializes in stolen valuable artifacts."

"Pleased to meet you," Rodriguez said, thrusting out his hand in greeting. "Seems our work overlaps yours."

"To some extent, perhaps. Primarily, I'm focused on the improper payment of, or in most cases the total non-payment of, taxes due on the sale of a stolen art artifact."

Without hesitation, Rodriguez quipped, "Similar to Al Capone being arrested for tax evasion, and not for all the dead bodies he left behind."

"That's certainly one advantage we agents have over you detectives. We deal in currency. Said another way, the crime at hand is reduced to a transactional amount equivalent to a sum of money. If we can come to terms on the sum, we can settle the crime. There is no crime because the tax is fully paid. Everybody wins. So it is, over the years we get to know both the buyers of high-value artwork as well as the sellers."

"And how long have you been an IRS Agent?" Leslie asked.

"It'll be ten years next month."

"For the record," Leslie added, "You work with Peter Jakowski, a police detective from Verona, Pennsylvania. Is that not correct?"

"Correct as far as it goes. His primary job is... by the way, this interview is on the record, but any transcript is to be released only on a need-to-know basis. Does that work for you?"

"I suppose it'll have to, won't it?"

"As I was saying, Jakowski's primary job with the IRS is to feed us information pertaining to the buying and selling of art objects of interest to the Seminal Society. In particular, he passes along the buying habits of Morris Dexter Stratis, a billionaire collector living in the Pittsburgh area. Jakowski, as you know, runs errands for Stratis. All, by the way, with the permission of his chief. Greasing the skids is how I would characterize his work."

"Would you consider Jakowski negotiating the payment of Income Tax on stolen artwork as *greasing the skids*?"

"Most certainly. There is nothing improper about that activity. In the end, both the government and his client Stratis are satisfied."

"I assume Jakowski performs this negotiating function for more than one buyer or seller."

"Most definitely."

"Care to identify his clients? I mean those folks he negotiates on behalf of."

"I'm not at liberty to do that, but I will acknowledge those that you ask about."

"Kumar?"

"From time to time."

"LBB?"

"Recently, yes."

"With respect to which artifacts?"

"Only two that I know. The Salvator Mundi and the da Vinci parachute."

"The da Vinci parachute. The one Tac used to jump with over at Miromar Lakes?"

"Only Tac never used the original. He jumped with a substitute that hadn't been waxed by da Vinci as far as we know."

Up to this point Ghana had remained remarkably calm. At the mention of da Vinci's name, her jaw tensed ever so slightly. Lewis apparently saw the same thing as Leslie had because his own jaw had tensed in preparation for asking a question. Instead, he remained silent.

"I'm sure you do know," Leslie said, "that we've found a fingerprint of yours in conjunction with that parachute, the one you claim was a *substitute*, in his garage."

"I have reason to believe you have. Yes."

"Care to explain how your print got there?"

"Wish I could. Truth is, I've never even been in Tac's garage. From what I've gleaned, your CIA, Lizbeth Hillard, lifted a single print from a cutting board. Index print to be more exact."

"Care to tell us how that print got on that cutting board at a Lee County crime scene?"

"I wish I could. As I told you, I've never been in that garage."

"I assume by that response you mean you have no memory of having touched a cutting board. Either in Miromar Lakes or anywhere?"

"Of course I've touched cutting boards! Let me correct that a bit. To be more precise, I've touched cutting boards, but not over here."

Rodriquez cleared his throat. "Please define over here, if you don't mind."

"In Lee County."

"Thank you."

"Here's the problem," Leslie continued, "your print is on a cutting board directly adjacent to a knife blade gouge. We have expert evidence that an opening was cut into a back-up parachute to make certain the back-up failed. As it did. We have every reason to believe the person whose print is on that cutting board is the person who used the knife to make that cut. That cut contributed directly to Tac's death."

"That's a lot of speculation, I'd say. But I repeat. I wasn't in Tac's garage."

"That's what experts get paid to do. Speculate. Only when they do it, it's not speculation. Believe me, we have every *i* dotted and *t* crossed on this."

"What's it prove?"

"The deceased, Tac Jacobi, had reason to believe the parachute that he bought was a genuine da Vinci. Somehow, he figured he had been duped into buying a fake. He was overheard arguing with Demetrious Andino about that. Then, unfortunately for him, his back-up parachute was tampered with and he had no chance of surviving."

"All I can tell you is that I had nothing to do with his untimely death. I did not cut the backup."

"If not, how the hell did your print get on the cutting surface?"

"No idea."

"Do you have the original da Vinci parachute?"

"I do not."

"If I told you that LBB claims to be the buyer of that artifact, what would you say?"

"Not surprised. He's been coveting that parachute for months now. Ever since Pax Skyler discovered it."

"If I went a step further and said that LBB claims you are the person selling the da Vinci parachute to him what would be your reaction?"

"Tell you he's nuts! Yes, I've been talking to him about valuation. That's so I can assess Skyler the proper amount in taxes. I've never known Bishop to be confused. But if he, in fact, says I'm the seller, then he's either lying to you or suffering from early onset dementia."

Leslie spent a long moment considering what she had just heard, then responded. "You know don't you that neither of those options makes much sense?"

"All I know is that I am not in possession of the parachute. Never have been. In fact, I have every reason to believe that Bates Aribah, granddaughter of Queen Bibi, has that parachute. I believe she was working with Donatello Andino before he was killed."

"You certainly didn't share your thoughts about the parachute with me, even though you knew I was working the Jacobi death."

"I had no reason to believe Jacobi jumping to his death had anything at all to do with the da Vinci parachute."

"You knew that Aribah is a good friend of Orion Skyler, Skyler's granddaughter. As you just said, you also knew that Skyler was into da Vinci, both fakes and genuine, and that Aribah was a courier for Skyler. You also knew I was trying to solve a death that had tentacles to Skyler, his granddaughter Star and to Aribah. Yet not a word."

Changing the subject, Ghana asked, "So how did Jacobi die exactly?"

"The fake da Vinci parachute was unable to slow his descent. Jacobi had guessed as much, so he used a second, or backup, parachute. Only someone, we believe it was you, cut a good-sized hole in that parachute, so he dropped like a rock. Poor guy, broke his neck when he hit the water."

"And it was my fingerprint on the cutting board that makes you think I made that cut?"

"What would *you* think given the facts we have?"

"As I said, I haven't cut any parachute on any surface!"

"Unfortunately, your fingerprint says otherwise."

"Impossible! There must be a mistake."

"It's your print. We've checked it several times."

"Now I understand why I've been put on Admin Leave! I have nothing further to say."

In anticipation of placing Ghana under arrest, Leslie nodded in the direction of her partner and then walked slowly toward the agent, studying her as she went. Something was wrong with the picture, but she couldn't put her finger on it. Stopping directly in front of Ghana, Leslie forced herself to say, "Agent Ghana, I'm placing you..." She took a quick step backward. "I know what's bothering me!" she blurted. "Rodriguez step away! Somethings wrong here! Really wrong!"

"Can't imagine what it is," the young detective said, following his partner's order. "Those prints are a match—"

"We've been duped! Give me a moment and I'll show you." It took longer than expected, but finally the file Leslie was looking for popped up on the screen. "Lewis, I know you've seen this and know what it is. But for Agent Ghana, before I run it, let me set the background. Billy Bob Bishop is as you know in the process of securing for himself the original parachute designed and constructed by da Vinci. As everyone involved also knows, and as you just confirmed, to him that artifact is worth a lot of money. As I told you a moment ago, he believes you, Agent Ghana, are the facilitator of that transaction. You have just denied that assertion of his."

"Right! I had nothing to do with any transaction to LBB!"

"I'm going to show you a few minutes of a Facetime call that LBB believes is between you and him. Until a moment ago, I agreed with him."

"I never had any such call!"

"You'll see in a moment why I believe you." Leslie tapped the start button. The screen came alive, filled with the now familiar pattern of Vitruvian Man drawn on the cloth portion of a parachute. Then suddenly the camera jerked, momentarily revealing Agent Ghana holding the material.

"Holy shit! That's me! But I've never even seen that parachute!"

Leslie froze the screen. "Look at the face."

"That's my face for sure. But that's not me! I don't know what's—"

"As I said. I believe you. And the reason why is because that image was captured just last night."

"Last night! The stitches are missing! I had stitches yesterday! After you dropped me at my car, the gash started bleeding again and, thanks to you I stopped at the NCH hospital. I needed five stitches!" Ghana tapped the bandage on her forehead. "No amount of makeup could cover this. No, that's not me."

"Who then?" Leslie quipped, all the while running through a mental database of possibilities. "I'm baffled."

"Sixty-four-thousand-dollar question," Rodriguez interjected. "Whoever it is, she's the spitting image of you! How your fingerprint got on the cutting board is a problem, but whoever it is, I like that person for homicide."

"How the hell am I supposed to know who it is? Whoever it is apparently fooled Bishop—as well as you."

"And seemingly, a lot of other people as well," Leslie conceded "We're back to square one, I'd say."

"Maybe. Maybe not," Rodriguez said, his fingers flying over his keyboard. "This'll take a few minutes, but we can eliminate Agent Ghana—or arrest her."

"What the hell you doing?" Leslie demanded, concerned her young partner was off the reservation and about to cause a big problem.

"Checking to confirm the story. I believe I can get into the hospital database and then we can see if, in fact Agent Ghana here actually received those stiches."

"Look, Lewis, I saw the cut myself. It was nasty."

"Call me a skeptic, but anything can be faked. Movies do it all the time. Unless I'm mistaken, you really didn't see her before you slammed on the brakes. Could'a been staged for all you know. You didn't see the stitches. Easy to confirm."

"You'll need my account info to get in," Ghana said. "I'm not disposed to—"

"Happens I got a work-around for that hospital. Oh, here it is! I'm in! Even has a picture of your forehead before the stiches. That's one nasty gash, I must say. I see an internal referral, but no mention yet of stitches. This'll take longer than I anticipated."

The thought flashed through Leslie's mind that her partner could just possibly be right. The *accident* in her car could have been staged to provide this seemingly iron-clad proof of Ghana being cloned.

"You asked to leave, so here's the deal. Promise me you won't leave the state and I'll end the interview. I must admit that should the medical records show that you received stiches, which, from the look of that wound I can't imagine not being stitched up, then that video becomes worthless."

"Sorry to disappoint you, Detective, but that video is worthless! Period. I'm terminating this meeting. Unless I'm under arrest, I'm under no further obligation to you."

Leslie allowed Ghana to leave. To do otherwise would have set off legal procedures that potentially interfere with a proper continued investigation. That decision didn't make her partner happy, but there was nothing he could do about it, except continue working the hospital records.

An idea came to her and she called LBB. "I just want to confirm that the woman in the video last night was the same woman who you've been dealing with on the da Vinci parachute."

"It is? Why do you ask?" Bishop answered, confused by the question.

"Just being certain we're on the same page. And how old do you believe that woman to be?" Leslie asked.

"Mid-thirties. No older than late thirties," he replied.

"You're certain she's not in her forties?"

"Almost positive. Why?"

"Tell you later. Thanks."

Leslie relayed her conversation with Bishop to her partner and added, "Government records show Agent Maxine Ghana to be forty-seven. If Bishop testifies that the Ghana he dealt with is, to his belief, in her thirties, even late thirties, the jury will rip us a new one! Simple as that."

"That would take one hell of a great custom-made mask, not to mention fantastic makeup!"

"As was said not long ago, when a billion dollars is at stake, anything becomes possible. How you coming with the hospital records?"

"Waiting to get a call back from a friend. That section of the file server went down and messed up the emergency room records. The emergency room nurse, the one who would have assisted, works the three to midnight shift today. I have a call in to her. I'll let you know when I confirm. One way or another."

"Until that file is located, or the nurse is willing to talk, we've got nothing. Well, maybe not nothing, but not enough to indict. Right now, our chances are near zero."

"That fingerprint haunts me, Leslie. How the hell it get on the cutting board?"

"That's all we really have. What else do we know about her? Physical traits?"

"She's five-nine, solidly built, wideset eyes with high cheekbones. She's from Trinidad and has short black curly hair."

"It's her hair that gives her face a round appearance."

"Interesting that you said that, Leslie. Would never have occurred to me that Ghana's short curly hair is what makes her face appear round."

"Why's that so *interesting*?" Leslie pressed, confused at Lewis's sudden animation. "Not following."

"Other than the short curly black hair, you just described Bates Aribah! I'd say she's between five-seven and five nine. Any difference would be easy to make up with shoe lifts. Her face is slender, as is the rest of her. But here again, padding can do wonders on her body. If you're right about the hair, a short curly wig could round out Bates' face. Voilà, Bates becomes Ghana. Skin tone's off I'll admit. But, hey, Iran for Bates, Trinidad for Ghana. We're dealing in variations. That's what makeup was invented for!"

"Lewis, sounds like you're going to bat for Ghana."

"Just running through the possibilities, is all. If the shoe fits kind of thing."

"You're forgetting one key fact. Ghana's fingerprint on the cutting board!"

"There is that. But as you know, the experts will testify that one print is not conclusive. A partial print at that."

A thought that had been nagging Leslie jumped back into her mind. "You know, it's more than just one print that's troubling. Where's the money trail? LBB says he made a down payment of a hundred million. Where'd all that money go? We've been searching Ghana's accounts for a while now—and nothing."

"True, but we've put that down to her being facile with accounts all over the world—and having friends everywhere." Lewis added, "I do believe she's capable of making it disappear."

"A hundred million? With hundreds more to come. I suppose you're right. But with that creep lawyer, Thunder, having his wings clipped, it'll be harder for her to make the money disappear."

"That's more money than anyone can spend! Can grease a ton of skids. No telling where the money is."

"Maybe, just maybe," Leslie speculated, "the deposit was never paid. Bishop may have wanted time to verify authenticity.

Didn't think to ask him. I say we put a close watch on both of them. Bates, as well as Ghana. If we get proof that Ghana had stitches, we focus on Bates. Until then, Gahana is our prime target."

Lewis was quiet for a moment, his jaw tight, his eyes closed. Then he suggested, "How about we request a search warrant for the Aribah residence? I know the judge denied the last one, but that was before we had a possible imitation going on. We're looking for shoe lifts, wigs and makeup. I bet that's specific enough to pass the judge's sniff test."

"You can try, if you wish. Be more specific on the makeup. Quantity might be helpful. Perhaps add a color range. I suggest including color photos of Bates and Gahana and limit the makeup to what would match Gahana. Judge should be okay with that. We may be fishing, but I agree, we have good reason."

THIRTY-FIVE

AN HOUR LATER LESLIE AND LEWIS were parked in front of the Aribah house, the search warrant open on the console between them.

"I've never seen one so limited," Lewis said. "Bathrooms, bedrooms, closets, dressing rooms. We're to stay out of the grandmother's space. And everything is to be video recorded, a copy of the video to be deposited with the court within two hours of the search. Think he means business?"

"Queen B's how the grandmother's known. Been in this country since 1978, a year before the fall of Iran. Well-connected at that time. I imagine she still is. Need to play this according to the book. That's why we're waiting for our video person. I requested Beth Hillard. She was at the crime scene. I said we'd wait."

"Wait no more, boss," Lewis said, opening the passenger door, "she's a minute out."

"Now, don't you go banging on the door until everything's ready. Judge said to tape it, we'll tape everything that happens. Beginning to end. No exceptions. That means we stay together. I want all of us visible in all scenes. We're doing this right."

"Show time," Lewis announced, seeing their Criminal Investigative Assistant turn the corner and roll to a stop behind them in the sprawling driveway.

Leslie repeated for Beth the instructions she had just delivered to Lewis. Beth nodded. "Ready when you are, Sergeant. You know if the old lady's home?"

"I don't. Guess we'll find out soon enough," Leslie replied, starting toward the front door. "Turn on the camera," Leslie instructed her CIA. "And don't forget the audio."

When Leslie was certain the camera was on, she pressed the doorbell. She also lifted the massive brass door knocker and let it fall. As was the situation the last time she came to this house, nothing happened. A full minute passed and still nothing.

Leslie repeated the process, remembering that she had timed almost two minutes that last time. "Two and a half-minutes have passed with no response. Lewis, call Bates. I'll call Pearl. Listen to see if we hear anything ringing inside the house."

Beth moved her camera assembly as close to the door window panel as possible, hoping the microphone would pick up sounds from inside the house.

Nothing registered on the sound meter.

Leslie then called as loud as she could, "Sheriff! We have a warrant for the Aribah house. Sheriff! Open the door!"

They waited a minute, then repeated the knocking and the calling. Still nothing.

"We going to get a locksmith?" Lewis asked. "Or should I get the crowbar?"

"I'm worried no one answered. From what the granddaughter told me, she's pretty much bedridden. Something could be wrong."

Lewis went to the car, popped the trunk and trotted back up the driveway, carrying a three-foot crowbar. One more ring, followed by silence. Leslie nodded in his direction. He inserted the bar just above the lock and threw his weight against the handle. The sound of splintering wood was followed by the door swinging open.

All three of them stepped inside and waited silently, listening. Hearing nothing, Leslie again loudly announced their presence. Several long seconds passed and still nothing. "I believe the owner's suite is back in this direction. Let's find Queen B and present ourselves."

Concern spread across Beth's face. "Don't we have to stay out of the owner's suite? Warrant says—"

"We're not going in, Beth. Just making our presence known. That'll pass muster."

Halfway to the back of the house Leslie paused, holding her arm up as she did so. "Judging from that smell, I don't think we're going to like what we find." Out of sight of the camera lens, she put her finger across her lips. The last thing Leslie wanted was to have to explain anyone's comments. The captured images could speak for themselves.

"You can say that again," Lewis answered, setting his jaw in anticipation of what they now expected to find on the other side of the door. "Well, here goes." He knocked on the door and announced their presence. Receiving no reply, he pushed the door open.

There was no doubt that Pearl Aribah was deceased. And had been for at least a day, most likely two or more. Leslie paused long enough to take in the scene, then instructed, "The search under the warrant is suspended for the moment. This is now a proper Lee County Sheriff scene. When we resume the search we will use the camera, although I now doubt if we even require the warrant. Please turn the camera off."

"It's off," CIA Hillard confirmed. "There's no question the old lady's deceased. Been so for a while anyway. I could be wrong here but judging from the angle of her head and the color of her neck, I'm thinking criminal activity."

"I agree, Beth. Let's not touch anything. The Medical Examiner can have the honors. Lewis, would you—"

"Already done. I also sent in an order to have the front door secured. I'm thinking we should continue the search while we're waiting."

"Good plan. We'll do it with the camera on just in case. No need to get crosswise with the judge. She's been good to us in recent months." When Beth signaled that the camera was again on, Leslie said, "For the record, the camera has been off for about four minutes. In that time, nothing was touched, but the ME has been notified of the death of the property owner, an eighty-six-year-old female who we believe to be Pearl Baribah, whose given name is Pearl Aribah. I believe her to be a member of the Pahlavi dynasty who ruled Iran before the revolution. We found Aribah apparently deceased in her bed. We will now conduct the limited search authorized under the search warrant, starting with Aribah's granddaughter's bedroom while we wait for the ME."

Bates' bedroom, bathroom and dressing closet appeared to be devoid of anything permitted to be taken under the warrant. At one point, Leslie commented, "If you ask me, I'd say there's more missing than what we're looking for. I saw only minimum cosmetics, no toothbrush or medications, and numerous empty shoe slots."

"Add to that list," Beth remarked, "blouses and slacks. I have more in my closet than we saw here. And that's not remotely possible. It's as if—"

"She blew the coop!" Lewis injected. "I think that much is self-evident."

"Before or after her grandmother passed is the question. If the ME determines we have a possible homicide, then all bets are off as to the search."

"Speaking of the devil," Lewis announced, "they're in the driveway as we speak. We'll have our answer in a moment."

Beth went to escort the ME team to the bedroom while the two detectives made their way back to Queen B's room. As Lewis had predicted, it didn't take long for Dr. Bratton Goodrich, the same assistant ME who had attended to the Miromar Lakes drowning of Tac Jacobi, to pronounce eighty-six-year-old Pearl Aribah's death as a likely homicide. Time of death was recorded as no less than ten, nor more than fifteen, hours earlier.

"The entire house, including the lanai, is a crime scene," Brat informed Leslie and Lewis. You and your CIA folks are welcome to join my team or leave as you wish. I'm thinking it'll be about four hours, give or take. Frankly, your help will speed up the process."

"Thanks Doc. For my part, I'll stay for the granddaughter's private spaces. Beth can remain for the rest if she has the time. That's her call." Turning to Lewis, Leslie elaborated, "What I'm concentrating on is anything that gives us insight into her friends. A diary maybe. Or a call log"

"A diary would be a home run," Lewis remarked, his gloved hand already probing in the bedside table drawer. He produced a note pad. "Something like this?" he called, holding the pad so Leslie could see writing scrawled on an open page.

"What's it say?" Leslie, who had been busy going through the drawer in the matching table on the other side of the bed, replied.

"Hair. George, question mark. Space. Leon, question mark. There's a diagonal line through Leon followed by three-thirty. Three-thirty is written in numerals."

"Okay. We'll deal with that when we're finished here. Keep looking."

Two hours later, Leslie stretched her back, trying to work the cramps out. "I'm getting too old for all this bending. Must have sorted through a ton of stuff and the only thing of value we found is that note you read me. Sounds like it's a hairdresser appointment. I don't use anyone fancy myself, so the names don't ring any bells. I'm sure Beth will track them down, but we might be able to shortcut the process. There's a crowd out front. I have to assume that if George is any good, someone out there will know him."

"Good thought. Worth a shot. How about me starting from the right? You take the left. Shouldn't take us that long."

The fourth person Leslie interviewed was a good-looking woman with perfectly groomed white hair holding the leash of a little white dog, the name Franco emblazoned on his harness. At the mention of the two names, her face came alive. "They're hairdressers. Lived for a while in Miromar Lakes. Moved a few years back."

"By chance," Leslie asked, "do you happen to know where they moved to?"

"Don't know where they live now, but this hair cut is a product of Leon," the woman said, turning in a full circle to display Leon's talent. "He's so busy these days he's hard to get. They're over at the Joseph Thomas Salon. On Forty-One. Behind Sprouts."

"Thank you," Leslie said, signaling to Lewis to cut off the canvas. They had what they wanted.

Fifteen minutes later, the detectives walked into the Joseph Thomas salon. As their white-haired informant had suggested, George was alone and finishing up a woman who looked to be in her sixties. "Sorry, we're closed after I finish up Debi here. Give me five and I can book an appointment for you. For both of you if you wish."

"We'll wait," Leslie said, taking a seat by the front window and motioning Lewis, who was pacing the salon, to do the same. The less attention they caused the better.

Seven minutes later, Debi pushed the front door open and walked out, but not before saying to the hairdresser, "You outdid yourself today, George. I'm pleased. See you in a few."

"Thank you, Debi. Enjoy the rest of your day." Turning toward the detectives, George said, "And what can I do for you two? I can fit one of you in tomorrow, around noon if that works. And maybe the other later in the day."

Leslie stood and walked over to the counter where George was standing. Lewis stood beside her. Both deputies held their credentials where he could see them.

"We're not here for appointments, at least not now we aren't," Lewis told the stylist, holding up a picture of Bates Aribah. "Know this woman?"

"Of course I do! Granddaughter of Queen Bee! Haven't seen the Queen in about a year. Nice woman. Tipped well. Always had a smile—and a nice word. Granddaughter, on the other hand, was a pistol! Talked my ear off about the high life, who she was seeing. She was never satisfied with what she had."

"And who was she seeing?" Leslie couldn't resist asking.

"I don't know about seeing so much. But she claimed to be engaged to a wealthy man from Texas. LBB she called him."

"When was the last time you saw her?"

"About a month ago. Came in for a hairpiece adjustment."

Both detectives came alert. Leslie took the lead. Lewis turned on his recorder. "Please recreate as close as possible exactly what was said by you and her during that appointment. Take your time."

George, realizing he had hit a sensitive topic, took a moment to gather his thoughts. "Well, as I recall it, she was even more demanding than usual. She said she had bought the hairpiece a month or two earlier, but that it wasn't holding its form. I asked her what she meant by that. She said that the intention was to make her face appear fuller. She said it started out doing just that, but that in the last week it wasn't working so well."

"What did you say or do?"

"I didn't say much. Only that I'd do my best to adjust the hairpiece to make her face appear round."

"Did you?"

"It took a full hour, but yes, I teased that bugger into submission. Then sprayed it solid. That sucker wasn't going anywhere. I suggested that I take a picture of it so I could fix it for her if it went out again, as she called it."

"How about a copy of that picture?"

"Never took it. She went even more crazy at my suggestion. Said she wouldn't be needing it much longer. I asked her why not. She said she had to wear it for a gig she was doing and never again."

"Anything else she say?"

"Not that I recall."

"Did she wear it out of here?"

"No. It was in a carry case."

"Anything further to add?"

"Nothing I recall."

"If you remember anything, please call either of us." Leslie handed George her card. Lewis did the same.

"Can you tell me what this is all about?"

"Not at liberty to right now. But you might want to stay close to your TV."

The first call Leslie made when she returned to her car was to Agent Maxine Ghana, who answered on the first ring. "I was about to give up on you," Ghana said. "Hope you have good news for me."

"This good enough? I'm now convinced you've been impersonated!"

"By whom?"

"Can't go into that at this point. But we have pretty convincing evidence of the impersonation—and a homicide as well. The FBI will be informed within the hour. I can't imagine why they won't immediately remove all restrictions. I'm personally very sorry for all the aggravation and trauma this has caused you."

"I'll just say this, Leslie. I don't believe my life will ever be the same. I suppose you'll be taking over in my place. That is, should you accept the Service's offer of employment."

"At this point, I think my answer is thanks, but no thanks."

"That is a shock! I can't imagine why you'd turn down an offer as good as this?"

"It's just not where I want to go with my life at this time. Sorry, but that's how I feel."

"Well, thanks for the good news on my front. I won't forget it. Wish we could work together. Talk soon."

THIRTY-SIX

LESLIE STEPPED OFF THE PENTHOUSE elevator directly into William "Little Billy Bob" Bishop's foyer. LBB was waiting for her. His smile was so broad it appeared to consume his eyes. From her brief phone conversation, he had gleaned that for all practical purposes she had resolved the issue of Ghana facilitating the sale of the da Vinci parachute to him. Of more importance, she had also resolved the homicide of Marino Jacobi. She was now in a position to resign from the Lee County Sheriff's Department and be with him full time. Almost from the instant they had met a few years back, that is want he had wanted. His preference was to marry her, although the only kiss they had ever shared was a quick peck on his check after their second dinner. In lieu of marriage, he was prepared to offer any terms she desired. He just wanted to have her as a full-time partner—and traveling companion.

"Leslie, did I understand correctly that you're about to arrest the killer of that guy Jacobi, the man who parachuted to his death using a fake da Vinci parachute?"

"You did."

"And you determined that the woman who I believe is IRS Agent Ghana is, in point of fact, an imposter."

"We did. And frankly that's why I'm here."

Bishop's smile slowly faded. Starting with his eyes and ending with the corners of his lips. His brain flooded with questions and concerns; all centered around a sense that his great plans of spending his life with this woman were somehow slipping away. Typically, he aggressively pursued what he wanted. But in this instance, he said nothing.

"When did you first meet Ghana?" Leslie asked, "I mean in person."

"About three years ago we had several telephone conversations pertaining to the value of a piece of art I sold. As you know from our conversations, I don't usually sell art. I buy what I want for my collection—what pleases me—and I have no intention of parting with it. That one piece, I came to realize, was a forgery, a pretty good forgery, but a forgery, nonetheless. My tax return had the exact amount I received for it. The taxable amount was almost nothing because I sold it for near what I paid five years earlier. It took a while to convince Ghana of that fact."

Leslie knew about that transaction. Bishop had bought the piece for seventy-five million in 2017 and sold it for eighty-five million in 2023. The tax rate he used on his tax filing was twenty percent, or two million dollars. Leslie also knew that Ghana had negotiated a twenty-four percent rate, meaning Bishop had paid an additional four hundred thousand. "If I recall right, you made a ten-million-dollar profit on the transaction."

"Ten million net," Bishop said. "Bought it for seventy-five. Sold it for close to ninety. But I had certain expenses. We agreed on ten as the profit. The point of contention was the tax rate. The capital gains tax rate increases to twenty-eight percent under certain conditions. We agreed on twenty-five."

"You saved three hundred thousand?"

"I look at it that Ghana collected an extra half a mil for the government. Not much, I admit. But that's more than zero."

"When next did you work with Ghana?"

"About a month ago."

"Pertaining to?"

"The da Vinci parachute. She said she could get it for me."

"Did she?"

"She produced it for inspection."

"Was it the real thing?"

"Passed all my tests."

"Why didn't you buy it? I assume you haven't yet."

"Price she's asking, eight hundred million, is too high. I didn't, and still don't, believe she could get that much from any of her other potential buyers. And, as it turns out, I'm right."

"How do you know that?"

"She called not long before you did, reducing the price significantly. She's in a panic to sell. Something must have happened."

"How much?"

"Five hundred. If we do it today."

"Are you prepared to pay that amount?"

"In a heartbeat."

"Can you have her deliver the parachute to you in person?"

"That's the plan."

"How about today?"

"That's what she suggested. Like I said, our friend Ghana's in a panic. Does she know she's no longer a suspect in the murder?"

"She does. Mind telling me how payment will be made?"

"So many questions, Leslie. I have a question of my own. Are you prepared to take me up on my offer of coming to Texas to live with me? You can set the terms of our relationship. I enjoy your company more than anyone I've ever been with. You can have your own allowance and, as I said, your own residence if you wish. My hope is that with time we can be together on a more permanent basis."

The offer of a lifetime! And because their time together had been in a professional situation, the two of them had never been romantic. Despite that, Leslie genuinely liked Billy Bob. Equally important, she also had a strong desire to spend quality time with him. "Please believe me when I tell you the feeling is the same with me. But until this matter is fully concluded, perhaps a day, certainly no more than two, I just can't commit one way or the other."

"I've waited this long. Another day or so won't change anything for me. I'll call Ghana and have her deliver the parachute. You had another question. Oh, yes. Payment. Same as we've done in the past. She'll give me an offshore account number. I'll transfer the money. If this works as it usually does, the money won't be in that account more than a few seconds. The bulk of it will go to Pax Skyler and perhaps to other *helpers* as well. Not all of them in this country."

Star's grandfather! Leslie thought. *What a tangled web*! "From my knowledge of the parachute," Leslie said, pausing to work on her pronunciation, "it was housed in Museo Nazionale Scienza e Tecnologia Leonardo da Vinci."

"I'm impressed. For a person who's never traveled, you nailed that. How about you and I drive over to the airport and fly to Milan tonight? You can see da Vinci's achievements firsthand and work on your accent at the same time. It'll be fun."

That would be fun! She thought. "You know I can't. In the middle of a—"

"Leslie, truth is you're always in the middle of an investigation. No time is good. This case you're working on is all but done. You said so yourself." Holding out his cell phone, LBB said, "Call your boss, resign. We can stop by your office and drop off your badge and gun and go right to the airport. You told me you always keep a spare day's clothes in your trunk. We can stop in Dallas, or even in Paris or Rome if you wish, and pick up a new wardrobe. What can be bad?"

Nothing can be bad! Never again worrying about money. Traveling the world. Doing whatever comes to mind whenever it comes to mind. Exciting. And doing it with someone I like to be with. The only person who even comes close to eliminating the pain of Junior's loss. Use that phone and I'll never again find myself fighting my way through a smoke-filled room trying to both save the life of a child and stay alive doing so.

Leslie forced herself to take a step back. "Exciting as that proposition is, I'm sorry, LBB, but I need to focus on the case I'm working on. Finish it up. After Ghana delivers the parachute, we'll talk. I promise."

"Okay, Leslie," Bishop said, his business face instantly returning, "but first I need a different promise from you."

"And just what will that be?" Her tone switched to match his.

"If Ghana delivers the parachute, as before, I need you to promise not to arrest me for possessing stolen property. Also, as before, you won't seize the parachute."

"Is it stolen?"

"It was in the museum. It's not now. That parachute was made by the hand of da Vinci. It's genuine alright. Provenance checks perfectly or I wouldn't buy it. Also, and this surprised me, the linen is in the same condition as it was when da Vinci treated it! That's over five hundred years ago! The museum refuses to reveal exactly where they found it, but they have certified it to be authentic and perfectly preserved. I have highly reliable reason to believe the parachute now being sold has recently been stolen. But not at my direction or control. That much I assure you."

"Interpol hasn't Red Noticed the parachute," Leslie informed Bishop. "Therefore, I have no basis to believe it has been stolen. Thus I have no basis to arrest you for possession of stolen property. Or, for that matter, take the parachute from you."

"Okay. I'll call Ghana and ask her to bring the parachute in person. I can't promise she'll comply."

"Do what you can."

Bishop walked across the room to the bank of windows overlooking the Gulf of Mexico and peered down at the beach a long moment before retrieving his phone and placing a call.

Leslie, seeing LBB put his phone to his ear, called her partner. In a voice too low for Bishop to hear, she said, "I assume we're ready to arrest Bates Aribah."

"I've briefed Boots and it's a go. She's already briefed Collier County and they've posted officers in the parking lot."

"Make sure their cars are unmarked and no uniforms in sight. Aribah has every reason to be on high alert. She's about to score big time, so I'm betting on her suppressing her natural prudence in favor of a big payday."

"Want me to join you?"

"That would be a good idea. You can supervise the lot and lobby. Also, we need a comms channel with Collier as well as a deputy up here in the penthouse. Gotta play this by the book. Hey, hold for a minute. Bishop's signaling for my attention." Leslie turned to LBB, who had his finger across his lips in the universal silence command. He mouthed, ONE HOUR.

She nodded her head then turned away from Bishop. Whispering into her phone, she instructed, "Need to be in place within thirty, forty-five minutes at most. Aribah says she'll be here in an hour. Get that deputy up here ASAP."

"Got it. I'm sixteen to twenty minutes out. Might spook her if I use lights or siren, especially given what she did to her grandmother and all."

"Agree. Let me know when you're in place."

When Leslie turned around, Bishop was standing directly behind her. "I couldn't help overhearing part of your conversation. I assume you're planning on arresting Ghana when she arrives. I thought you said—"

"This won't affect you—or the parachute—if that's what's concerning you."

"Then what's going on?"

"I suppose there's now no harm in telling you. The person who is bringing the parachute is an imposter. She's made herself up to look like Ghana."

"If she's not Ghana, then who?"

"We have every reason to believe it's Bates Aribah."

"Can't be! I know Bates. She's much shorter. Not even the same build. Bates is much more slender."

"Make up. Wig. Padding. Lifts."

"Are you positive?"

"As positive as I am of anything in life."

"I can't believe—"

"Bring up that snippet of an image you played for me yesterday. The one of Ghana's face when she shows you the parachute and I'll show you why we're certain it's not her."

Before Bishop could locate the short video file on his phone, the elevator opened and out stepped an over-weight man in his fifties, holding Collier County Sheriff Deputy identity credentials in his hand. "For the record, I'm Detective Craig Wittington. I was asked to help you with an arrest."

"Thanks for coming up so quickly, Detective Wittington," Leslie said, producing her own credentials. "I'm Detective Sergeant Leslie Hodges, based in Lee County. And this is William Bishop. We're in Mr. Bishop's apartment. A woman will be arriving soon who I plan to arrest. Mr. Bishop here was just about to play a brief clip showing what she looks like. Take note of her forehead."

Bishop, holding his phone where the three of them could see, said, "Watch carefully. She'll only be visible for a very short time. Seconds at best." He touched the start button and almost instantly the facial image of Ghana came and went.

"Did you catch her forehead?" Leslie asked.

"Nothing to catch," Bishop said.

"I agree with that," parroted Wittington.

"That's just it! The day before this image was captured, the real Ghana cut her forehead. In *my* car no less. She had several stitches. Which, by the way, were just confirmed. So, this image we just saw could not have been Ghana. FYI, Detective, Ghana is an IRS agent out of Palm Beach."

"So," the detective quipped, "we're here to arrest a woman who forgot to sketch on fake stitches during an impersonation. That what we got going?"

"Only she didn't know about the stitches." Leslie said, trying not to get into it with her counterpart. "The arrest will be for homicide. Of her grandmother, as well as for that guy who jumped out of a plane over in Miromar Lakes and who died when his parachute—parachutes—failed to open. The woman we're about to arrest's real name is Bates Aribah. There's evidence she suffocated her grandmother, woman named Pearl Aribah. Grandmother's also known as Queen B. Iranian royalty."

"Now that's better," Detective Wittington admitted.

"What? Murder!" Bishop exclaimed. "You didn't tell me anything about a murder!"

"Would it have made a difference if I *had* told you?" Leslie questioned, wondering if she was making a mistake in considering his over-the-top offer of moving in with him.

"I suppose not. But it is disconcerting knowing Ghana—I mean Bates—murdered her grandmother."

"I must caution you not to communicate that information, or any information concerning law enforcement, to her in any manner."

"Wouldn't dream of it. You know me better than that."

"That's why we're doing this here. Because I trust you." *Now I'm lying to him. This is the only way I can think of to catch Bates without a national hunt.*

"Will she be alone?" Wittington asked. "I don't want to be caught short handed."

"She'll be carrying a bulky package," LBB chimed in. "I can' imagine she could manage it on her own. In any event, at a minimum, she'll have security."

Leslie's communicator vibrated. Touching the LISTEN button she heard Lewis say, "In position. The radio channel for our friends is eighteen. I'm switching over at the end of this."

"Ten-four." She dutifully switched her comm to the proper channel and watched as Wittington did the same. "Now we wait."

"Waiting is what we do the most of," Wittington volunteered. "Takes practice like anything you do. You get good at it after a while."

"Don't think this will be long," Bishop called from across the room. "She just requested the codes for the money transfer."

"Oh, shit. We're screwed if she doesn't show! What if—"

"Hold tight. The last code's given to her *after* she's here. These preliminary codes verify the links and allow her to confirm that the funds are in the account and available. That last code I give her allows her to withdraw the money. That's how I know she'll be here."

"She could call you for the code *after* the delivery."

"She would never trust me that much. No, she'll come in person and the transactions will be essentially simultaneous."

Leslie's comm again sounded. Answering it, she heard Lewis' voice. "Ghana, who I assume is Bates, is leaving her car. I have to say that disguise is good. She appears to have a large male carrying the package. Walking together."

"Message received. Thanks."

A few moments later, Leslie's comm announced, "Elevator just closed. They're both on their way up."

Turning to Wittington, Leslie said, "You take Bates into custody and arrest her for manslaughter of Queen B. I'll separate the muscle. Unless he acts up, we have nothing to hold him on."

"Please protect my valuable artifact, whatever you do," Bishop called from several feet away, his voice stressed, his face red.

The light above the elevator came on. They heard a slight whoosh of air as the elevator stopped. The door didn't immediately open.

Leslie pushed the call button several times, still no movement. She pushed it again. Still nothing. Then, without warning, it slid open. Wittington positioned himself in front of Leslie, prepared to nab Bates the moment the door opened far enough.

Seemingly standing by itself was a large bundle of fabric with what appeared to be bamboo framework surrounding it. Then Leslie saw a large man standing off to the far side, holding the bundle upright. What Leslie did not see, was Bates. Then, as if totally disconnected from reality, she heard herself exclaim, "Where the hell's the girl?"

It took her several seconds to realize what had happened, at least partially. She called her partner. "Lewis! Did you yourself see Ghana enter the elevator?"

"I did. Why? Is she not there?"

"Only the muscle's here with the parachute. Ghana's—Bates'—gone!"

"Elevator didn't stop on the way up! Only place she could possibly go is the elevator ceiling."

From across the room she heard Bishop stage whisper, "Good for her!"

Wittington stepped into the elevator and grabbed the man holding the parachute by the front of his shirt, pulling him toward the door.

"Watch the material!" Bishop yelled. "Watch the material!"

The Collier County detective separated the man from the material, saying, "Get your ass out of the elevator and sit down with your back to that wall. Move from that wall and I'll put a hole through your leg! Now move!"

The man did as instructed.

Leslie turned to LBB, who was now busy tapping his phone screen. "I hope you're not releasing the funds! We'll never see Bates again if you do!"

Bishop held the phone up so that he could talk into it. Then said, "Done. Good Luck."

Leslie grabbed the nearest chair and jammed it in the now closing elevator door. Turning to Wittington, she instructed, "get a couple of deputies up here to check the top of the elevator. Bates had to go somewhere. I'll bet my partner's right!"

Pushing the comm button, she called, "Lewis, you there?"

Silence.

On the third call, she got a response from Lewis. "Sorry I didn't answer. Was a bit busy. I watched our target get on the elevator and made sure she remained on until after the door closed and the elevator started up. After I spoke to you I remembered the elevator stopped on the third floor. Took me a moment to realize what had happened. By the time I got up there she had disappeared. I figured she could only have gone into a room or down the other stairwell. If she went down, one of the deputies would snag her, so I concentrated on the rooms. As luck would have it, as I went down the hall, I heard the safety lock on a room near me snap closed. That meant someone was inside. I banged and announced myself. No answer. Made no sense, so after a few more tries, I broke the door."

"Hell, now we have an unlawful search issue on our hands!"

"Cool your jets, boss. Boots ordered a search warrant for a suspected murderer here at the hotel. Judge had no problem. We can search anywhere!"

"So?"

"Bates is on her way to Collier County Jail."

Leslie took a moment to catch her breath, then said to Wittington, "Would you please get the contact info for that guy over there. If he gives you a hard time, arrest him for possession of stolen property. We can deal with him later."

"I ain't going anywhere without this here package," the man spat. "Unless Ghana says it's okay. You hear me?"

"I paid for it," Bishop interrupted, his face now deep red. "Ghana, or whoever's down there, is no longer the owner of that parachute. It belongs to me, and to me alone!"

The guy sitting on the floor, snarled, "Not 'till the woman I'm working for says so! You'll have to come and get it."

"We'll see about that!" Bishop snapped back, grabbing his phone and punching in two digits. An instant later he said into the device, "Get in here! Your services are required."

Facing Deputy Wittington, Leslie said, "We're leaving. This isn't our rodeo. Let them work it out. Here, help me remove this package from the elevator. I believe it belongs to Mr. Bishop, but that's between them to work out."

The big guy on the floor, realizing he was no longer of interest to the cops, climbed to his feet, but made no move toward the elevator.

When the parachute was off the elevator and in the living space, Wittington said to Bishop, "With all due respect, sir, as I see it, the sides aren't close to even! You're no match for this thug. He means business. You'd be wise to allow him to take this here package with him. Otherwise, you and your boy'll get yourselves hurt."

"First of all, the man I just spoke with is anything but a boy!" LBB shot back. "He's a former highly decorated Texas Ranger! If this thug, as you call him, doesn't join you on that elevator, he'll receive an up-close and personal demonstration of what Texans mean when they say, "One riot, one Ranger!"

The End

Thank You

This book was edited by my daughter-in-law, Brenda Goldberg Tannenbaum, as well as by Debi Bass, Kathlyn Auten and Charles Ryan. As I have said many time before, I am blessed to have these wonderful people in my life. I deeply appreciate their tireless effort.

As always, thank you again to my wonderful wife, Mary Tannenbaum, who for the past thirty-five years has always been there for me. I love you.

Books by

David Harry Tannenbaum

The Seminal Society Series

Edison's Phonograph

Chladni's Euphon

Newton's Laws

Galileo's Telescope

da Vinci's Parachute

General Fiction

Standard Deviation

Out of the Depths

Adventures in the Law

Mystery/Thriller (under the pen name David Harry)

Jimmy Redstone/ Angella Martinez Series

the Padre Puzzle

the Padre Predator

the Padre Paranoia

the Padre Pandemic

the Padre Poison

the Padre Phantom

the Padre Phony

the Padre Pirate

the Padre Puppets

About the Author

David Harry Tannenbaum and his wife, Mary, have a home in Miromar Lakes, Florida. David enjoys swimming, bocce, model train building, walking Franco—and searching for characters to be exploited in his next novel.

In Memoriam

Dr. Stephen Tannenbaum (no relation) – I have known Steve since high school. In college, at the University of Pittsburgh, Steve and I were Kappa Nu fraternity brothers. After college we drifted apart; he graduated from Pitt Dental School, married his college sweetheart, Shirley Cohen, and continued to reside in Western Pennsylvania. I moved to Columbus, Ohio, graduated from Law School then moved first to New Jersey and then to Dallas. After retirement, Mary and I returned to Pittsburgh (part time) and my friendship with Dr. Steve resumed as if we had never been apart. We discovered that our lives had unfolded along parallel paths. Both of us were past synagogue presidents, and both of us love to write. Steve enjoyed writing, and publishing, short stories with deep character interest, while I enjoy writing longer novels. Steve passed on March 5, 2025, and his memory is indeed a blessing. He is very much missed.

John Douglas Madeley – I met Doug about eight years ago when he and I were randomly seated next to each other at a Lee County Library Association dinner reception for Nelson DeMille. Before the meal was served, he and I (total strangers) got into a political discussion broken up only by the placement of the food plates before us on the table. Both Nelson and his son Alex spoke about the process of writing a fiction novel together. The program ended and our private discussion resumed. A few moments later Doug asked me my name. He followed that question with a request for my address. I drew the line at that point and demanded to know why he needed my address.

"To pick you up in the morning," he replied, adding, "Be out front of your house at eight o'clock."

"Why?"

"Because, like I said, I'm picking you up, that's why."

"Should I eat breakfast or what?"

"No need. I'm buying breakfast."

"Where are we going?"

"You'll see. Just be out front!" With that Doug walked away.

At eight the next morning I was standing in front of my house, curious as to what adventure awaited me. Doug rolled up and off we went to the back room of a restaurant roughly four miles away. He proceeded to introduce me to at least twenty men, mostly retired, who ate breakfast and discussed various topics every Wednesday. The group is called Tertulia and has been meeting for well over twenty years. What a great group of men! Lead by Doug until a few months ago when he passed away while traveling in Turkey.

At 8:30 on Wednesday mornings I look toward the door to Haney's backroom expecting—hoping—to see a tall man ambling in, several newspapers carefully folded against his leather purse, his smile lighting up the gathered Tertulians. Doug, your spirit lives on as we exchange thoughts on life. I trust you know that you are very much missed.

www.ingramcontent.com/pod-product-compliance
Lightning Source LLC
LaVergne TN
LVHW010652110826
845149LV00014B/3051

* 9 7 9 8 9 9 8 5 1 9 2 3 9 *